shrinking violet

shrinking violet

danielle joseph

Pocket Books   MTV Books

New York   London   Toronto   Sydney

Pocket Books
A Division of Simon & Schuster, Inc.
1230 Avenue of the Americas
New York, NY 10020

First MTV Books/Pocket Books trade paperback edition May 2009

POCKET and colophon are registered trademarks of Simon & Schuster, Inc.

For information about special discounts for bulk purchases, please contact Simon & Schuster Special Sales at 1-800-456-6798 or business@simonandschuster.com

Designed by Renata Di Biase

Manufactured in the United States of America

10 9 8 7 6 5 4

Library of Congress Cataloging-in-Publication Data

Joseph, Danielle.
   Shrinking Violet / Danielle Joseph.—1st MTV Books/Pocket Books trade paperback ed.
      p. cm.
   Summary: Painfully shy, eighteen-year-old Teresa dreams of becoming a radio disc jockey, but when her big break comes it threatens her budding relationship with the first boy ever to notice her, as he speaks of honesty while she hides her on-air identity.
   [1. Bashfulness—Fiction. 2. Disc jockeys—Fiction. 3. Mothers and daughters—Fiction. 4. Secrets—Fiction. 5. High schools—Fiction. 6. Schools—Fiction. 7. Miami (Fla.)—Fiction.] I. Title.
   PZ7.J77922Shr 2009
   [Fic]—dc22   2008054694

ISBN-13: 978-1-4165-9696-7
ISBN-10:   1-4165-9696-8

Much love goes out to my husband Delle and my two curly-haired angels, Marley and Makhi.

shout-outs

I would like to thank the following people:

You all rock for helping make my dream come true!

Delle, my husband, for always believing in me and for your unwavering support.

Marley and Makhi for sharing my love of stories and being silly!

Rosemary Stimola for being a fabulous, savvy agent and for snagging me this on-air gig!

Jen Heddle for connecting with Tere and for not allowing me to broadcast dead air. You are an amazing editor!

The Cohen Clan for being quite a mix! My dad, Rodney, for understanding that technical writing was not my calling. My mom, Sharon, for reading to me every night. My siblings: Cindy for sharing her stories and the secret knocking code. Kenny for shaking up the string of girls. Nikki for always asking why and Emma for being the best teen editor!

My mentor Joyce Sweeney for sharing her expertise and

cheering me on the whole way. Adrienne Sylver for being a wonderful and speedy critique partner.

Gaby Triana, Marjetta Geerling, Linda Bernfeld, Christina Gonzalez, Liz Trotta, Marta Magellan, Mary Thorp, Tere Starr, Elaine Landau, Ruth Vander Zee, Susan Shamon, Saundra Rubiera, and the rest of the Wednesday Critique Group for your invaluable feedback. Also Debbie Reed Fischer and Joyce's Friday Critique Group for being great listeners.

My first and second grade teachers, Betty Peterson and Judy Shannon, for telling me that I could write whatever I wanted and then for telling me it was great! Eva Adler, my high school English teacher, for fostering my creativity. Emerson College professors, Jessica Treadway, Kevin Miller, Andre Dubus III, and Eric Arnold, for all your encouragement and for teaching me the craft of creative writing.

The following people for your technical support: Beth Cameron for showing an intern how it works behind the scenes. Joe Plett for helping me with my audition tapes. Rob Robbins at The CALL FM for providing me with up-to-date radio information.

Copyeditor Ela Schwartz-Hnizdo for her super-organized, impressive copyedits and the rest of the MTV/Pocket Books Crew for all you do.

In memory of Granny Gladys and Granny Billie, wish you both were here to share this with me.

Never bend your head. Always hold it high.
Look the world straight in the eye.

—Helen Keller

chapter ONE

You're listening to Sweet T on 92.7 WEMD SLAM FM. It's after dark now, so don't change that dial because here's where killer tunes explode through your speakers, leaving you wanting more. I'll take you through the night and feed your soul. Call me at 1-800-555-SLAM and let me know what's up, Miami. Now check out the new Juice Box track I've been promising you.

★ ★ ★

Until a few years ago, I always dreamed that a radio station would be a sleek glass architectural gem on Ocean Drive. Flashing neon lights with the studio's call letters would adorn the top of the building, large enough to be spotted miles away. Don't get me wrong, SLAM FM has a good setup five minutes from the beach in North Miami. But they occupy the second floor of an office building, nestled between a law firm and a bail bondsman, hardly in the midst of all the South Beach revelers staring at the disc jockeys through the huge windowpanes.

The only good thing about Mom marrying Rob Fandango, radio bigwig, is that he owns a top-forty station. But while he whisks Mom off to celebrity-wannabe parties every weekend, I'm holed up in my room, downloading all the latest tunes on my iPod and scanning the dial for the next overnight sensation.

There are a few local celebs, like the hottest up-and-coming rapper, PJ Squid, that I'd like to meet, but I'd have nothing to say to him. More like I'm afraid I'd open my mouth and nothing would come out, or even worse, I'd say something stupid.

Might as well admit it—I'm shy. Not the kind where you blush when someone compliments you, but the kind that results in feelings of nausea when meeting new people. When I was little, I thought I was Shy Adams. People would ask my name, and my mother would immediately answer for me, "She's shy." She even did it three weeks ago when we met up with some of the radio people at a restaurant. It was so embarrassing because I can no longer hide behind her; rather, she can hide behind me. I'm five inches taller than her and a good thirty-five pounds heavier—I'm the evergreen tree to her palm.

"Teresa, you can wait in the car if you like." Mom's ID card pops out of the slot and she zooms into her reserved space in the station's parking garage.

My seat belt is already unbuckled. "No, I'm cool."

I walk a step behind Mom toward the elevator. By the time we reach the second floor, my stomach is whirring. I cross my arms against my chest and inhale. I can do this. I've done it before. We'll only be inside for five minutes, tops. Mom has to drop off a birthday present that Rob asked her to buy for his lawyer. Then we're off to my Friday afternoon dentist appointment. Joy.

When you open the heavy glass door to the station, the first thing you see is a gigantic red and blue SLAM sign hanging over a large U-shaped desk. In addition to the receptionist's area, the entrance is large enough to fit two red couches and a table filled with *Rolling Stone, Vibe,* and other music industry magazines. There's a small guy with a goatee and shades sitting there now. He's speaking in a hushed tone on his cell. I don't recognize him. Maybe he's a promoter. I hope he's here for PJ Squid.

Patty's up front answering the phones. She's in her midforties, is the proud owner of a seventies feathered hairdo, and plays solitaire in between calls. She gives us a half smile as we waltz by.

We round the corner and walk past the on-air studio. My heart thumps. I'd give anything to be inside there, broadcasting live, instead of doing mock shows from my bedroom.

Derek, the drive time DJ, is leaning against the outside of the door. "Hi, Delilah." He throws Mom a crooked smile.

"How's the show going?" Mom asks.

"All good." He winks. "Do you like your new ride?"

I'm standing next to Mom, but he doesn't even acknowledge me. We've met several times before but have never spoken to each other. It has always been at the end of a long table at a restaurant or at a few station parties filled with models and other women that don't eat for a living.

"I love the Lexus. It drives so smoothly," Mom coos.

Derek puts his hand on Mom's shoulder. His knuckles are really hairy and so is his chest, for that matter. I don't think the first three buttons on his shirt have ever been used. "You deserve it."

I try to peek into the studio, but Derek's blocking the glass pane in the door.

"I like to think so." Mom laughs. "Rob knows what makes me happy."

Okay, this is about all I can handle. This guy gives me the creeps. I clear my throat and point down the hall toward our original destination.

"Right." Mom nods and says good-bye to Derek.

We continue down the carpeted hallway to Rob's window office, facing the bay. When we're a few feet away, I hear him talking to someone.

Mom reaches for the doorknob. "Maybe he's in a meeting," I say.

"Nonsense. He knows I'm stopping by." She whips open the door.

DJ Wipeout is seated across from Rob. "I'm sorry to hear that—" Rob stops midsentence as soon as he spots us.

Both men are sporting poker faces. Call me crazy, but it looks like they're busy.

Mom strolls right in, while I linger at the entrance.

"Here you go, honey." She plops the gift bag onto Rob's desk and gives him a big smooch on the lips.

He smiles but doesn't budge. Mom looks at Rob, then DJ Wipeout. "Excuse me. Did I interrupt something?"

"Aaron's leaving us," Rob says.

What? No way. He's got a great show, *The Love Shack*, "where lust is always in the air."

"For how long?" Mom slides her wedding ring back and forth.

Rob taps his coffee mug with a gold pen. "He quit."

Mom's jaw drops. I inch closer to the desk.

"I'm going to work on my uncle's cattle ranch in Texas." Wipeout runs his hand over the top of his shaved head. I catch a glimpse of the tattoo stretched across his forearm that says *Rock or Die*.

Double no way. He's going to waste his sexy voice rounding up cows all day and stepping in manure?

"That's nice." Mom smiles.

"*The Love Shack* won't be the same without you," Rob says. "I have no clue who to replace you with."

Me! I want to shout. *I can do the show blindfolded!* But instead I stand there deader than a stuffed moose.

"I'm sorry, bud." Wipeout lets out a huge sigh. "But this is my calling."

Yeah, me, too.

This is Sweet T live on The Love Shack, *hoping all your dreams come true . . .*

chapter TWO

TERESA ADAMS!" Mom's standing in front of me in full lobster glow. She went overtime at the tanning salon again.

I roll my eyes up and yank out an earbud. "Yeah?"

"Pamela Oberlong will be here in fifteen minutes."

"Okay." I nod and stick my earbud back in. There's nothing
like the sweet sounds of PJ Squid. With his fresh lyrics, he'll be
number one on the charts in a few months. Rob's given him
some airplay, but he's crazy if he doesn't do more—like a live gig
before other stations snag PJ.

I glance up again. Mom's still there. Her eyes have narrowed,
and I think she's even a shade redder. I remove an earbud again.
"What?"

"Take that thing off for a minute." Mom's lobster claw pulls the other side out.

"Ouch." I rub my ear and stare up at her.

"Go change before Pamela gets here. That outfit makes you look lazy."

Oh, but a miniskirt and tube top is more appropriate. Mom has five of those sleazy shirts. She thinks the more skin you show, the better.

"But it's Saturday."

Mom throws her hands up. "So it's okay to look like a slob on the weekend?"

"Can't I just stay in my room then?"

"No, that's rude."

"Fine. I'm going." I increase the volume on my music and clunk up the stairs. I slide off my favorite jeans and black Rapfest tee and peer into my closet, searching for the best *Pamela Oberlong* outfit. Why we have to impress the Mary Kay lady every time she comes over is beyond me.

I settle on a pair of black capris and the pink button-down tank that Mom says shows off all my good parts and hides all my bad parts. Pamela better be happy. She didn't know me when I was a fat snowball. "Snowball" has been my nickname since I moved to Miami in the fourth grade. First off, I live in Florida, so that name is pretty dumb, and even though I lost thirty pounds three years ago, I can't shake the name. Everyone still looks at me the same. Like they expect me to blimp out any minute.

I blame the shape of my body on my dad, but since I don't even know who he is, I can only guess. Mom doesn't know either. She says she was young and stupid. That she went to a couple of wild parties when she was a teenager and did a few things she shouldn't have. *No shit.* It doesn't take Scooby-Doo and his gang to figure that out.

Actually, come to think of it, she was eighteen, my age, when I was born. I'll be happy if I score one date.

I picture my dad as a lumberjack with broad shoulders and a big butt. I'm definitely not built like my mom. She has a petite frame and long legs like a flamingo. Next to her I'm Shrek.

It doesn't help that my stepfather, Rob, is a small guy, too. He's only a couple of inches taller than me, barely five foot nine, but he tries to appear bigger by wearing cowboy boots. You'd think he was tall when you hear his booming voice on the radio, but that's the thing about the radio—it's a mask.

I often dream about the mask I'd wear to school. It has long auburn hair, not the shoulder-length ultra-thick mop that I sport. It has bright blue eyes instead of my musty greens and full red lips. If it comes with a bodysuit, I'd wear that, too, flat tummy, long legs, and smaller, firmer boobs. Then the guys would notice me, for sure.

The doorbell rings. Mom opens the door and shrieks, "Oh, Pamela, it's nice to see you. Have you lost weight?"

"And you, Delilah—you look amazing!"

Somebody shoot me, quick.

I only have two minutes, tops, before Mom calls me down. I know she'll want me to talk to Pamela—I just can't think of anything to say. We have about as much in common as my mom and a nun.

I stretch out on my bed and practice. "Hi, Pamela, you look really nice." "Hi, Pamela, new car?" "Hi, Pamela, new lipstick? I heard red is back." Wait, was it ever gone? I sound so lame. I don't even care about this stupid woman.

"TERESA!" Mom calls from downstairs.

I pop up from my bed and take a quick peek in the mirror. Ugh, new pimple forming at six o'clock. Great, now I'll have to buy some coverup from Pamela. To her, every imperfection is a chance for a sale. Ka-ching! I can see her square face adding up the math in her head. Zit, ten dollars; thin lips, twelve dollars; small eyes, fifteen dollars; shy—can't help that.

"Did you hear me?" Mom yells again. I slam my door and trudge down the stairs.

Mom sits on the living room couch while Pamela sets up her products on the coffee table. Mom picks up a tube of lipstick and flips it over to the bottom. "Hot Stuff. Perfect for me." She laughs. But she didn't even open it yet.

"Hello, Teresa," Pamela greets me. "I love that color on you."

"Um, thanks." I shove my hands in my pockets. "Your teeth are really white." Did I just say that?

Pamela rubs her hand over her mouth in a fanning motion and

smiles. "I'm glad someone noticed. I spent six hundred dollars to get these pearly whites."

I plop down on the suede couch opposite from Mom. It's so stiff that I bounce. When I design my own living room, all the furniture will be comfy.

"I noticed, too." Mom sets down Hot Stuff and picks up Vixen Prowl.

Pamela finishes setting up, then takes a seat in the wicker armchair next to me. She leans over and pulls my face toward her. "What beautiful skin. You should use a medium to light base."

Geez, what do people with really bad skin need? A double coat?

She fishes through her obnoxious pink suitcase and holds up a bottle to my face. "This has avocado in it."

I don't even like to eat the fruit. Why would I want to wear it on my face?

"Teresa's looking for something that will give her some pep," Mom chimes in.

I am?

"Ohh, I'd love to do you up," Pamela squeals.

Man, this is a total setup. Ambushed by Mom. I should've seen it coming.

While Pamela rummages through her stuff, I plead with Mom by frantically shaking my head. I don't want to be anybody's little project.

Mom's still fiddling with the lipsticks. "It's just what you need, honey."

You don't *need* makeup to be on the radio. I'd much rather have every hair on my head plucked out one at a time with tweezers.

Pamela gathers up an armload of supplies and tells me to sit down in the kitchen. "Are you ready for the new you?"

"Um, no," I manage to say. I follow her to the table but just stand there, eyeing the staircase that leads to my bedroom. My sanctuary.

"Don't worry; I won't bite." Pamela laughs and pushes me down into the chair. Her teeth blind me.

Before I know it, she owns my face. She dabs a Q-tip in some brown gunk and applies it to my skin. "Watch how much I use. You don't want to overdo it."

Trust me, that's not a problem.

Next she moves on to some blush and after that, she uncaps a few sleek-looking pencils. "Look up so I can apply some under your eyes."

"Maybe a little more." Mom hovers over Pamela.

I feel like one of those pathetic clowns standing outside the flea market on US1 holding a huge sign directing you inside for major discounts.

Pamela rests a hand on my shoulder. "Relax. Trust me. You'll look great."

"Okay." I slouch, hoping to appear relaxed.

Mom pulls herself away from the freak show to brew a pot of coffee. "I want the finished product to be a surprise."

I hope she likes it because then maybe she'll leave me alone for a few days.

We're on to the eye shadow. First white, then purple. Pamela starts with the lower lid. I tilt my head and watch the time on the clock change. Three, now two minutes left until two-time Grammy winner, Maltese, will be on VH1 talking about his up-coming hip-hop album with DJ Wild. The album drops March 15—that's in two weeks. I can't wait.

It's weird having someone this close to me. So close that I can see her nose hairs and smell her cucumber hand lotion. I wonder what Pamela is like under all her makeup. Does she like wearing her mask?

"Which color?" She holds up two different lip liners.

"This one." I point to the lighter of the two. It matches my shirt.

"Good choice." Pamela smiles.

I don't know how people reinvent themselves every morning. Primping takes way too much time and effort. Mom's the master of reinvention. She changes for every guy she's sweet on. I'm glad she finally settled on Rob because I'm tired of watching her transformations. Every time she brought a new guy home, I'd have to prepare for his arrival. The worst was when she made me don a cowboy hat for Ted from Wyoming. He showed up at our house in a baseball hat, and there I was in a dorky suede cowboy hat. At least now I can pretty much be myself. Well, except for today, apparently.

Pamela finishes off with my lips. I'm now wearing Hot Stuff. Maybe it holds magical powers and attracts guys like I attract mosquitoes in the backyard.

"Oh, I love it. The mascara and eye shadow really open up your eyes." She hands me a small mirror.

I hold it, but don't pull it up to my face. I take a deep breath and close my eyes.

"Well, go on . . ." Pamela nudges me.

I slowly bring up the mirror and peel open my eyes, one at a time.

Wow, I *almost* look pretty.

Mom sets two cups of coffee down on the table. "Nice job, Pamela. Now if only I can find someone to fix up the rest of her."

Almost.

chapter THREE

I grab a handful of cotton balls and run the water in the sink until it's warm. I wipe at my eyelids, then my cheeks. I have to press down hard to remove the gunk, especially under my eyes.

Why didn't I just say no to Pamela? It couldn't be worse than what Mom will say if she sees my streaked face and pile of soggy cotton balls. What's the point in making yourself up if you'll still be treated the same?

Mom jiggles the handle on the bathroom door. "Open up. I want to take a photo for the scrapbook."

No way in hell. I'll stay in here for the rest of the year if I have to.

I turn the faucet on full blast, hoping she'll catch the hint and leave. Instead, she pounds on the door. "It'll only take a minute."

Hasn't she humiliated me enough for one day?

She pounds again.

"Not now!" I yell.

"Stop being difficult and let me in." Mom uses two fists to knock against the door this time.

Finally I relent, opening it a crack. I quickly drop the cotton into the wastebasket. But I cannot save my face.

Mom pries the door open all the way. "Oh, God." She puts a hand up to her mouth. The camera hangs around her neck, swaying back and forth. Her red acrylic nails stare at me like daggers.

I peer into the mirror. My face looks like a child's watercolor painting left in the rain. It's a mess of brown, black, red, and purple.

"It's hard to take off," I say.

"You could've at least kept it on until you went to bed."

"Why?"

It takes Mom a few seconds to answer. "Because Pamela worked hard to make you look nice. And I wanted a decent picture of you."

Geez, thanks, Pamela, I'll move you to the top of my Christmas list.

I don't respond. I can't. I'm concentrating too hard on keeping all my emotions inside.

"I'm only trying to help you," Mom adds some sugar to her voice.

Then why does it always end up about you?

I promised Mom I'd lose the weight for her wedding, and I did. She wanted the photos to come out perfect because she'd never had a proper ceremony before. She never bothered to try and find my dad, and she got hitched to her first husband, Tony, when I was five. That one was in his parents' backyard.

Well, I did it that summer. I went to Weight Watchers and ran on Mom's treadmill almost every day, and by December I squeezed into the pink strapless dress she had bought for me. I've kept most of the weight off, only letting about ten pounds creep back, but I still feel like people stare at me at Ridgeland High. I hope when I go off to college that people will look at me differently.

"Hmm." I frown into the mirror, not convinced.

"Here, this is yours." Mom thrusts a pink plastic bag at me and starts to walk away, but quickly turns back around. "I don't know what's wrong with you."

Me neither.

Her stilettos click-clack down the hallway.

I slam the bathroom door and dump the contents onto the counter. Different-colored bottles and tubes spill out. I pick up a blue bottle with a gold top. Eye-makeup remover. This could've saved me a lot of pain. I dampen another cotton ball, close my eyes, and wipe away every shred of evidence. Then I scrub my face until the only thing I can smell is Dove soap.

Mom calls me down to help with dinner. She tries to stay away from ordering takeout because Rob is used to home-cooked meals. His first wife was a chef. We don't make eye contact. We just assume our usual dinner roles. She makes the tossed salad, and I sauté the chicken breast. She always complains about cooking. I don't see what the big deal is.

Before we moved in with Rob, we were strictly the *white food is evil, go green* type of family. But I dreaded most of those meals because it gave Mom all the time in the world to point out what's wrong with me. It would take us about five minutes to chew and the next fifteen were spent on how I could get more involved in school social activities. The other nights I was left alone with an elderly babysitter who fell asleep before me, while Mom jaunted around town, dating one guy and then the next. That's where I really got used to being alone. I had no one to answer to. Of course, I had no one to talk to either.

The radio fills the dead air that lies between us. I'm singing along in my head and Mom's bouncing around the kitchen.

"This girl can carry a tune." Mom wields her vegetable knife in the air. "What's her name again?"

I sprinkle some more chili powder on the pieces of meat and flip them over. "Maya Jackson."

"I'm sure she'd be fun to party with."

"She's sixteen."

"So what, I'm too old to hang out with the *young* crowd?" Mom swings her hips and tries to sing along, *"You think you know me, boy, well just wait and see . . ."*

"*American Idol* worthy," I mutter.

"Oh, no, I was thinking more like MTV." She laughs.

The front door swings open and I can hear Rob toss his keys onto the table in the foyer. Mom drops the salad spoons and rushes to greet him.

Hi, babe," she says.

They move into the other end of the kitchen, and then all I hear is them kissing. I don't turn around. They could be at it for a good five minutes. You would have thought, him being close to fifty, that things might slow down a bit. Oh, no, not this cowboy.

The chicken is done before they are, so I put it in a serving dish and place it on the table. It smells good.

Mom comes up for air. "Teresa, can you set up the rest of the food?"

She doesn't even wait for me to answer before she locks lips with Rob again.

I snatch a cucumber from the salad bowl. A little dry, so I add more dressing and toss the vegetables again. I'm suddenly thankful that I still have homework to finish for tomorrow. The lovebirds are going to be pretty busy tonight.

I sit down at the table and wait for them to join me. I pick at the salad.

Finally Rob breaks free and walks toward the table. "Oh, hi, Tere. How was your day?"

"All right."

"Good." He motors right past me and grabs a beer from the fridge. "Finding a new DJ isn't going to be easy."

"Why?" Mom gasps like she even knows what he's going through.

"I tried to lure Captain Pete, the midday guy from SUN, but he's locked into a two-year contract." Rob thumps down at the table and kicks off his cowboy boots.

As much as I really don't like SUN, SLAM's competitor, Pete is a good DJ. If it wasn't for him, the Ravers wouldn't be playing at Tobacco Road now and Giant James would still be delivering pizzas.

"What are you going to do?" Mom asks.

"Garrison will pick up his shift on Monday night, but we need to find a replacement. Get them groomed before sweeps." Rob takes a huge swig of Bud.

"What about that Feather guy we met at the Delano last week." Mom passes Rob the salad, but he waves it off. "He was cute."

"Cute doesn't cut it on the radio. There's a reason he's a catalog model." Rob spears the biggest piece of chicken from the serving dish.

"Oh." Mom bites her lip. "Do people really listen to the radio at night?"

Garrison's good, but he's not a night guy. He's morning show all the way. He's always hyper and gets people moving. I love waking up to him. It's like jump-starting your day with a cup of coffee. But not many people drink a large cup of joe right before they go to bed. I have enough trouble falling asleep as it is. I usually listen to the radio for a couple of hours before I nod off.

That's one good thing I got from Mom. When we first moved to Miami, I tossed and turned half the night. After about the third night of me waking up bleary-eyed, Mom bought me a hot pink radio and told me to let the music help me fall asleep. After the first night I was hooked. The radio really gave me peace and settled my worries about being in a new city, having to make new friends. Miami is nothing like Orlando, but now I'm so used to living here. It's a great place to be if you want to discover new artists.

"Yeah," both Rob and I say at the same time.

"When do your friends, er, classmates listen to the radio?" Rob asks me.

A sliver of sunlight shines through the French doors and makes the diamond stud in Rob's left ear sparkle.

"On the way to school. But mostly at night." The morning drive may be the most popular time slot, but most high schoolers are doing homework when they listen to the radio or just cruising around.

"So we need someone young and fresh." Rob shoves a mound of mashed potatoes into his mouth.

I nod my head. He's totally right.

The phone rings. No one moves, so I shuffle over to the counter. I check the caller ID. "It's for me."

"Go ahead." Mom waves me away.

I answer it and head to my room. "Hi, Audrey. Thank God it's you."

Audrey is the only person I can confide in. Like me, she's a not-popular, which is a step away from the dorks. I didn't meet Audrey until sixth grade. We were in PE together, both endur- ing the torture of Kevin Parker. He called her Beak (on account of her larger than normal nose) and of course, me Snowball. We were both ecstatic when he got suspended for ten days freshman year for fighting and was sent to an alternative school.

"Why, what's wrong?"

"I got attacked by the Mary Kay lady this afternoon." I plop down on my bed and kick off my Skechers.

"Ohmigod. Did you call the police?"

"I should've." I laugh. I think of myself all made up and then Mom's face when she caught me washing it all off. I can't stop laughing. I fall to the floor and laugh some more. It feels good.

"Tere, what is it?" Audrey gasps.

I think I'm scaring her, so I stop. My stomach muscles are kill- ing me. "No, my mom just had her do a makeover on me. It was okay, but of course not good enough for the Princess."

We call my mom Princess behind her back because she always coaxes men into doing whatever she wants. She's an ex-Realtor, sold Rob the biggest house in the neighborhood, then two months later, when it came time for him to move in, we moved in, too. She hasn't worked a day since. Now, I'm not complain- ing, because this McMansion makes our town house look like a dollhouse. Rob is definitely her best score yet.

"I'm sorry. That sucks."

"Nah, it's okay. I went to the station with my mom after school yesterday, and DJ Wipeout quit while I was there."

"In front of you?"

"Yeah, pretty much. Now Rob's all worried he won't find someone decent to replace him." I look up at the collage of musicians that I made on my bedroom wall. I need a photo of PJ Squid up there. It'd be nice to have some new hottie to say good night to before I go to sleep. And let's face it, PJ Squid is flawless, with his dark brown curly hair, green eyes, and the build of a Greek god. He designed his own workout studio in his house and the investment was totally worth it.

"You're good, Tere."

"Me?"

"Yeah, you'd be a great DJ. You know the music better than most people, and you've got a deep, sexy voice. I'm sure you'd sound awesome on the radio."

I never thought of my voice as sexy. Deep, yeah, but not something guys would swoon over. I was an alto in mandatory eight grade chorus and I don't think Mr. Baxter stuck me with mostly boys because I sounded sexy.

"No way. I'd freeze up."

"You'd be all alone in the studio. Not much different from you hanging around in your room doing those fake countdowns all the time."

"I'll stick to broadcasting from 11441 Blanche Drive, thanks."

When we hang up, I crank the volume on my stereo and wait for the Saturday night countdown to begin.

Even if I was remotely interested in filling in for DJ Wipeout, there's no way Rob would go for it. Audrey's crazy.

* * *

Hello, South Florida, this is Sweet T and I'm back and ready to blast you away with some slammin' tunes on the top twenty countdown. First off, if you're feeling a little lonely tonight, give me a call and let me know who you think should be number one. In at number twenty is Ram Z with "You Get What You Pay For"...

chapter FOUR

I'm glad this is my last year of high school. If I can help it, I won't sign up for any college classes that start before noon. Luckily, I got in early decision at the University of Miami and avoided the whole college search hassle. So many people at school have been freaking out for months about whether they'll get into any of their top choices. My top choice was to get out of the house. Come August I'll no longer have Mom breathing down my neck all the time.

Mom makes me walk to school even though I have my license because she says it's good exercise. It's not the twenty-minute hike that bothers me, it's the fact that everyone passes me in their cars and just looks the other way.

The weather report said it was going to be a breezy morning, so I throw on a hoodie and hook myself up to my iPod. Music is definitely my wake-up call. I grab a raisin bagel and a bottled water and wave good-bye to Mom.

"I won't be home until after eight tonight." Mom cinches the belt on her pink bathrobe. "Eat without us. There are Lean Cuisines in the freezer."

I nod, clasping the bagel in my mouth.

"If you have to start your day with carbs, you should only eat half." Mom holds out her hand to collect the *bad* half.

Instead, I rip off a piece of bagel with my teeth and chew. Then I'm out the door. Can't she just lay off the whole carbs thing? I don't think anyone has died from eating a raisin bagel for breakfast.

Today won't be so bad because I don't have a class last period, meaning I can walk home before most people get out of school. I was psyched when I ended up with a bunch of seventh-period study halls. Somebody out there must like me, or not like me, depending on how you see it. *Thank you, Schedule God!* All I had to do was cough up a note from my mom saying that I could "study" at home.

I try and match my steps to the beat of the music, but midsong PJ Squid is rapping like crazy, and there's no way I'm breaking into a jog. Tracy Kramer whizzes past me in her red Jeep on Oak Bluff Drive and has to brake quickly for the light. When I reach the intersection, she's still waiting to turn. I can tell she's listening to SUN 101.2, because they're playing crap music again. I think the owner of the station must be sleeping with Holly Lemon because her one hit single, "Lemon Drop," is polluting the street. Why anyone would want to listen to her high-pitched, nasally voice sing about her spiritual awakening after seven months of rehab is beyond me. I guess it doesn't hurt that her hair is as yellow as the sun and her boobs are so perky that they can carry on a conversation without her.

I cross the street and enter Ridgeland through the back by the teacher's parking lot. When they first repainted the building my freshman year, it looked like a nice ripe peach. Now, four years later, the peach has lost its color and is starting to mold around the edges.

As soon as I spot the security guard, I sling my school ID around my neck. When they took the pictures at the beginning of the year, the new guy in the front office didn't know how to use the camera properly, so everyone whose last name started with A–C got stuck with a stretched out photo that easily adds twenty pounds to your face. Now I'm reminded every day how I'll look if I gain all the weight back, and I guess so is everyone else.

I swing by the science wing and pick up my literature book from my locker. A mob of girls are crowded around some volley-ball player, and are admiring her belly-button ring. "Hey, you're in Ms. Peters' class, right?" Stacy Barnes shouts in my direction.

We've only been in the same class for over six months.

Stacy sits in the second row next to the window. Frank Williams, the guy behind her, likes to play with her long golden-brown hair and watch her shake her ass every time she gets up to sharpen her pencil. She's all cheer and no depth.

I turn around to make sure there's no one behind me. Nope. And when I turn back, Stacy's still staring at me. "Can you tell her I'll be a few minutes late because I'm in a volleyball meeting?" Stacy relubricates her lips with shimmer gloss.

By now the whole group has turned their attention from the belly-button piercing to me. My face goes red. All she wants is for me to say yes. So I nod, hoping that's good enough.

"Thanks." She flashes me a quick smile.

I try to smile back, but by the time I do, Stacy's already fussing over the new navel ring.

"Does that girl speak?" I hear one of the others ask, but no one has time to answer because the warning bell rings.

Ms. Peters is writing on the wipe board when I walk into Room 121 and everyone else is shuffling to their seats. I stop next to her and clear my throat, hoping she'll turn around, but she doesn't. She's too busy writing out a quote, which I'm sure will lead today's discussion.

I clear my throat again, but then Tim Connors cuts in front of me. "Hey, Ms. Peters. I'm back."

She turns around. "Feeling better?"

"Yeah. Wanna see the damage from my motorcycle rollover?" He lifts up his shirt before she can answer. I look away but still catch a glimpse of the nasty red scar. Nice abs, though.

The last bell rings and Tim rushes to his seat. I, however, haven't moved.

Finally Ms. Peters notices me standing in front of the board. "Hello, Tere."

"Hi," I say softly.

"What can I do for you?" She recaps her marker.

"Stacy's late."

She leans in closer. "Speak up."

I don't, but still repeat myself. "Stacy's late."

"Yes, she is, isn't she?" Ms. Peters grabs her attendance book off her desk.

"No, it's, just that—"

"Don't worry, I know, one more late and she has in-house suspension."

Oh, God. That's not what I meant. I don't need to make an enemy because once you screw with a member of the volleyball team, you're, well, screwed!

I take a deep breath. "Sh-sheee—"

Ms. Peters cuts me off, "Thanks, Tere—now take your seat."

I don't move. I'm frozen like a snowman. What can I do? I'd have to yell at the top of my lungs to get her attention now, but my mouth is as dry as the before-person's hair in a dandruff shampoo commercial.

"Good morning!" Ms. Peters bellows over the classroom chatter. Immediately the place falls quiet. Now, that is a good radio voice. Except I don't see Ms. Peters playing hip-hop and top forty.

No, she's all about string music. Apparently, teaching English was her second choice. Playing the violin in the symphony was her first. Poor Ms. Peters got stuck with us.

Defeated, I take my seat in the third row and eye the door. If Stacy comes in now, maybe Ms. Peters will give her a break.

Ms. Peters reads the quote on the wipe board. *"Friendship is certainly the finest balm for the pangs of disappointed love."*

"That's deep, Ms. P," Frank yells from the back. "You're a real poet."

"And she don't know it!" Tim reaches across two desks and gives Frank a high-five.

Ms. Peters ignores them. "This quote is written by Jane Austen from her book, *Northanger Abbey.* I want everyone to take five minutes and free-write in their notebooks about what they think it means."

"Love sucks," Amy, the girl sitting next to me, mutters.

I wouldn't know. I've never loved anybody. Yeah, I've had plenty of crushes, but they haven't gone any further than that. Unless you count the time in ninth grade when this girl, Sophia, overheard Audrey saying that I thought Johnny Dawson was cute and she decided to tell her friend Ruth, who told anyone that walked by her that day. And by the end of school, half the freshman class thought I liked a guy that was serious with Emily Lawrence, the most popular cheerleader in our class.

Emily cornered me at my locker the next morning and told me if I ever looked at Johnny again, she'd hang me from the flagpole by my eyeballs. Revenge happened two years later when Johnny founded the school's gay and lesbian theater group.

I write the quote at the top of the page and stare at it. The word *pangs* reminds me of pangs of hunger. Definitely painful. I know love is painful, too. You get all wrapped up in somebody, then they disappoint you. Leave you. Screw with you. Ms. Austen was definitely saying that having a good friend, someone to confide in when you're down, is the best medicine. I'm glad I have Audrey to talk to, but I still can't share everything with her. Not the depths of my soul.

I look up from my paper and see Stacy stumbling in the door. Ms. Peters confronts her and hands her a yellow tardy slip, already filled out.

Stacy rolls her eyes. "That's *so* not fair."

"Sit down," Ms. Peters says sternly.

"It's all that girl's fault." Stacy points to me, then tries to hand the yellow slip back to Ms. Peters.

"If you don't want another one, you'd better get to your seat." Ms. Peters points to Stacy's desk.

I slink down in my chair, wishing I were invisible. Stacy stomps past my desk, even though it's not on the way to her seat. "Thanks for covering for me," she snarls. "Now I'm stuck with Mr. Bradley tomorrow."

My face turns red again. I want to tell her I tried, but I can't pull the words out of my mouth fast enough. Instead, I peer down at my notebook and focus on the word *disappointment*. I overheard Mom using that word once on the phone. I'm not positive, but I could swear she was talking about me. "It's a real disappointment, especially after all the effort I put in. I tried to lead the way," Mom said.

"Okay, class." Ms. Peters claps her hands together. "What do you think Ms. Austen was saying?"

Amelia Samuel's hand shoots up. If I ever had a complete opposite, it would be her. She has curly blond hair, could practically fit in my pocket, and talks incessantly. "I think Ms. Austen was telling us that you have to surround yourself with good friends because they are the ones that can really help you through heartache. And believe me, love is no picnic. Even when you're little, like the time in second grade when I was in love with . . ."

I eye the class and notice that most people are either staring at their own notebooks or whispering to their friends, but just about no one is listening to Amelia. So maybe we do have one thing in common.

I darken the letters. D–I–S–A–P–P–O–I–N–T–E–D. It's a very long word, a word that does not fall easily off your tongue. I cover the first three letters with my thumb, *dis*, and instantly it becomes a neutral word. The word *appointed* carries no feelings. That means *dis* is the culprit.

"What stands out to you in this quote, Tere?" It's not until she says my name that I realize Ms. Peters is standing right in front of me. Her stubby hand rests on the corner of my desk and the tips of her maroon loafers are nestled underneath.

Why is she calling on me now? She knows I never have anything to say. What did I do? She's left me alone for over a month. I glance up at her bright red lips. She cracks a smile and moves her hand to my shoulder.

The whole class is silent. They're waiting for the death of me. I know I shouldn't be so dramatic, but whenever I'm forced to speak aloud, I like to at least have a little notice so I can mentally prepare.

Time seems to have stopped as Ms. Peters waits for my answer. The rest of the class waits, too. I look down at my paper, lick my dry lips and close my eyes. If I don't see all those eyes staring at me, then it's like I'm alone. Finally, I open my mouth, "Disappointed."

Ms. Peters waits for me to say more, but there is no more. She gets the hint and walks to the center of the room.

"Disappointed. When is love a disappointment?" she cheerfully asks the class.

Stacy's hand goes up. "When Frank dumps you."

Everyone laughs. Frank turns red because he dumped Stacy's best friend and volleyball captain, Laurie, last week.

I should raise my hand and say, *I have no idea what they're talking about.* That I've never had the chance to be the dumper or the dumpee. That it's nothing to laugh about or take for granted because not everyone gets a chance to experience love. But saying all that would definitely constitute public suicide.

Pretty soon people's hands shoot up, and they mention first

loves, broken marriages, Jerry Springer guests that cheat on their lovers—but no one says anything about actually being a disappointment.

Gavin Tam, the tall, slim guy on my right, with straight black hair and dark brown eyes, taps me on the shoulder. "I know what you mean. Love is a lie."

He does? I instinctively flip my notebook over to a fresh page. I force a smile from my lips. Maybe he really does.

He smiles, then goes back to giving himself a tattoo of weird squiggly lines on his arm. Besides me, he's probably the next quietest person in the class. But I don't think he has trouble speaking, he just chooses not to. Ms. Peters moved him next to me a month ago when she rearranged the seats. He's cute, but I've never had the nerve to ask him for more than a sheet of paper.

Ms. Peters tells us to use our free-writes and expand our thoughts into a two-page essay about an incident where a good friend really came through for us. She uses an example from her own childhood when a buddy looked out for her. Her ballet teacher said if she forgot her tights again for rehearsal, she wouldn't be in the show. Well, she forgot them. But her best friend Kate thought she might, so she spent her own allowance on a second pair of tights and kept them in her ballet bag as a spare for Ms. Peters.

I really can't think of anything like that. I stare at my blank page. Audrey is a good friend—don't get me wrong—but we're in the same boat. Neither of us asks for much and we try to stay out of the spotlight. I write her name up top of the page, hoping that will spark something. I look over at Gavin's paper to see if he's started the assignment. Man, does he have a lot to say. He's abandoned his tattoo art and is scrawling away in his notebook. I can't read a word of it, though, because his writing is small and slanty.

I check to the other side of me and see that Amy is busy writing, too. She has built a wall with her arm and has her nose to the paper, like someone might steal her response. *I'm sorry, Audrey. You really are a good friend.* I need to think harder, but I got thrown for a loop today. First I pissed off Stacy, then Ms. Peters called on me and I answered her question like a moron. Ugh. I shake my head back and forth. I need to let everything go. It's really no big deal.

I could make up a story. Write about all my best friends. How we have each other's backs. How we'd risk ruining everything just to help a girl out. I could have Ms. Peters in tears at the end of the essay, wishing she had a group as tight as mine. But I can't do that to her. To me.

Finally, I end up writing about the time my mother royally pissed me off because she said I dressed like a slob and that's why I didn't have any friends. Nice, huh? After I used up a box of tissues, mopping up my tears, I called Audrey and she had her dad come pick me up. We spent the night scarfing down pizza and watching TV. We didn't talk about my mom once because we had agreed long before that when we were mad about something, we needed to escape, not rehash what happened. She gave me the biggest hug when I left the next morning and told me if it wasn't for me, her one true friend, she'd be the most depressed person in the world. That made me feel important.

The bell rings as I'm still writing, and Ms. Peters tells us to have the papers typed up for her by Wednesday. I wait for Stacy to leave before I desuction myself from my plastic seat, but she doesn't even look at me. She's too busy flirting with Frank on the way out.

"Cool shirt," Gavin says as he shoves his books into his backpack.

I look down at the picture of the Escalade on my tee with the words *PJ Squid* written on the side in gold letters. Gavin knows who PJ Squid is? I thought he only listened to heavy metal and music about death.

I say "thanks" and look up, but Gavin's already at the door, tucking a piece of his chin-length hair behind his ear.

chapter FIVE

I'm starving when I meet up with Audrey for lunch in the court-yard. I usually have first lunch (since all the students can't fit into the cafeteria at once, we have three lunch periods at Ridgeland), before English, but our whole schedule was screwed up today because we had an all-school assembly during second period this morning on the Everglades. We've had the same monotone speaker for four years, and his speech hasn't changed a bit. He wouldn't last a second on the radio. Everyone would fall asleep at the wheel listening to him drone on about wildlife.

It's eighty degrees out, so Audrey and I sit near the coconut trees but not directly beneath them just in case a coconut decides to fall. Plus, one year a bird pooped on Audrey's head, and I had to help her wash it out. Not a pretty sight, especially in a bathroom full of dopers.

Audrey unwraps her ham-and-cheese sandwich. "Did you ask him?"

"Who?"

"Rob. Did you ask him if you could fill in at the station?"

"No way." I pull my string cheese apart like a wishbone.

"What's the worst thing that can happen?"

Three softball players rush past us. One's yelling into her cell phone, another is telling her what to say to the caller, and the third is sobbing. They're headed to the parking lot.

I unscrew the top to my water bottle and take a sip. "He could say no."

"Exactly my point."

"Or even worse, he could say yes." Then I'd have to face all those people, thousands of them, at their homes, jobs, sitting in traffic, jogging along bike paths, hanging around with friends. I would be a part of all of their lives and I wouldn't even know who they were. Frightening but also fascinating. Radio holds a lot of power. But how could someone as weak as me play such an important part in people's lives?

I pull out my iPod and hand one of the earbuds to Audrey. "Check this tune out. It's pretty fresh."

She sticks it in her ear. "Who's this?"

"Maltese. He's the guy with the six-pack. And a really good dancer."

"Ah, now I see why you like him!" She laughs.

A couple of populars walk by, salon-style hair dancing in the wind. I survey the area to make sure there are no cameramen filming a Pantene commercial. Both girls are talking on their jeweled cell phones. It would be funny if they were talking to each other just to seem important. That's something my mother would have done in high school. If I were one of the jeweled girls, she'd be thrilled. But even then I'm sure she'd find something else to complain about.

I notice that Gavin's sitting with a few friends against the side of the building. Two of them are talking, Gavin's listening to his iPod, and another guy's playing some little handheld game. But Gavin and the handheld guy are in the middle, so the other two have to talk over them. It's funny to watch.

"What do you think of Gavin Tam?" I nudge Audrey.

"The metal guy over there?" She points to the side of the building.

I slap her hand down. "Yeah. But he likes rap, too."

"Okay, the rap metal guy. What about him?"

"Oh, nothing. He's in my English class."

The corner of Audrey's lip goes up. "You like him?"

"No." I turn up the music a notch.

Audrey gets the message, and I cue up another hot jam. Neither of us wants to go back to class. Back to life. The way I see it, there are three parts to me. The way my mom wants me to be, the way I'm expected to act at Ridgeland, and the way I want to act.

I haven't figured that last part out yet, but I know it's not the way everyone else wants me to be.

Only two more classes left after lunch, then I'm home free. Audrey has band practice, otherwise I would've dragged her home with me. She tried forever to get me to join the band, but since I don't play an instrument, I thought it was a ludicrous idea. She said if I chose something like the clarinet, I could pretty much fake it because there were four other clarinet players. She, however, is a star French-horn player and certainly doesn't fake it.

After lunch I go left to sociology and Audrey goes the other way to Spanish. Ms. Collins makes us sit in alphabetical order. She says it's easier to take attendance, but I think it's just one of her cruel little experiments to see if I survive sitting in the first row. All my life, with the last name Adams, I've hated alphabetical order with a passion. I'm always first, unless Alison Abel or Phillip Abraham is in my class and then I'm second or third. My worst fear, that I've had ever since I entered high school, is that if Phillip and Alison are both sick the day of graduation, I will be the first person to walk up onstage in front of hundreds of people. To have so many eyes staring at me at once will make me go blind.

Luckily, Phillip is sitting next to me today. I peer over at him. Looks healthy, pink skin, no rings under the eyes, definitely no problem eating. Good, hopefully he can stay that way for the next few months. I'll cook his meals and do his homework if I have to.

Ms. Collins takes attendance; then Phillip raises his hand.

"What is it, Phillip?" Ms. Collins reaches for a stack of papers on her desk.

"I feel like I'm going to hurl. Can I get a pass to the nurse?"

Okay, so much for him being invincible. After he leaves, Ms. Collins hands out a pop quiz. Did Phillip have a premonition? Well, I'm happy to take the quiz if that means I won't be called on.

The quiz is easy. A few questions about societal norms from last week's reading and an essay question on how we would feel if we had an arranged marriage right after graduation. First off, if my mom chose the guy, it would be totally hopeless. No doubt he'd be hot, but his brain would be malnourished. He'd probably spend all day flexing in the gym mirror, and it'd only be a matter of months until he cheated on me.

But what if by some stroke of luck my mom happened to come across a guy that was good looking and intelligent? That would be amazing. I would never have to drool over guys again, wishing I had the courage to speak to them, wishing that one would ask me out.

Before Ms. Collins has even collected all the quizzes, some of the girls are already chatting about the essay question.

"I'd, like, slit my wrists if my parents chose a guy for me." Beth, senior class vice president, twirls a strand of hair.

"Yeah, my dad would pick the geekiest guy on the planet," another girl says.

Not my mom. She'd show up with a guy that's hotter than

Brad Pitt. She'd pull him out of a mental ward if she had to. To Mom, looks and first impressions are everything. That's probably one of the reasons why I'm such an introvert. I never wanted to say something wrong when I was little, give the wrong idea. I didn't want to make Mom angry, so I figured it was better to keep my mouth shut and let her do the talking. I guess after a while I just got used to it. I was comfortable with my role as the quiet observer.

Ms. Collins passes out a magazine article on arranged marriages. On the cover is a picture of a couple in their wedding attire, holding hands. Their smiles are so supersized, I'm afraid they might crack the page. The headline reads *American Christian Organization Promotes Arranged Marriages to Help Combat STDs.*

"Man that sucks. He's ugly," Beth whines. With her as our VP, we're *so* doomed.

"Yeah, if my parents made me marry a fat ugly chick, I'd be freakin' mad." Ken, the guy behind me slams his fist on his desk. I sink down in my seat and suck in my stomach. I look into the faces of the couple on the magazine cover. Nobody thinks about how the *unwanted* one feels. To get up every day and know that the other person is only with you because they have to be must really suck.

I read the story about Tom and Karen's arranged marriage in Indiana. About how Karen was really shy as a kid and how Tom helped her to open up. About how they are growing to love each other more every day. About how their church has adopted many

Indian customs to arranging marriages. I wonder if you can sign up for one of these services if you can't find a spouse. Or do you have to be enrolled by your parents?

The bell rings and I shove the article into my bag. I want to take it home and read it some more. I jet outside, missing most of the masses, and slip on my iPod. I roll up my sleeves and take in the afternoon heat.

★ ★ ★

This is Sweet T taking over the airwaves on 92.7 WEMD SLAM FM. It's a scorcher out there this afternoon, but don't worry, keep it locked here and I'll ice you down. Call me up at 1-800-555-SLAM and let me know what'll cool you off, Miami. Now grab a tall glass of sweet tea and blast your radio. Here's Maltese with "Put Your Finger on the Money" . . .

chapter SIX

I jet home in a record eighteen minutes; for once I didn't have to press any walk lights. The first thing I do is grab a Diet Coke and a box of Cheez-Its and crank up the music in my room. I love catching the end of Jack Cruise's show. He's the oldest DJ at the station, almost sixty, but one of the funniest guys. He's constantly cracking jokes about artists and how they misuse their time and end up getting busted for petty crimes.

"Love Wrecked" comes on the air, and I turn the volume up even louder. It's about a scorned guy that will never trust another woman. This topic fits right into Ms. Peters' Jane Austen quote today in class. Even though Panick is on top of the charts, I'm not sure Ms. Peters would appreciate me bringing the song in as an example of the message *love sucks.* I sing along with him, *"I sheltered you through the storm, you complained I could not perform, and left me out at sea."* Still, I think Ms. Austen would approve.

I slide on my wireless headphones that Rob gave me for my birthday. They bring me closer to the music. It's like the songs are being pumped into my veins. Rob usually gets me better gifts than Mom. I'd prefer a pair of surround sound headphones over a minimizer bra and a curling iron any day. These headphones transport me miles away from Earth. At least, that's how I feel when I'm wearing them.

* * *

Coming up next is the mad hot new release by Coil. Coil will be at Club Bed next Thursday on South Beach for a VIP party. When you hear their song, "Tempted," call me up at 1-800-555-SLAM. Caller number nine wins two tickets. Good luck, Miami!

* * *

I could do this gig—alone in my bedroom, that is. I love when people call in to win and they're champagne-toast excited! They scream into the phone and act like it's the best thing that's ever happened to them. I want to feel that ecstatic about something one day, even if it's winning tickets to a local show or complimentary laser hair removal. The only thing I ever won was a free bag of M&Ms, when I was eleven, but Mom wouldn't let me redeem my prize because she said I needed a free bag of candy like she needed another loser boyfriend. Total buzz kill.

I lie down on my bed with every intention of writing my English paper, but instead take a little catnap . . . okay, more like a brontosaurus nap. But I'm totally refreshed when I wake up. And hungry.

The TV's on downstairs, so I know Mom and Rob are home. I think about staying in my room, surviving on Cheez-Its and now flat Diet Coke, but my stomach pleads with me and I make my way to the food zone.

I nod hello to Mom and Rob in the family room and head to the kitchen. I think Mom's saying something to me, but I really can't hear anything with my music pumping. A commercial comes on the radio for Pizza Hut, and I fall prey to the advertising, only we don't have a steaming pepperoni pizza sitting on the counter, so I warm up the frozen Lean Cuisine veggie version.

The lovebirds have the MTV video countdown on, so I sit with them. They're cuddled up on the leather sectional together, her legs tucked under his side.

"Eating so late?" Mom asks me.

It depends on how you look at it. If we were in Australia, I would be eating very early. I say this all with my eyes, but my lips never move. Then I plunk down on the other end of the sofa.

"How was school?" She leans in closer to Rob.

"Okay. Got an A on my pre-calc test."

"That's nice." Mom smiles. "Any talk about the prom?"

"It's not until May." I cut my pizza into fours and take a bite.

"Yes, and that's in two months. These things are planned well in advance. I have a zillion ideas for the decorations."

I finish chewing. "They already have a decorating committee. Of seniors."

"Well, I'm sure they could use my help." She turns to Rob. "How about one of your DJs playing there?"

That would be cool.

Rob peels his eyes away from the bronze supermodel, Iola, on the TV. "Yeah, I'm sure we could work something out."

"Maybe Floss," I say. Diana does overnights at the station. She got the nickname Floss because she always gets between people and brings up the dirt. I like her because she doesn't take crap from anyone. She's made of steel.

"Diana, really? I thought you'd have chosen Garrison or Dave." Rob pulls Mom's foot out from under him and gives her a massage.

I sip my water and try not to look right at them. "Yeah, you're right. They'd want a guy."

"Who's they?" Mom asks.

"The prom freaks."

Mom wrinkles her forehead. "Freaks?"

"I'm talking about the popular girls. They always get what they want."

Mom shifts her body so Rob can massage her other foot. "What do you want, Teresa?"

"If I went, I'd want the best music. Not the bubblegum crap they play on Sun."

Rob laughs. "Yeah, I don't know what Mitch's been up to lately, but they've been playing a lot of training-bra artists."

"Huh?" Mom turns her head from Rob to me.

"Exactly!" I shove the last bite of pizza into my mouth.

Rob pulls Mom closer to him. "Just talking about our competition, babe. Maybe I should steal one of the weekend DJs from over at Sun to fill the evening slot. They're not under contract." He shakes his head. "Nah, they've probably been too warped by Mitch already."

I could do it. I practice saying it in my head but can't get the words out.

"So what are you doing about the prom?" Mom glares at me.

"I don't know." I thought that conversation was over.

"What do you know?" Mom takes a swig of her Miller Lite. "You don't care about the prom. You don't care about how you dress. You don't care—"

Rob elbows her in the stomach. "Enough."

My face is red. I turn my attention toward the TV. To Holly Lemon being interviewed poolside at her decked-out crib.

"That's not true," I whisper. My blood is boiling inside. What does she know about me? "I do want stuff," I shout.

"To burn around?" Mom's voice is iced over.

The camera pans to Holly making out with her boyfriend on her enormous canopy bed with red satin sheets. She says good night, blows a kiss to the camera, and the shot fades.

"I want to be a DJ," I say directly to Holly. I've wanted to be one since I was twelve. If Mom ever paid any attention to me, she would know this. I live, breathe, and dream about music.

"What? You can't even carry on a normal conversation," Mom snaps.

"I know more about songs than most people." I pull my iPod from my pocket. "See this? It's filled with all the new artists."

"You'd be better with something out of the public eye," Mom says.

"You don't have to be a prom queen to be on the radio, Mom. You just have to have passion for music." Even if she doesn't get it, it feels good to have said it out loud. Maybe if I say it enough times, it will finally stick. "I *want* to be a DJ."

"Yes, you said that." Mom fingers the sapphire choker around her neck. An early birthday present from Rob. "But I've never seen anyone in media that doesn't have at least some sort of sparkle."

"What matters most is what comes from inside." My heart is thumping hard. I place my hand on my chest to silence it.

"All I'm saying is you need to be realistic." Mom sighs.

Since when has *she* ever been realistic?

Rob grabs his BlackBerry from the coffee table. "Are you serious about this, Teresa?"

"Yes." I sit up straight.

He scrolls down the screen. "Okay, then. Come by the station at four tomorrow. You can sit in with Derek during his show. See what it takes to be a DJ."

"Really?" My face lights up. Maybe Rob was sent from up above to watch out for me and get Mom off my back.

Mom groans. "This could be humiliating."

"For who?" I hug myself tight.

"She's not doing anything after school anyway." Rob strokes Mom's face. "It'll be good for Tere to check out the real world."

Mom softens at Rob's touch. "Okay, but tell Derek if she gets in his way to send her home."

I smile at Rob. Then glare at Mom. I won't disappoint.

I don't even wait for her to throw more insults my way; I just run up to my room and scream into my pillow. I don't know how to feel. Half of me is dancing on air; the other half is ready to kiss the toilet and puke out my guts. This opportunity is the best and worst thing that's ever happened to me. I pick up the phone and call Audrey. Maybe she can make sense of all this.

"Good evening, this is Audrey speaking, how can I direct your call?"

Audrey always answers her phone with some kind of secretarial greeting. She's done this ever since she started helping out at her dad's dentist office the summer before seventh grade. What's even worse is that I have to listen to the whole greeting before I can say anything.

"Yes, can I speak with Audrey Craven please?"

"She's in a meeting right now. Can I take a message?"

"Yes, tell her that Sweet T called. The number one DJ for SLAM."

I've had my on-air name planned for a couple of years now. Well, ever since Great Aunt Bertie died. She was the one who gave me the name Sweet T. She'd brew a batch of tea and keep on adding more sugar until I told her it was enough. She used to say, *You love your sugar, girl. You're sweet tea.*

"No way!" Audrey screams into the phone. "You asked him? See, I told you that you'd make an awesome DJ."

"Calm down. Rob said I could come by the studio tomorrow and hang with Derek during his show. That's it."

"So cool! I know you can do it."

"Well, that makes one of us." I stare into the oval mirror over my bureau. I wonder if I'd be cuter with curly hair. I push up a clump of hair, let it go, and watch it fall right back down.

"Hey, maybe he'll let you make a shout-out."

I look up at my wall. Maltese is the first person I make eye contact with.

Ugh, what did I get myself into?

★ ★ ★

Good evening, Miami. This is Sweet T on 92.7 WEMD SLAM FM. It's Monday night and I've got plenty of slow jams lined up for you. If you're down, here's one that's sure to get your heart pumping again, "Believe in faith" . . .

chapter SEVEN

I hardly slept last night. My stomach was doing the limbo. I can't believe I told Rob my dream of being a DJ and he actually asked if I'd like to go to the station. I know he didn't do it for Mom because she made it quite obvious that I'd be better off working in some office basement than showing my face on-air. Which is a total joke because on the radio you can remain faceless.

I didn't choose radio because I want to hide. If that were the case, I would've said I wanted to work as a computer guru or something else that you can do from home. Some people think that shy people don't like interacting with others, that we're anti-social. But that is so not true. It just makes me nervous to be put on the spot, to have to talk to a large group or even people I don't know. So while I might not want to be a tour guide or the president, I've always loved radio. Music is great for any occasion. If you're sad, it cheers you up, and if you're happy, it helps you celebrate. Being a DJ allows you to provide the music that can guide people through good and bad times. And who hasn't been touched by at least one song in their lifetime?

As I walk through the halls of Ridgeland to first period, I wonder if anyone will remember me a year after we graduate. Five years? Ten years? My existence here is pathetic. It's not like I want to be prom queen and have my image emblazoned in everyone's mind for decades to come, but I want to be somebody. I think.

I wrestle with the lock on my locker and pull out my pre-calc book and the couple other books I need for the day. I see Stacy and her friends, Laurie and Valerie, walking toward me. They're all wearing short bouncy skirts and tight tops exposing some serious skin that I'm sure more than tempts the limits of the dress code. I duck my head into my locker in an attempt to hide.

Stacy stops next to me. "Boo."

I cringe and look up at her out of the corner of my eye. I shut my locker door and try to step around her and her crew, but they block me in.

"You heard me." She laughs. "I've just got one question. Are you retarded?"

My face heats up like a stove top, and I feel like I've got a spoonful of peanut butter lodged in my throat. I don't even bother formulating an answer.

Her friends burst out laughing. Then Laurie says, "If she is, how's she going to answer you?"

They laugh some more, until they sound like one of those overzealous laugh tracks on a failing comedy show.

The peanut butter thickens. I can hardly breathe. I don't look at their faces. Instead, I push through them, letting my stack of books serve as a shield.

Their cackles follow me as I speed-walk to class. I hurry to my seat in Ms. Peters' room and chug my water bottle until the peanut butter dissolves. I've gotten through three years of school without running into Stacy and her crew, and now two digs in one week. I must be getting lamer by the minute. Even if I could get out the words to let Stacy know how hard I tried to tell Ms. Peters she was going to be late, she'd never understand.

I take out my notebook and doodle, mostly flowers. They don't start out dead, but by the time I'm done drawing, they're all wilted. Gavin is drawing, too. His doodles actually look like abstracts. He's back to squiggly lines, but there's a definite pattern to them.

He's wearing another all-black outfit today. I can't make out what it says on his shirt, but there's a silhouette of a guy on a skateboard on the front.

"You skate?" Gavin lifts his head from his masterpiece.

Me? Oh, great, he thinks I was staring at him. I wasn't! Okay, maybe a little, but I was just trying to make out the words on his shirt.

I shake my head and point to him.

"Yeah, I got a board."

I picture him sliding down the front steps at the regional library, with the security guard a few feet behind him, yelling at him to get lost, while Gavin's black hair flies in the wind like a flag of defiance. I never noticed how dark his hair is before. I mean, it's really black. Some people would kill for hair like that!

I smile at him and quickly look away. He seems oblivious, so I immediately go back for seconds. I can't help myself—he's such a cutie. The type of person who, the more you get to know them, the cuter they are. And trust me, smiling directly at a guy is a lot for me.

I sneak a few peeks at Gavin all through the Jane Austen reading. He has one eye on the book and the other on his notebook. I can't believe we've gone to school together for the past four years and this is the first year that my radar has picked up on him. Freshman and sophomore year, I spent most of the time drooling over Patrick Olsen, the guy with the English accent. He had such a sexy voice, and the funny thing is I never spoke to him, not even once. He moved away at the end of sophomore year. And the next year was a real toss-up. I went out to dinner with Audrey and a couple of band guys. But Gerald, my date, was a strict opera buff. We were such music polar opposites that I don't even know why Audrey bothered setting us up.

Ms. Peters reads most of the chapter and calls on a few volunteers. Luckily, I'm spared for today. At the end of class Gavin has filled a whole notebook page with his geometric design.

I stand over it as I zip up my backpack. Something about all those lines and shapes pull me in.

"If you stare at it for long enough, you'll go blind," Gavin says with a straight face. His dark brown eyes look like onyx. I watch as a smile tiptoes across his face.

"I like." *I like it.* Okay, now he must think I'm an idiot. Maybe Stacy's right. I am retarded. I walk briskly out the door and don't even bother peering back. The first real words I say to Gavin put me back in preschool. Maybe I'd have better luck talking to a toddler.

I don't see Gavin for the rest of the day, and that's fine with me. It's only right that I keep away from him, for at least twenty-four hours, to make sure this stupidity virus isn't contagious.

I head off to pre-calc. I've got an A so far in that class and don't want to screw it up by speaking.

Pre-calc's a breeze because we work on our own most of the class, and in sociology we have a sub and watch a short documentary about arranged marriages. The whole idea of marriage is kind of freaky. I mean, I don't have the best role model, that's for sure. I hope Mom stays with Rob forever because he's way better than all her old boyfriends and definitely better than her first husband, Tony. I wonder if my dad is married. He probably lives in some huge mansion on the beach with a wife and five kids. I'm sure he has no idea I exist. Definitely no room for me in his perfect world.

Next is my free period. I decide to spend the time de-moronizing myself after my speech flub with Gavin. If I'm hanging out at SLAM today, I have to not only be able to speak, but speak properly.

Maybe if I loosen my vocal cords, I'll feel more comfortable on Derek's show later. I can try some of the exercises that the chorus teacher had us do in middle school, but all that comes to mind is "moo." Somehow I don't think me standing in the court-yard mooing will help my social status.

I lean against the concrete wall between the cafeteria and the library, trying to come up with an idea. I could read a book aloud, but the thought of anyone hearing me clamps my mouth shut. There has to be a place around here where I can rehearse with-out being labeled a nut. The library? No, too quiet. Mr. Sanchez lets kids hang in the ceramics studio, but no one *reads* in there. People practice in those little booths in the language lab. That might be a good place. I mean, how could it possibly be full? It's not high on the popular hangout spots, so it should be safe. This just might work! I head down the hall, snacking on pretzels, my lunch leftovers.

The room is lined with small booths and chairs. At the front Mrs. Tripp is thumbing through a catalog, marking certain items. On her desk is a sign-up sheet. I fill out my information.

"What would you like to work on?" she asks.

The peanut butter is there again, but I swallow hard. "Pronunciation."

"What language are you taking?"

"English."

"Excuse me?" She puts down her stack of mini Post-its.

Okay, wrong answer. I took Spanish in middle school and my first year of high school and German last year. Just enough to fill the school's foreign language requirement. *"Deutsch."*

"First year?"

I nod. I hardly remember anything.

A minute later Mrs. Tripp comes back from the supply closet with a CD and a companion workbook. I choose a booth in the back and plug in the headphones. These hard plastic clunky things are nothing like the soft leather ones I have at home.

At first I let the disc run and don't say anything, listening to the thick German accent. It starts off pretty easy, counting from one to twenty. I don't know how they communicate with all those hard K sounds. I'm afraid I'd accidentally let loose some flying spit and hit someone in the eye. Not so attractive for a speech-deprived girl.

I glance around the lab. There's only one other student in here and she's on the other side of the room. I doubt she can hear me with her headphones on.

I breathe deep. *I can do this.*

I begin the lesson again and whisper, *"Eins, zwei, drei . . ."* One . . . two . . . three. Short and sweet. That wasn't so bad.

I quickly scan the room again to make sure nobody else has showed up.

Coast is clear. I move on to short sentences. *"Ich habe eine gute idee."*

I have a good idea? I'm not so sure about that. After a while I pick up the momentum and am repeating every word after the speaker.

Wo ist die Toilette?

Ich fühle krank.

Where is the toilet? I feel sick. Those are two sentences I should definitely hold on to in case I ever travel to Germany.

I take a break and look around again. It's pretty sparse except for the posters of Spain, France, and Germany on different walls. It's really strange to be here willingly. Most people are sent here begrudgingly by their foreign language teachers. At least no one knows my true mission—me giving up my free period to practice German. Yeah, I'm cool.

Finally Mrs. Tripp comes over to my station and tells me that school is over.

I practice my verbal skills on her. *"Danke."*

She smiles and takes my materials back, and I head off to the library to do my homework. I have to hang around the school for over an hour. I stay until it's time to catch the Number 16 bus downtown at three-fifteen. It's only a twenty-minute ride to the station, then I'll be driving home with Rob. I told Mom that it'd be a whole lot easier if I had my own set of wheels. She said,

"We'll see about that after graduation." But that's almost three months away and doesn't help me now.

The whole bus ride I practice speaking in my head, but after a few minutes I find myself counting in German. For some reason it's more soothing.

A couple of stops away from the station, an old guy nudges me in the side. "Welcome to Miami," he says.

I jolt my head back. Who does he think I am? I certainly don't look like any famous celebrities.

"Do you like living in Germany?" he inquires so loudly that the couple in front of us turns around.

"Ahh," I point to myself.

"Your accent is very nice. I heard you counting the stops. Lived in Berlin as a teenager." He grins like a kid. "My father was in the military."

I smile and nod. I can't believe the words slipped out without me even knowing.

The bus screeches to a halt and the man stands up. "Miami's a big city; watch out."

"Danke," I whisper.

There's nothing like the truth.

chapter EIGHT

I've never been to SLAM alone before. There's no one to hide behind today. Maybe Mom's right. I'm not ready for this. My whole body's shaking by the time I reach the station. I feel like an earthquake victim. Maybe I should turn around, forget the whole thing, and catch the next bus home. Mom would be happy, but I would not.

I clutch my backpack with one hand and grasp the handle to the front door with the other. If I hold on to something, maybe the trembling will stop. I take small steps until I reach the security desk in the middle of the lobby. The sign-in sheet glares at me. I write down my name and where I'm going, then hand the guy my driver's license.

"Here to pick up a prize?" he asks me.

"My dad." I point to the elevator. I can't believe I just called Rob my dad, but there's no way I'm correcting myself.

"Oh, you're here to pick up your dad." He nods.

I nod back so he doesn't think I'm some psycho. Then I take off to the second floor before I change my mind about being here. I open the glass door and step inside. The station seems a lot bigger than it was last week.

There's a new girl sitting at the front desk answering phones. Maybe Patty's solitaire addiction finally got the best of her. New Girl can't be much older than me. She's wearing a supertight, low-cut SLAM tank. Her boobs look like Pop-Tarts sticking out of the toaster.

Pop-Tart snaps her gum at me. "Can I help you?"

I swallow hard. "Derek."

"What?" She cups her hand over her ear.

I open my mouth wider but don't look directly at her. "Derek."

"What about him?" The phone rings and she answers it, "SLAM 92.7 . . ."

It's not easy dealing with the dense ones.

I look at the carpet and wait until she transfers the call. "Tere Adams," I say.

"Nobody by that name works here." She wrinkles her nose.

I point to myself.

"Oh, *you're* her. I get it." She picks up the phone. "I'll let Derek know you're here."

I play with one of the loops on my jeans. I sneak a quick glance at the red couches. Two old ladies armed with clipboards are sitting there with a large plastic jar stuffed with dollar bills nestled in between them. I wonder what they're collecting money for. I squint to read the label on the jar. It says *Edna's College Fund*. Okay, I guess it's never too late to realize your dream. I wonder which one is Edna.

Pop-Tart puts down the phone. "He says to go right in."

I start to walk away but she yells, "Wait."

I quickly stop. What's wrong? My face goes beet red. Is my fly down or something?

She leans over the counter. "It's so cool that you're here."

Really? Rob told everyone I was coming? How sweet.

Pop-Tart leans over even more, letting it all hang out. "This is incredible. I've never met a deaf person before."

Oh, brother, this girl needs more than Hooked on Phonics.

A lady in a black suit passes me as I walk down the hallway. She must work in the sales department. Those are the only people that really dress up around here.

I stand outside the studio and wait until the on-air light goes off. The hallway is filled with photos of the DJs and celebs that have come by the station. In front of me, I'm staring at a picture of Rob and Gracie May at the New Year's Eve bash. I've never seen Rob smile that widely before.

The light goes off, but my stomach is back to the limbo. I just stand there for a moment. *I can do this. I have to do this.* I grasp the door handle before I change my mind. Derek's at the board with his back to me.

I don't move from the door, hoping he'll eventually turn around. But instead, he leans over the laptop plugged in next to him. The lights on the request lines are blinking, but I know he has two interns down the hall answering those calls.

I shuffle to the center of the studio now and rustle the keys in my pocket. Finally Derek swings around. "Oh, hi. Tere, right? Rob told me you'd be stopping by."

Derek reaches out his hand and shakes mine. His palms feel like sandpaper. I quickly pull away.

He's wearing the same orange shirt as last Friday, with the first three buttons undone. A gold chain rests between the hairs on his chest. It's a figure of a woman with huge breasts. Actually, it would be more accurate to say, it's a pair of gigantic boobs with a woman's body attached to them.

So I shouldn't be surprised that he's staring at my chest right now. I let go of his hand. If he needs someone to drool over, Pop-Tart has a pretty nice set.

"Like what you see?" He laughs. "They don't call me Dynamite Derek for nothing."

I cringe. There's nothing dynamite about this guy. Yeah, he still has his hair and is in good shape for forty, but if he walked into a room full of high school girls, we'd all think he was some lounge singer hired to entertain the teachers at a retirement party. He's got a good on-air voice, though. I'll give him that.

Derek goes back to his laptop, so I just continue standing in the middle of the room like a coatrack. I need to talk to him. Otherwise, he'll tell Rob I hung around here like a fungus.

"Thanks," I mutter.

He doesn't answer me, so I try it again. "Thanks . . . for letting me chill here."

"Damn," he says to the computer. At least I think he's talking to the computer.

Finally he turns around. "Sorry, thought I had the wrong commercial loaded. Those plastic surgery people are always counting to make sure all their slots run." He plays with a few levels on the board. "Oh, and you're welcome. Anything for the boss's kid." He laughs. "Sit down." He points to the chair a few feet away from him.

I sit. It's one of those swivel office chairs. It'll make a good getaway vehicle if needed.

"You want to be a DJ?" he asks.

I nod but realize he doesn't have eyes on the back of his head, so I clear my throat and say, "Yeah."

"Got to pick out a name first. What do you want to be called?" Derek turns around to face me and leans back on the console, exposing even more chest hair. Something I didn't think was possible. "Trixie? Bubbles? Baby?"

Wait, is this a strip club or a radio station? I instinctively pull up the neck of my scoop tee. "Sweet T."

If I had a turtleneck with me, I'd put it on right now.

"That'll work. A name and a voice is all you got out here in radio land." Derek fades down the Maltese track and brings up Gracie May.

"Now that's a sexy woman. I wouldn't mind getting into her pants." Derek grins.

I don't say anything and it's not because I don't have anything to say, it's just that I have nothing nice to say.

"You don't talk much," Derek says.

"Nope." I cross my arms.

"That can be a good thing, too." He winks at me. His brown eyes are soulless.

God, I know he's good at his job, but one dose of him is enough to send anyone into cardiac arrest.

Just when I think he's done talking, he swings his chair around again. "By the way, you're in violation of the dress code."

"Huh?" I look down at my Little Miss Trouble tee and jeans. Since when does anyone other than the salespeople dress up at a radio station?

He points directly at my breasts and laughs. "So you're trouble? That's a provocative statement. You can't wear anything *suggestive* here."

Does he really think he's funny? I'm trashing this shirt as soon as I get home.

Jason, Derek's producer, busts into the studio with a box of Krispy Kreme doughnuts. "Here you go, dude." He slaps them on the console next to Derek. Unlike Derek, Jason's very clean-cut. He's tall, with blond hair and hazel eyes. He's GQ to Derek's Unpopular Mechanic.

"Man, you're good." Derek pulls out a glazed and takes a huge bite. Before he's even finished chewing, he asks, "You want?"

"No." I grab my bottle of water to clear out my throat. He is so gross.

Derek's halfway through a second doughnut when the song ends and he has to go back on the air. "Good evening, South Florida, it's Dynamite Derek helping you survive the drive home . . ."

Jason mouths to me. "Who are you?"

I make a *T* sign with my hands.

He mouths, "Time-out?"

"Intern," I say softly. It makes things easier.

"Ahh." He nods and jumps onto the computer. As soon as he's finished, he swivels around to face me. "Since I'm sure Derek didn't tell you what a studio intern's duties are, I'll fill you in."

"Thanks," I say and pull a small notebook and pen from my backpack.

Jason brushes away the paper. "Nothing formal. When you get here, just check the commercials loaded on the computer against the printout for the show. You'll find the printout next to the console."

That's all?

Jason continues, "You'll help on phones as needed and any-thing else that comes up during the show, promotions, giveaways, etc. Any questions?"

"No." I shake my head, and before I can think of anything else to say, Jason is back to the computer, pulling up a song for Derek.

That's what I like about radio, there's no downtime. You talk, listen to music, do a few shout-outs and before you know it, it's time to sign out and hand the mike over to the next DJ. I still don't know how I got the guts to talk Rob into letting me give this radio gig a try. But I'm glad I did. Despite the fact that Derek is a major slime dog, I think I'm going to like it here.

chapter NINE

Gavin looks different today. I'm not sure why, though. Piece of hair hanging over his left eye. Check. Dark brown eyes. Check. Faded jeans. Check. T-shirt. It's red. *Whoa, back up.* That's like me showing up to school in a string bikini. I lean forward and notice that it's a Speed Bump tee. Not exactly alternative music but definitely good stuff. They're one of the groups that Rob's trying to get to play at the SLAM Summer Bash in July. This is the fifth year in a row that the station is sponsoring a huge outdoor concert at Bayside with over fifteen different artists. The concert starts at noon and goes until eleven at night. I've been for the past three years, and it's such a blast! Of course, it would be better if I could go without my mom, but I can't complain because we always get backstage passes.

I wait until Gavin looks up from his paper.

"Nice," I whisper to his shirt.

"Thanks. My mom was just happy that I wore a color other than black."

I laugh.

"I'm going with my brother to see them play in May."

"Really, when?"

"I think it's the second or third weekend. I know it's a Friday."

"Oh." My heart sinks. The small venue on the Beach. They're already sold out. I should've asked Rob for tickets, but Mom always tells me not to be too greedy, that the tickets need to go to his staff, too. Of course, when she wants to go to a concert, she doesn't waste a second to ask for not only the tickets, but also the best seats.

Ms. Peters asks everyone to quiet down and takes attendance. Stacy's absent. *Darn.*

We hand in our homework. Then we're instructed to break up into pairs. After being called on to speak in class, pairing up is the next kiss of death for me. I immediately go into invisible mode and stare down at my notebook, my hair covering as much of my face as possible.

Waiting for everyone else to pair up always seems like an eternity. I know the drill: there are a few seconds of *do I have any friends in this class* panic, followed by excited voices calling to each other across the room. Then, when there's only one person left, they can come and grab me. I resume doodling to look busy, while people crisscross in front and back of me to find their perfect match. I don't look up because I don't want anyone to see me, feel bad for me. I'm used to being picked last. The only time it sucks is when we have an uneven number and the teacher has to place me with two people who chose each other, leaving me the third wheel. Or worse, I have to partner with the teacher. That thankfully hasn't happened since freshman year science when I burnt the tip of Mr. Cronin's pinkie.

Okay, time to work out the logistics. At the start of the semester there were twenty-eight students in this class, but three got schedule changes and then we got a new guy from another school. That makes us an even twenty-six, which is great except if Stacy's absent that would mean, she'd be . . . my partner. No way! I can't let this happen. Being her partner is like having all my eyelashes plucked out by a tiger.

Gavin, what about Gavin? I like him; he talks to me. I tap his desk and point to him, then me.

"Sorry." He shrugs. "Kayla already asked. We're in history together."

A funny acid taste rises to my mouth. Being Stacy's partner is not an option. I'll have to tell Ms. Peters, forge a note from my mom. Anything.

I close my eyes. I imagine Stacy laughing at me uncontrollably after she has told the whole class that I'm retarded. This is not happening.

"Okay, is everyone paired up?" Ms. Peters asks the dreaded question.

"One extra." Amelia points to me. God, can't she keep her mouth shut?

I sink into my seat and grab hold of the legs of the desk. My hands are sweaty. My head is spinning.

"Stacy's absent," Beth says.

Remind me never to vote for her for student office again.

"Yes, but we're starting the project in class today." Ms. Peters looks at me with sympathy in her eyes.

"You could be her partner," Frank yells.

He might as well shout, *Loser alert, aisle two!* I bite the insides of my cheeks and close my eyes.

"Tere could join us," Gavin offers.

A sympathy vote from the cute guy—I'm so humiliated.

Ms. Peters claps her hands. "Excellent. Now get into your groups and I'll pass out the assignment."

"But that means you'll have two groups of three, then," Beth whines.

"That's fine," Ms. Peters says. "And the rest of you will stay in pairs."

I don't move. Chairs are being dragged all around me. I don't want to mess up Gavin and Kayla's perfect twosome. I would give anything to be invisible right now.

"Come on, Tere. Move your desk up." Kayla found a seat in front of Gavin and has turned herself around to face us. She doesn't look like his type. She takes photos for the school paper and is really upbeat. She's wearing all pink, even her shoes.

"Okay, I'll do it for you." Kayla shoots up and grabs hold of my desk. I stand up inside it and walk as she slides it closer to her.

Ms. Peters places the assignment on Kayla's desk. Kayla reads aloud, "Each of you needs to pick an author, living or dead, that you admire. Of course, each choice is subject to my approval . . ."

"Geez, even teachers have disclaimers these days," Gavin grumbles.

Kayla and I both laugh—she like a lion. Me like a kitten.

Kayla continues reading, "The next step is to read one of their books and find out as much as you can about them. You will prepare your finding in a two-page paper. See attached handout."

Kayla stops reading. "What does this have to do with a group project?"

Ms. Peters is walking around the class and stops in front of her. "Read on."

"Oh, right." Kayla smiles. "You will then become this author and decide what would happen if your two choices met in person. You can perform a short scene, write a poem, sing a song, but whatever you choose, it needs to be done orally. Twelve to fifteen minutes for each project."

Okay, my brain froze when she said perform. No. Way. Do they have any mute authors? Because otherwise I'm not doing this assignment. I can't.

"This'll be fun!" Kayla puts down the paper and pulls a book out of her bag. "I'm Judy Blume, all the way." She holds up the author's photo to her face. "See, we even have the same haircut."

Scary.

"What about you guys?" Kayla asks.

"Definitely Stephen King." Gavin pushes a strand of hair from his face. I watch it fall right back.

Kayla makes a gagging sound. "That guy is gruesome."

"I know." Gavin grins.

Kayla and Gavin definitely don't like each other. I grin, too.

"So what about you?" Kayla jabs me lightly with the corner of Judy Blume's *Summer Sisters.*

"No performance." I shake my head.

Kayla looks at Gavin and rolls her eyes. "I hope there's not a problem here. I need to keep my 5.0. I'm still waiting to hear from Duke. It's my first choice."

Maybe they shouldn't have let me in their group. I don't want to be the reason that Kayla has to go to community college instead of her dream school.

Gavin doesn't catch her eye rolls because he's busy drawing. Looks like he's as thrilled as me about this project. "Well, I'm already in at the University of Central Florida, so I'll just take the F." He looks up from his paper with a smirk.

Kayla narrows her eyes. "Not funny."

"We'll figure something out," Gavin says.

"Like what?" Kayla asks.

"Mute," I offer.

"No, you're not." Kayla sighs.

Gavin stifles a laugh. "Helen Keller."

"You want her to be Helen Keller?" Kayla points to me, like she can't figure out who Gavin's talking about.

I don't know why I never thought of Helen Keller before in all my years of losing sleep and throwing up over oral reports. "Okay." I tap my hand on my desk.

Gavin looks up from his drawing. An enormous dog is spread over the page. It's eyes are fierce. "Cujo."

"God, help us," Kayla murmurs and flips to a fresh notebook page. She writes down the names of our author picks in big bubbly letters. "This is going to be one weird meeting."

I stare down at the dog. It's a Saint Bernard.

* * *

Good evening, Miami. This is Sweet T on 92.7 WEMD The SLAM. It's Wednesday night, hump day, and if you've made it this far, you can survive the rest of the week. Still in doubt? Be caller number ninety-two and I'll hook you up with a pair of tickets to see Maltese on Saturday night at Club Zen. Here's Maltese with "Melt Down." He can melt me down anytime. Have you seen the abs on this guy?

chapter TEN

It would be cool if I could fast-forward the school day to English class. We're working on our group projects today. That means no one's going to call on me and hopefully no one's going to humiliate me. I know eventually we'll have to stand up in front of the class to deliver our presentations, but as long as I don't have to talk, I can hack it. And in the meantime, I get to scoot my desk next to Gavin—the highlight of my day.

My morning classes blur by with a sub left over from the Dark Ages in pre-calc and a sociology pop quiz designed to stump even the reigning *Jeopardy!* champ. I hope Ms. Collins pities us and uses a huge sliding scale when she grades the quizzes.

I'm not looking forward to lunch because Audrey's absent today, which means I have to eat alone. How dare she get a sore throat? Definitely poor planning! I should really think about getting a backup friend. There are a couple of girls in my pre-calc class that I could sit with, but they usually end up droning on about the homework. Not a relaxing way to spend lunch.

I chow my blueberry muffin at my locker. Now what? I still have twenty-eight minutes left until class starts. It's time to loosen my vocal cords so I can talk to Gavin and Kayla. I want to seem at least halfway intelligent in our group discussion, so I head to the language lab.

On the way, I pass the band room. Maria, one of the French-horn players, is standing at the door. She waves me over. "Hi, Tere. Where's Audrey?"

"Sick."

"Is she okay?" Maria's brows connect. I mean, really connect.

I fold my arms. "Sore throat."

"We need her to prepare for competition this weekend." Maria sighs. "Hope it's not strep."

Doug pops his head out of the band room. "I called her last night. She sounded bad."

"Hope you don't get it." Maria smirks. Doug asked Audrey to the prom months ago. Not that he needed to ask her, because they've basically attended every school function together since they met in ninth grade band. It's like they have a mutual understanding that unless one of them finds their soul mate, they're going to be together. I wonder what will happen next year when they're at separate colleges.

Doug makes kissy sounds and steps closer to Maria.

"Gross." She shakes her head. I swear the band geeks are one incestuous group!

And on that note, I say good-bye and keep on walking. I guess I could've eaten lunch with them. But then I'd probably have to hang in the band room, and that's usually filled with people jabbering nonstop.

When I open the door to the language lab, Mrs. Tripp is seated at her desk, eating a salad. I wonder if she counts each bite that she chews. Not a paper is out of line on her desk. Her hair is neatly slicked back in a low ponytail. She looks so methodical.

I fill out my info on the sign-in sheet and clear my throat. She sets down her fork. "German again?"

I nod.

I'm the only one in here today, which is good because I really have to work on enunciating. I was reading a report online last night that said if you enunciate well but speak softly, people can still understand you easier than someone who speaks loudly but slurs their words together.

I flip the German workbook to page five where I left off yesterday. Days of the week. I can handle this.

Sonntag. Montag. Dienstag. Mittwoch. Donnerstag. Freitag. Samstag.

I pause the CD and repeat each word slowly again, making sure I pronounce every syllable. I don't stop until the corners of my mouth are wet. I fish in my bag for a tissue and wipe my lips. I wonder if the Germans go through more tissues per person than Americans. Even the work *Kleenex* sounds kind of German.

"I'm a dorkstag," I hear someone whisper.

Did someone record over the CD? But it's on pause. I fiddle with the buttons just to make sure.

I hit play and repeat the days of the week. This time a little softer. *"Sonntag. Montag . . ."*

"Dorkstag. Geekstag. Freaktag . . ."

There it is again. What the hell is going on? I double-checked to make sure no one else was here when I came in. Maybe if I ignore it, it will go away.

"Mittwoch. Donnerstag . . ."

The other voice speaks again, "Loserwoch. Dogstag . . ."

I'm afraid to turn around. My ears are burning like red-hot pokers. Is there a Kick Me sign on my back? I reach over my shoulder blade and feel around to make sure nothing's there. I know it sounds like I'm paranoid, but it's happened before. In the seventh grade I wore a Kick Me sign half the day until the custodian pulled it off my back. I knew this kid named Heath put it there in homeroom because he used the other side of his detention slip.

I turn my head slightly. Out of the corner of my eye, I spy a long tanned leg stretched out from the booth behind me. Well, it's definitely not a guy.

I tilt my head around even farther, hoping Mystery Bitch will go away, but she speaks again, "I'm a dork, I'm a dork . . ."

I lean back a little more, trying to catch a glimpse of her.

She leans forward, her straight golden-brown hair framing her face.

Damn, it's Stacy. I should've known. What's she doing here? Doesn't Mrs. Tripp hear her creepy voice?

I turn to the front of the room, but Mrs. Tripp isn't there. I wouldn't be surprised if Stacy swallowed her whole.

I pop out the German CD and pack up my stuff. My cover has been compromised; I have to motor out of here.

"Leaving so soon?" Stacy laughs.

I don't move, but I can feel the heat from her eyes burning holes in the back of my head.

She screeches her chair on the linoleum. "At least we know you're not mute."

I will not turn around.

I make my way up to the front of the room as Stacy throws one last dig at me. "A mutant, maybe." She laughs big this time.

I leave my book on Mrs. Tripp's desk, sign out, and quickly zip out the door before Stacy comes up with any other award-winning insults.

I spend the last ten minutes of lunch in the bathroom stall reading my sociology book. I have to remind myself that people like Stacy have nothing better to do with their time than make fun of the unpopular. But it still hurts.

I make sure I'm in Ms. Peters' class before Stacy. If I'm nestled between Kayla and Gavin, then she can't bother me. Besides, she joined Frank's group, and it seems like he's her latest conquest. Hopefully he'll keep her away.

Kayla plunks down with her monstrous pink backpack. "Where do you guys want to meet?"

"We're meeting right now," Gavin says.

"Yeah, but that's only for half the class period." Kayla rolls her eyes like Gavin has no idea what he's talking about.

"The project isn't due until May first. That's six weeks away," he says.

"Great, that gives us a lot of time to make sure it's perfect." Kayla smiles. "Besides, it's spring break next week and I'll be out of town."

Gavin sighs, then turns to me. "Have you gotten your book yet?"

I shake my head.

"Well, if we meet first, then we can have an idea of where the project is going. Anyway, how long does it really take to read a book?" Kayla pulls out her laptop.

"I know King pretty well already," Gavin says.

"And I finished *Summer Sisters* in a weekend." Kayla holds up the paperback again.

They both stare at my face. Great, now it's all up to me. I bite my lip and nod.

"We could meet on Sunday. You can get the book today and

finish it by then, right?" Kayla leans in close and speaks real slow, like she's talking to a three-year-old.

When her gaze doesn't move from me, I respond, "Okay."

"Whose house?" Kayla asks. "My grandparents are visiting, so mine's out."

How convenient. Well, I can't have them at mine. Mom would be hovering over us the whole time. Then after they left, she'd tell me how I should've sat up straighter, spoken louder, and acted peppier. No thanks.

I remember once when I was in seventh grade this new girl, Daria, came over to my house to work on a science project. She talked more than a TV commentator and ended up chatting with my mom the whole time. I felt like I was invisible that day and ended up finishing the whole project myself, while Daria gave Mom a tutorial on Internet shopping. It was like I wasn't even there.

"My mom's sick," I blurt out.

"Is she okay?" Gavin asks.

"Yeah." I twist the drawstring of my sweatpants.

It's not a total lie. Mom could quite possibly be sick by Sunday. After all, she is sick in the head.

A voice comes over the PA asking for Stacy Barnes to report to the main office. I hope she's suspended. Indefinitely this time.

"My place is fine," Gavin says.

We agree to meet at Gavin's house at three, after Kayla goes to church and plays two hours of tennis. After I wake up at noon and watch MTV until it's time to throw on a pair of sweats.

I wonder what Gavin's mom looks like. All I can picture is a smaller version of him with the same black hair. Maybe she has tattoos and piercings and wears all black. Too bad I can't find out in advance and dress accordingly.

Right after school I check out Helen Keller's autobiography, *The Story of My Life,* from the school library. There are a few biographies, too, and a book she wrote with someone else, but I want the real deal. I want to know how Helen did it. How she conquered life being deaf and blind. It's a nice day, so I climb up the bleachers and read until it's time to catch the bus to the station. I read for almost an hour without taking a break.

Helen has so much to say that it seems like she hardly ever had time off. She took the crappy deal that she got out of life and actually made something out of it. Even after only reading the first few chapters of her story, I already feel guilty. Guilty for thinking that there's no worse fate in life than having to stand up in front of my English class and present an oral report.

I close my eyes as I make my way down the metal steps, but I stumble on the second step and snap them open. I don't know how Helen did it. Entered a world she couldn't see or hear.

When I was little, around four or five, I sometimes used to walk around the house with my eyes closed, feeling the walls. It drove my mom crazy. She said it gave her the heebie-jeebies.

That's one of the things I like about music, you don't have to see to feel it. I whip out my iPod and let the sounds of Gracie May pump through my veins. I wonder how Beethoven composed music deaf. How did he feel the beat? My sneakers move to the rhythm as I make my way down Marlin Avenue. I picture myself in a music video, gliding down the street, surrounded by fancy cars. I move, one foot at a time. One beat at a time. Until I see the bus pull up and I'm still about one hundred feet away. This time I have to motor faster than the beat or I can kiss getting to the station on time good-bye. My foot hits the last step as the door hisses to a close. I slide my bus pass through the turnstile and slowly catch my breath.

chapter ELEVEN

Pop-Tart doesn't disappoint. She's at the front desk in a skin-tight Lycra tee with the word *Huh?* stretched across her breasts. She's moving her hands back and forth at a rapid pace like she's directing airport traffic. If only the person on the other line could see her now. Of course, if it's a guy, he'd be frothing at the mouth.

She finishes her call and waves to me. "Sorry, they didn't understand my directions. What's up?" she says slowly as she elaborately mouths the words, her lips stretched wide.

"Nothing." I sign in with her fluffy purple pen. Definitely not radio station issued.

"You read lips?" Pop-Tart asks.

"No." I squeeze past her.

"Oh, sorry," she says. "I don't know sign language."

I turn around to face her. "Me neither."

"Okay." She tilts her head to the side. Her big clunky hoop earrings swing back and forth like pendulums. "This is going to be hard."

The phone rings and she breathes a sigh of relief. Wouldn't want her to think too long; her lightbulb might burn out.

Jason's walking out the door when I reach the on-air studio. "Red Bull run."

I just nod. Does this poor guy do anything else besides play fetch for Derek?

I slide my book bag off my shoulder and lean against the wall. Derek's bound to turn around soon. I stare at my raw cuticles in the meantime. I could definitely use a cleanup. Next time Mom's on the attack, I'll let her fix up my nails.

Derek rolls his chair back. "Oh, I didn't see you there. You're like a cat. You just slink right in."

He's staring at me like he's waiting for an answer, but I don't have one.

"You like cats?" he purrs.

Ew. That is so nasty.

I nod.

"Bet you're a real kitty cat in . . ." He wheels his chair closer to me. "Wait, are you eighteen?"

"Yes," I mutter.

"Still. I better stay away." He stretches his legs out in front of him. "You have one?"

I grit my teeth and try to spray some venom on him. "One what?"

"Cat."

"Mom's allergic."

"Me, too. I knew your mom and I had something in common. She's a cougar." He laughs.

Ugh, if he were my stepdad, I'd slit my wrists.

The song "Doomed Tuesday" is fading out, so Derek quickly turns back to the console. He slides down the tune just in time and brings up an old Thwart song. This one's before the band went mainstream, when they still had a lot of grunge to their sound. They had a different bassist back then who was known for performing amazing impromptu solos at many live venues.

"Old Thwart." Derek points to the console.

"With Al Montana," I say.

"I'm impressed." Derek picks up the playlist and runs his finger down the paper. "I'm doing a flashback hour."

"How far back?" I ask.

"Just this decade. What do you want to hear? Maybe we have it?"

"Juice Box or Mintpaste."

"So you're a post-punker?" He winks.

What the hell's that?

When I don't reply, Derek reads my face, "People that like artsy, alternative bands."

He grabs the mike before I can respond and the on-air light goes on. "Dynamite Derek here on 92.7 WEMD, The SLAM, giving you a taste of the good old stuff with a miniflashback. Started off the hour with back-to-back Fizzle songs from when they shook the house, had some PIN in there with Heart and No Soul and Thwart with "Rocked Out" when Al Montana was still with the band. Got an intern in the studio tonight. She was wearing diapers when Juice Box hit number one with 'Spill Proof.' . . ." He brings up the song.

My face is flushed. Nobody can see me, and Derek didn't even say my name, but still I'm totally embarrassed. He must think I'm some dumb kid, post-punker, wannabe DJ. Well, that's not true. Okay, so I want to be a DJ and I do like punk tunes, but I really do know about music.

Jason bursts into the room with a couple of Red Bulls. "Want one?" he asks.

I shake my head. "No, thanks."

He hands them both to Derek. Derek pops one open and chugs. "Satisfy me, baby." He laughs, but no one else does.

I wouldn't be surprised if he tried to be a comedian before he got this radio gig. He's always spouting one-liners and laughing at his own jokes, even when he's on the air.

I try to ignore him and get to work checking to make sure that all the commercials for the show are lined up. I focus on the Juice Box song playing in the background. *"Tip it up, Turn it round, drop it on the ground . . . spill proof . . ."* The lyrics are pretty silly if you pick them apart, but as a whole they really work.

When I'm finished with the computer, Jason jumps on it. "Derek, need me to upload any other tunes for the hour? I think we're going to be short, about two minutes."

"What are they requesting on the phone lines?" Derek pulls at the chain around his neck.

"A lot of the stuff you already played. Some Jungle Crew and Lint but most of those tunes you can't play on the radio."

"I'll pick up a couple of lines and see if we get anything good," Derek says.

I'm leaning on the side of the console like a dork. "Can I do anything?" I ask no one in particular.

"Just watch Derek man the phone," Jason says, "something you'll be doing soon."

Gulp. I have to answer the phones in public? Why can't they stick me in a little closet?

Derek reaches for the receiver. "SLAM, what's up?" He does that three or four times and then puts down the receiver. "Man, I'll have to pick something myself. All they want is Thwart. Round up a few hot dudes and you have a band."

Man, that's sacrilege. I can't believe he said that. All those guys have tons of experience. They're anything *but* bubblegum. Just because they're all cute doesn't mean they're not talented.

He turns up the volume, and "Spill Proof" blasts through the air.

I turn up my inner DJ. *Good evening, Miami, there's nothing like listening to Johnny Lipton from Juice Box, his voice melts your soul, seeps into your pores. This guy sings from the heart. Are you with me?*

"What's going on in here?" A booming voice breaks my music-induced trance.

I look over. It's Rob. I sit up straight. Am I in trouble? Am I supposed to be doing something?

"Listening." I point to the console.

Derek and Jason burst out laughing.

"This girl's real serious." Derek eyeballs me.

"Well, she doesn't get it from me." Rob laughs, too.

How stupid. I don't get anything from him. We're not even related.

Rob puts his arm on my shoulder. "Watch Derek carefully. He's a master."

Mastur*bator*, I want to say.

chapter TWELVE

I'm glad we're meeting at Gavin's house to work on the author project and not mine. I can just see Mom hovering over us and answering questions that aren't even addressed to her. Then halfway through the meeting, she'd grab a pair of kitchen scissors and try to snip Gavin's bangs. She'd like Kayla, though, with all her pink crap—probably invite her to a Mary Kay party.

I hope Gavin's mom likes me. I figure she's got to be pretty open-minded if she has a son that dresses in all black and is a huge fan of Stephen King. Just in case she doesn't, I throw on a pair of capris and a light green tee. I don't want to frighten her. But I don't want to gross out Gavin either. I figure this outfit is neutral territory. Besides, my sneakers are black. His favorite color.

Mom gives me the once-over after she comes down the stairs smelling like a perfume factory exploded on her.

I sit on the bottom of the stairs and put lotion on my legs. I don't want to show up with scaly alligator skin either.

Mom steps around me. "That's a nice color on you, Teresa. Matches your eyes."

I wasn't expecting that. "Thanks."

"Something's missing, though." She rubs the side of her cheek.

Really? I'm wearing a push-up bra. I got a pair of socks on, both black, and my sneakers match. Pants. Got those.

"A necklace. That's what you need. Something midlength with stones. I'll be right back." She races up the stairs.

"I'm fine," I say, but my voice is buried by the click-clack of her spiked heels.

A minute later Mom's downstairs with a string of glossy beads that are a mixture of green and silver stones.

"Let me put it on for you." She lifts up my ponytail and closes the clasp. She motions for me to stand up and spins me around. "Much better. Gives you some style."

I catch a glimpse of myself in the mirror on the way out. It's a bit gaudy. I have to find a way to ditch it before I get to Gavin's house.

We climb into Mom's Lexus and she immediately turns the radio onto SUN FM. She'd never tell Rob, but she likes their music better. It's more pop-oriented, filled with artists that are either going to be in rehab soon, are convicted felons, or have several baby daddies by the time they turn twenty-one.

"Up to number three, it's Maddie Miracle with 'How Can You Not Want Me?'"

"Oh, I love her voice," Mom squeals. "I hope Rob gets her for the summer concert."

"I'm praying for Maltese or PJ Squid."

"Funny names."

"Maltese is one of *People* magazine's Most Beautiful People. He's always on MTV bare-chested."

Mom stops short at the light. She's not what you'd call an exemplary driver. She doesn't calculate the moves of others or account for the unexpected. That's why she sideswiped the mail truck last year when she was parallel parking on South Beach. The year before that she nearly killed a peacock that was crossing the street. She swerved at the last second and hit a bench instead. Don't worry, none of the accidents were *her* fault.

"Oh, I think Maltese was at the Versace party last month." Mom puckers her bright red lips, then runs her tongue over her front teeth.

"And you didn't tell me?"

She makes a right onto Coral Street, Gavin's street. She slows down, and we both search for 14201. "I didn't know you were interested in Maltese."

"Interested? Megacrush, more like it." I have four pictures of him on my bedroom wall. Hasn't she noticed?

"Well, here we are." Mom pulls into Gavin's driveway.

There's an orange Saturn in front of the garage. I bet that's Kayla's car. She would definitely drive something practical but flashy.

"Okay, remember to be polite and friendly." Mom repositions my necklace.

"I know." I unlock my car door.

"That means you have to open your mouth," Mom calls after me.

Not if I'm Helen Keller, I don't.

Gavin's house is the color of sand, which is like many of the houses in South Florida. It's a two-story and looks pretty big from the outside. There's a plaque next to the doorbell that reads, *My House Is Your House.* That is so un-Gavin-like.

I run my finger over the illuminated light of the bell. Before I ring, I turn around to make sure Mom has left. I don't need her rolling down her window again and yelling something embarrassing. I quickly slide off the necklace from QVC hell and stuff it into my backpack.

I ring once and wait, but no one comes to the door. Maybe I didn't press hard enough? But if I ring again, I'll seem like a pest. I peek at my watch. I'm only five minutes late. I'm sure they're waiting for me. I reluctantly ring again and mentally prepare my speech. *Sorry for being a serial ringer.*

Okay, is this some kind of joke? Were we supposed to meet next week? Is someone looking through the peephole and doubling over with laughter? Am I a paranoid mess? It's just that I don't go to other people's houses much, except for Audrey's. And that place is anything but normal with her twin seven-year-old brothers running around the house yelling "Freeze, put your hands up!" and her mother and father singing show tunes while they make dinner together.

I take a deep breath and knock. If no one answers this time, I'll go down the street and call Gavin's house from my cell. Then I'll explain that I'm running late but will be there in a few minutes.

The door opens. I'm armed with apologies. "I'm sorry—"

A petite woman with short curly hair greets me. Has to be Mrs. Tam. "I'm glad you knocked; the doorbell sticks sometimes. Come in, Tere."

She holds out her hand. "I'm Gavin's mom. It's a pleasure to meet you."

"Hi." I know I have to say more if I ever want to get to know her son better. I can't just stand here, looking dumber than a turkey with its head cut off. I take her hand and shake. It's tiny. Her bones feel like they're made of chalk. I don't want to crush them.

"I've heard lovely things about you," she continues.

She has? Gavin's talked about me? "Thanks." I blush. "You, too. You're lovely."

She smiles. "Thanks, dear. Kayla and Gavin are in the den. Follow me."

We walk through the foyer, past a cranberry-colored office

and into the pale yellow den. Kayla and Gavin are sitting on opposite couches, separated by a wooden coffee table. Kayla has several colors of pastel paper spread out in front of her. Gavin's holding an electric guitar. Above his head is a framed needlepoint that reads, *People always make time to do the things they really want to do.*

If my mother had a crafty bone in her body, I would've thought she'd sneaked in here and hung that sign up. But since she throws out a pair of pants if she loses a button, there's no way she could even thread a stitch.

"I'll be in the kitchen if you need anything." Mrs. Tam grabs a couple of empty cups off of the coffee table.

Gavin just nods. Kayla says thanks. I don't say anything.

Where am I supposed to sit? If I sit next to Gavin, then it might be too obvious that I like him, and if I sit next to Kayla, he'll definitely think I don't like him. So I stand there like an ice sculpture.

Gavin smiles at me.

I melt.

Before I can return the smile, he turns his focus to his cell phone vibrating on the table. He looks at it but doesn't pick up.

"I'm setting up a planning tree for the project." Kayla numbers the papers with big, bubbly print.

"Nice," I say without fully parting my lips.

She takes out a glitter pen and shakes it. "Sit down, will ya."

Gavin plays a few chords on his guitar with the amp off.

I chicken out and slide into the stuffy plaid armchair between the two couches. "You play a lot?"

"Every chance I get. Drives my mother crazy." Gavin wipes the hair out of his eyes with his palm. God, he's so rock-star cute!

I laugh. That would be a great way to get back at my mom for being so annoying, play a loud instrument. She'd probably find a way to soundproof my room, though.

"What kind of music do you play?" I slide my backpack to the floor.

Kayla looks up from her planning neurosis sheets. "Wow, two whole sentences. She speaks."

I roll my eyes at her. I try never to do that because it makes me look all cross-eyed, and slightly freakish, but I couldn't help myself.

"Anyway . . ." Gavin taps out another beat. "I like some older punk stuff and a lot of local urban bands. I'm even into rap and some jazz."

Kayla pops her head up. "I love jazz. And country."

"Not me," I say to the powder-blue carpet. "I'm a post-punker. I like hip-hop and edgy alternative tunes."

"Like what?" Gavin stares at me with his dark eyes.

My skin is hot and prickly. "Thwart, Mintpaste, Juice Box."

"Man, you should've listened to SLAM yesterday. They had a whole flashback hour. They played Thwart, Mintpaste, and a lot of other amazing bands. Sweet." Gavin nods.

"Really?" I lower my head. I don't want them to see me grinning. Gavin's basically calling Derek's show cool, and technically I was a part of the coolness factor. I mean, I was there, in the studio, breathing the same oxygen as the Masturbator. Okay, not a nice visual.

"Yeah, they play good tunes." I pictured Gavin listening to smaller, grungier stations like MAD 100.2 or SCARY 88.9.

So he thinks my station is sweet. We have even more in common than I thought.

"I hate to break up the music party, but let's get this project rolling. I have a foreign language meeting at five," Kayla informs us. "They're thinking of cutting the department budget for next year so I'm meeting with some students to see how we can stop that from happening."

Is that before or after she saves the world?

Kayla hands us each a sheet of paper and has us brainstorm ideas for the project. She sets the timer on her cell for five minutes.

I want to write:

Reasons I'll be unable to attend the presentation:

1. Stomach poisoning caused by unknown items in school lunch.

2. Jaw suddenly clamps shut due to morning overload of peanut butter.

3. Cat got my tongue, literally. Cat got scared by neighbor's

dog and latched onto my tongue. Note: Need to pur-
chase or borrow cat before said event.

4. Since I'll be in character the day of the presentation, I
will in fact be blind and deaf, therefore making it nearly
impossible for me to find my way to school.

What I end up writing:

1. Dress up as our authors and have tea.
2. Present our authors in different media and set up like an
art showcase.

I'm stuck on number three when Kayla calls time. Neither
Gavin nor I volunteer to go first, so of course Kayla does. She has
six ideas. *Show-off.* I peek over at Gavin's paper. It looks like he has
three ideas, but one is crossed out. Good, I don't feel so bad.

Kayla starts off with some elaborate plan about baking desserts
that would best represent our characters. Almost as if on cue, Mrs.
Tam brings us coffee cake and lemonade. Kayla doesn't even take
a break. She loses me on number three, when she talks about
hiring actors from a local production company to act as extras
during the time period when our authors were alive. I wonder if
she goes this all out on every school project. Just thinking about
all this work gives me a headache.

Gavin's on his third glass of lemonade, and I'm picking at the
crumbs on my plate. My calorie counter, I mean, mother, isn't

here so I have to enjoy every morsel. "Cake is for the weak," Mom always says. Funny, I thought it was for birthdays.

I nod every few minutes, and Gavin keeps saying, "Yup." So I shouldn't be surprised when Kayla says we have to show up for class in costume. Then she turns to me. "Since you have speaking issues, I racked my brain and came up with a great idea . . ."

Gavin rolls his eyes at me, and I roll mine right back. Ohmi- god, I can't believe we just had our first eye-roll together. I can't wait to tell Audrey. Maybe being crossed-eyed and slightly freak- ish is a good thing after all.

"What?" I say reluctantly.

"When you're introduced to us, you can feel our faces, just like Helen did. The best thing is that you can speak like her by stuffing your mouth with cotton balls."

Is she for real?

All of a sudden, Gavin slams down his glass. "That's crazy!"

"Whoa, chill," Kayla says looking as startled as me. "We can figure out the details later."

This girl is out of hand. "No cotton," I mumble.

Gavin reaches over to my side of the table and grabs my list. I would've stopped him if he didn't graze my boob in the process and send shivers up my spine.

"Sorry." He blushes.

I'm not.

Gavin glances at my paper. "Tere has a great idea. We should present our authors in different media and set up like an art showcase."

Kayla slumps down in her chair. We've definitely thrown her for a loop. She takes a deep breath. "Okay, we can incorporate that. I can wear roller skates. Judy loved to skate as a kid."

Gavin picks up his guitar again. "Looks like King will play his guitar."

Kayla looks at her watch. "Any questions?"

I twist my lips, trying to think of something to say, but I'm just along for the ride.

"What about you, Tere?" Gavin turns to me. "What's your art form going to be?"

"Still thinking . . ." of a way to get out of this assignment.

I leave Gavin's house at five o'clock with a vile image of me in a 1920s flowered housecoat. Why didn't I pick someone hipper, more modern? I love Helen, but for God's sake she was a blind and deaf woman living during the First and Second World War. She couldn't have possibly been a fashion icon. I know I'm nobody to talk, but even my sweats look better on me than an old curtain. *God, if you're going to strike me with lightning, now would be the perfect time.* I quickly add that to my mental list as the fifth reason I might be unable to attend our presentation.

When I get home, I plop down on my bed and delve right back into Helen's story. She talks about her soul's sudden awakening at the age of seven. How she would walk around all day discovering new things—flowers, animals, the river. And through all of this she learned how things grew and thrived. Anne Sullivan, her teacher, was amazing. I try to think of the things that Mom had taught me at seven. At the time she was boyfriend-less and on the prowl. She encouraged me to play with her makeup. I would drape her jewels around my neck, slide on her heels, and prance around her room. She would remind me to stand up straight and flip my hair and smile. Thinking back, that was probably a lesson on how to snag a guy. I'm afraid I wasn't a very good pupil because not long after that I retreated to the living room instead to watch TV while she spent hours primping.

* * *

Hola, Miami. This is Sweet T on 92.7 WEMD The SLAM FM. It's Sunday evening, and the first thing I want you to do is turn up the volume. Let the sweet tunes take you through the night. The eleven o'clock lineup will soothe your soul and put your mind at ease. I'm starting off the set with Powdered Sugar and their top ten hit "Carefree, Baby." This one's for you, Miami . . .

chapter THIRTEEN

Derek's back to the regular music format today. I hope Gavin's listening. Actually, I kind of wish I didn't know he listened to the station because now I'm even more nervous to speak on-air if Derek ever asks me to. But I know I'll have to sometime if I want to be a real DJ.

Thank God this is the last day of spring break. I've been in Gavin withdrawal all week. Why did Kayla have to go on a church retreat? Forget planting trees in Kentucky, we could've been rehearsing for our presentation. I tried to think up a couple of excuses to go back to his house, like maybe I left my favorite pen there or we should really get a head start on this project before Kayla gets back. But everything sounded lame, and for even more torture we had an extra day tacked onto the vacation for teacher planning. We start back on Tuesday. I just pictured Gavin on the other side of the radio all week.

I'm trying to stay away from Derek as best as I can. He wears really strong cologne, like *that* will attract the ladies. I know he receives tons of calls from listeners that are totally infatuated with his voice, but spend a few hours with him and he'll turn you off the male species altogether.

"Hey, T, baby, can you pick up a couple of the lines and see what the people want to hear today?" Derek elbows me in the gut.

Ugh, that would involve me talking.

"What do I say?" I whisper to Jason.

"Just give the station ID and let them do the talking. If they ask to hear a specific song, the answer is yes."

I grab a notebook and a pen out of my bag and shuffle over to the phone. I have to pretend that it's just Audrey calling or I'll faint. I hold on to the console for support. It could be anyone on the other line. Even Gavin.

At first I stare at the flashing lights. I know the interns down the hall are answering most of the calls. I've seen them with their big spreadsheets, tracking which songs are the most popular. I used to have Audrey call in requests for me and then we'd listen forever for them to be played. When we didn't hear one Thwart tune for over three hours, Audrey called back and whined to the DJ until he put it on. She made up a whole sob story about wanting to cheer up her sick sister. She even put me on the phone, but I totally clammed up and could only let out a whimper. I think I sounded like a dying seagull. The DJ cued up the song right after that.

My palms are all sweaty so I wipe them on my jeans. I turn around to make sure no one is breathing over my shoulder, but Derek has "gone to take a leak" and Jason is cueing up the music. I pick up the phone and hit line three. "SLAM 92.7."

"Hello, is this SLAM?" a guy with a light Spanish accent asks.

"Yeah."

"I can hardly hear you. Probably my cell. Let me turn up the volume."

I clear my throat.

"Can I make a request?" the man asks.

"Shoot."

"Can you play Maddie Miracle?"

"Sure." Excuse me while I go hurl.

I hang up the phone and go immediately to the next line. "SLAM 92.7."

"Hey, I thought the DJ would answer."

You wish.

"Nope," I say.

"Okay, honey. I'm hanging around with the guys, kicking back a few, and we want to hear some Gracie May."

"Sure."

Answering phones isn't as bad as I thought. If you agree to the listener's request, you can keep your wordage at a minimum of two and a maximum of four. Not bad for a phone conversation.

"Thirty seconds." Jason sticks his head outside the studio door.

I hang up the phone. Derek rushes in. "Sorry, caught up in the john."

Way too much info.

"92.7 The SLAM. Derek's in the house. Got an announcement here, PJ Squid will be playing on South Beach at Mack's, Sunday night at nine. We'll be giving tickets away within the hour. Be caller number ninety-two when you hear 'Squid Stylin.' And where are all the females? Give me a call, ladies . . ." He switches off the mike and pulls up a Ravers track.

He turns to Jason. "Every once in a while you have to give a shout-out to the broads. Know what I mean?"

"Oh, yeah." Jason leans back in his chair. Then when Derek has his back to us, he whispers to me, "I'm sure my boyfriend would love to hear that."

Boyfriend?

Right, he's cute, sweet, meticulous, and thoughtful. Of course, he's taken. I wish I could say my boyfriend would love that, too. Instead, I just nod my head.

Derek blows on his hands. "Watch the master." He picks up the phone and gives the station ID. He quickly hangs up and goes to the next line. "I don't want to talk to no dude. Ladies only."

Puhleese. I roll my eyes. I've got to stop doing that. Ever since

Gavin's house last week, it's become habit forming. Mom would not approve.

"That's better," Derek says into the phone. "What can I do for you, baby? You sound like a kitty cat." He purrs. Whoever told him that was a turn-on? "Are you hot? Come by Mack's on Sunday night so I can see the goods."

I don't get it. She could be Bigfoot's sister. How does he know?

They should really equip these studios with barf bags because I'm truly queasy. Fresh air would be good. I excuse myself to go to the bathroom.

On my way back, I pass Rob in the hall chatting with Derek. "Can you stay for Garrison's shift?" Rob asks. "He's got the flu."

"Man, normally I'd do it, but my mother's seventy-fifth birthday party is tonight."

Something about Derek at a seventy-fifth birthday party makes me crack up.

"I don't know what I'm going to do. Juan G. is on vacation. And since that show hasn't had a producer since Lambert crossed over to AM, there's no one." Rob plays with his cell phone case. "Hey, what about Jason? You think he can handle the show?"

"Oh, yeah. He doesn't miss a beat." Derek moves his hands in and out of his pants pockets, fidgets with his money clip. At least, I hope that's what it is.

I walk up from behind them and speak directly to the beige

wall with a picture of Rob and Prince in a shiny purple frame. "I can stay. To help."

Rob nods. "Okay, Tere. I'm sure Jason could use a hand."

Yes, hanging with Jason is going to be fun! No Dynamite Derek leaving his sleaze all over the studio.

Derek and I go inside and he fills Jason in. You can tell Jason's psyched. Not only is it a chance to break free of Derek, but this opportunity is his on-air audition.

A couple of minutes later Simone from the production office brings in Garrison's playlist. Jason has to do *The Love Shack* show, so there are a whole bunch of gushy songs on the rotation. I don't know about him, but it makes me happy.

Rob calls Jason to his office to talk. I'm sure he'll give him the big *I know you'll do great—don't mess up* speech. And that leaves me alone with Derek the Cat Tamer.

Derek strokes his coffee cup and smirks. "So T, I bet this love show is your thing?"

"Yeah, a lot of people my age listen to it." I tuck a stray piece of hair behind my ear.

"Where do you go to school?"

"Ridgeland."

"Your cheerleaders are smoking!"

I pull at a ragged hangnail. "Wouldn't know."

"Where's the prom this year?" Derek plays a little pocket pool and adjusts himself. Gross. Does he think I didn't see that?

"Downtown Marriott."

"Sweet. Mine was at a Holiday Inn."

Like a hundred years ago. "Oh."

"So who are you going with?"

I bite the inside of my cheek and look to the floor. Derek's wearing brown cowboy boots similar to Rob's. Did they score them at a two for one sale? "Not going."

"What?" He slaps the console. "When is it?"

"About a month from now. May fifteenth."

"No, you have to go. You have time to find a date. The guys are relying on you. It's the best night to get laid."

I hope he's not expecting a response to that. I turn my gaze toward the door.

"There's got to be someone you can ask," he continues.

I wish. I already looked at Speed Bump's tour schedule and found out they're playing Miami the same night as prom. Even Gavin's not an option now. I guess he'd rather do a stage dive than throw on a tux. "Nope."

There's twenty seconds left on the "Spill Proof" track. Derek slowly fades down the song and says, "We'll find somebody for you."

"Please don't," I whisper. He might as well form a pity party with my mom. Their catchphrase can be *we'll pay you to date this poor helpless girl.* Insert photo of me, moping on the couch in my sweats.

We make it through the last half hour of Derek's shift without mentioning the prom. Good, I hope he forgot. Jason's back. He smells like early morning rain, and his hair is slightly wet with gel. He makes me feel like I have to prep for the love show, too. Maybe if I at least throw some water on my face, it'll help calm my nerves. I grab my stuff and excuse myself to the bathroom again.

As I'm walking out, Jason says, "Loosen your vocal cords— you're going on-air tonight."

He might as well call the ambulance now. My heart's beating like crazy. I don't know if I'm ready. Maybe I need a few more days or years to let everything sink in.

I swing open the bathroom door and dump my bag on the counter. I scrounge around and come up with a stick of Big Red and an ancient tube of ChapStick, encrusted with sand. Who am I kidding? I don't even have a brush with me. I turn on the faucet and wet the top of my head.

The bathroom door swings open. It's Pop-Tart. "Hello!" she shouts.

I'm standing here like a wet dog. "Hi," I mumble.

"You okay?" She frowns. She actually looks concerned.

"Yeah."

She doesn't move. A few squiggly lines appear on her forehead. She parts her lips, but no sound comes out.

It's weird to be stared at. I quickly check the mirror to make sure I don't have any boogers hanging out of my nose. "What?"

"There's nothing wrong with your hearing, is there?"

"Nope."

Pop-Tart scratches her head. "But you said—"

"I never said anything."

"Oh." She cocks her head to the side. "Well, what is going on?"

"Just freshening up." I tousle my thick hair like I know what I'm doing.

"I can help." She dumps out the contents of her shiny gold kitchen-sink bag.

She could definitely give Pamela Oberlong a run for her money. She pulls out a compact and dabs powder on my face.

"Not too much," I say, feeling myself panic.

"Let me tell you a little secret about being on the radio. When you look good, you feel good."

"Huh?"

"I heard you're doing the show with Jason tonight."

"Yeah." I gulp.

"Hold still." She grabs my chin and runs a tube of glittery pink lipstick on my lips. "Don't worry, I know you're a natural girl, but a little makeup never hurt anyone."

I didn't know there was a name for it, but Natural Girl sounds much better than Dork Girl.

Pop-Tart makes me look up to the sky and coats my lashes with mascara. We wait a minute for it to dry, then she has me bend my head down and flip back my hair. She grabs a can of hair spray and sprays like she's competing at the Raid championships.

I cough.

"Sorry." She steps back. "I can get carried away. But you have great, thick hair."

"Really?"

"People pay money for volume. I blow mine out every day or I look like crap."

That's hard to believe.

I'm afraid to look up, so I peel open one eye at a time.

I glance into the mirror. Wow, not bad. Pamela might really have some competition. "Thanks, ahhh . . ."

"Kelly."

"Tere."

"I know." She smiles, then shoves her emergency makeup kit back into her bag.

Whoa, one point for Pop-Tart and zero for me. She remembered my name and I had no clue she even came with one.

I look at my watch. Damn, we've been in here for almost twenty minutes. I don't want Jason to think I flaked out on him. I toss my crusty ChapStick into the garbage, mouth *thank you* to Pop-Tart, and head back to the studio.

Thankfully, Derek's gone and most of the staff has left for the day, too. Jason's at the console with one hand on the mike and the other scanning songs on the computer. Hopefully he won't notice my over-do.

He swings around a second later. "So this show is going to be fun." He does a double take. "Wow, you look different."

My face heats up like a cracked egg on a Florida sidewalk. "I know. I ran into Kelly in the bathroom."

"No, it's a good thing." Jason smiles.

"Thanks." I smile back. Too bad he's taken. There really could've been something. Ha.

I rub my hands up and down my jeans. "Okay, what do you need me to do?"

"I already checked the commercials, so slide a chair up here and relax."

I can do that. I think. We sit there for the first fifteen minutes, chilling to the tunes. Jason's the kind of person you can just sit next to and enjoy your own space. Not like with Derek. I feel like he's always watching everyone, like dead air is a sin. I imagine the sign in his house reads, *Idle time is wasted time.* I imagine how my needlepoint saying would read: *Woman of few words* or *A day without blushing is a good day.*

At seven-fifteen, like clockwork, the song "Love Stinks" (don't ask me how that actually qualifies as a love song) fades down.

"Wish me luck." Jason reaches for the on-air button.

"You'll do great," I say. I shove my hands under my legs. I'm shaking, and I'm not even the one who's going on-air. This is crazy.

"Good evening, South Florida. This is Jason Stevens, and you're listening to *The Love Shack* on 92.7 The SLAM. I'm filling in tonight, so I hope you'll give me a call and tell me what you're

dying to hear. I have my friend T in the studio helping me out—"
I elbow him and whisper, "Sweet."

He continues, "Sorry, Sweet T, and believe me, she lives up to
her name. We're just kicking back and letting the tunes roll. Here's
Maltese with 'All Over You . . . '"

I'm in full blush now. So what if Jason's gay and is in a committed relationship? He called me sweet.

Sweet T.

chapter FOURTEEN

The phones are lighting up, and I'm jotting down the love requests like a waiter taking orders at IHOP on a Sunday morning. Most interns leave at seven, so it's all me. It's pretty much an even amount of girls and guys calling. One guy kind of sounded like Gavin. Okay, maybe two guys, but one said his name was Randy and the other Kevin.

Jason pulls as many of the requests as he can, and people are loving it. A couple even call back and thank us for throwing their jams on the air.

"I can't believe Garrison didn't have any help." I tally up my requests so far. Forty-five.

"And he is still doing his own show, too. Angie from sales helped him out some nights, but otherwise he runs solo," Jason says.

You'd never know he does all this work himself. He is so smooth.

Jason swivels his chair around to face me. "So, Sweet T, are you ready to make an appearance?"

"What do you mean?" I flip my hair back in my best imitation of a clueless girl.

"Just a live station ID. Something small to get you revved up."

"I don't know . . . um . . . " I've only been dreaming about this day for the past six years, but what if I croak? Or worse, what if I blurt out something so moronic that I send the whole of Miami bursting into hysterics? I already feel the peanut butter lining the inside of my throat.

He gently grabs my shoulder. "You have a great voice. It'll be fine. I'll do my thing, then point to you."

Easy for you to say, you didn't just swallow half a jar of peanut butter. But I nod anyway. There's something soothing about Jason. Something about him I can really trust, like he'd never let me fall.

I reach for my water bottle and chug. Forty seconds left to find my voice. I have a whole show prerecorded in my head. All I have to deliver is one line. *This is Sweet T and you're listening to* The Love Shack *on 92.7 The SLAM.*

I move closer to Jason and close my eyes. *I can do this.* Small breaths. One at a time. I hear my ninth grade English teacher, Mrs. Pine, in the back of my head. "Smile when you deliver your speech, and your voice will come across as happy. Frown, and no one will want to listen to you."

"Give it up for Trena Bay with back to back love songs." Jason draws out the word *love,* letting each letter linger in his mouth. I can picture the girls swooning over him, cuddled up in their beds or driving along the expressway blasting the volume. "We want to thank you for sharing the love tonight with all your calls. Keep them coming . . ." He points to me.

Ohmigod, this is it. I take a deep breath this time and close my eyes, then remember that Helen Keller said to look the world straight in the eye. *I can do this.* I open my eyes wide and stare at the mike, my entrance to the world. I stretch my lips into a smile and let the words spill out. "This is Sweet T hanging out with Jason Stevens tonight and you're listening to *The Love Shack* on 92.7 The SLAM."

I don't exhale until I feel the beat of the next tune. It's Maltese, with "Melt Me."

"You did it!" Jason breaks my trance. "You're a pro."

"Yeah, right."

"No, really—you have a knack for radio."

I'm just glad I didn't mess up. He persuades me to go on a couple more times during the show, a few station tags and the phone number to the request line. We take turns grabbing the calls.

Halfway through the show, I kick off my sneaks and pull my legs up onto the chair. It's almost like I'm at home, much different than when Derek's here or even the rest of the staff. When it's only Jason and a couple of engineers hanging around the building, I can chill. Plus, he actually lets me do stuff, which makes me feel important.

Jason picks up a line, then whispers into the phone. "Yeah, I think she's single. Hot, definitely. That, I can't tell you. She's a woman of mystery." He looks over at me and winks.

I wave my hands back and forth *no. Please, don't tell them anything else. It'll ruin everything.*

He hangs up the phone. "Why do you look like you just saw a ghost?"

"It's weird. People talking about me. I'm not used to it."

"You better get used to it. They like you."

"But I don't want them to know anything about me." I pull the zipper all the way up on my sweatshirt.

"Don't worry. I'll keep your identity a secret. I know the truth."

Instant goose bumps populate my skin. "You do?" I gulp. *You know I'm a former Snowball, two-time loser?*

"Yeah, sure. You're a super kick-butt spy working undercover as a narc."

I can't stop myself from cracking up. Jason knows I'm full of it. But even if he does scope me out, I know my secret is safe with him.

I end off the show with, "Sleep tight, Miami, You never know where love is hiding . . . "

Jason arranged with Rob to drop me home and it's almost midnight when we pull in, but I have to call someone, and let's face it, the only someone I have is Audrey. Mom and Rob are out at some fashion show, so I don't even have to sneak by them.

I plop down onto my bed and whip out my cell. "Hi, Aud."

"Hello," she says groggily.

"Sorry, did I wake you?" I whisper, like that will help.

"No, I was just studying for Señora Garcia's test from hell. Crazy lady has to give a test the day we get back from break."

"That sucks." I don't know why, but I'm totally out of breath. "I did it. I was on the air tonight."

"You got your own show?" she squeaks.

I spring up and down on my bed. I feel like I'm back in the fifth grade, the time I came home all high from the cotton candy and elephant ears at the county youth fair. "No, not exactly. Garrison called in sick, and Derek's producer, Jason, took over. Halfway through, he had me talk on the air."

"What did you say?"

I close my eyes and let the words dance in front of me. *"Hi, Miami, up next is the Hot Tees with 'Sweet and Sticky.'"*

"That's it?"

"Well, I got to end off the show, too."

"That's great!"

"Yeah, but the whole time I thought I was going to hurl all over the console."

"You didn't, did you?"

"No, of course not. But do you know how many people listen to *The Love Shack*? Like a quarter million."

"Wow, probably more people than tuned into *Dance Craze* tonight. The show sucked, and they voted off Ollie. The cute swing dancer." That's one thing Audrey and I don't have in common. Swing dancing.

"That sucks." I try to muster up as much sympathy as possible. Audrey's a reality TV show junkie, and if she doesn't get her weekly fix, she can be really moody.

I let out a yawn. "See you tomorrow."

"For sure," Audrey says.

"Oh, and don't tell anyone about me being on the air. Ever."

"Never ever, best friends forever." Audrey recites our mantra.

I slip into my pj's and put on my iPod. It takes me a long time to fall asleep. I didn't even tell Audrey the best part. That they liked me. The people. The audience. Okay, really only two people called in, but, still, they called in about me. Sweet T. I can't believe I'm expected back tomorrow to do it again. Garrison will be out at least until the end of the week.

I step into the kitchen to grab some breakfast before I head off to school. Mom's busy with the blender, attempting to make a smoothie. What is she doing up? And even more suspicious, what is she doing using an appliance? I guess Smoothie King isn't open this early in the morning.

She squeezes some lime into the machine. "How was it last night?"

"Way cool." I pour myself a bowl of cornflakes. I can still taste the words on the tip of my tongue. *This is Sweet T on 92.7 The SLAM . . .*

"You didn't mess up?"

I can't even remember the last time she was proud of me. It was probably back in eighth grade when she took me to the hairdresser and the owner of the store asked if they could take a photo of me for a presentation they were doing at a salon trade show. Apparently my hair had the perfect balance of natural shine, highlights, and body. For months after that Mom was after me to stay out of the sun, so as not to ruin my *perfect* hair. Not such an easy feat in Miami!

"Did you even listen?"

"No. I was on the phone with Karen forever, and then we had to go to the fashion show." Mom opens and closes several cutlery drawers until she comes up with the small paring knife. "But Rob listened before we left. He said it went well."

I nearly drop my spoon. "Really?"

"Yes, but don't get all crazy." She waves the knife in the air. "This is his reputation on the line. So if you screw up, he screws up."

She doesn't think I know that? "Is it so crazy to believe I was a success?" I shove a spoonful of cereal into my mouth before I say what I really think.

She starts the blender, but apparently the top is not on properly and fruit sprays onto the counter. Serves her right. She quickly turns it off and tightens the lid. "Just don't make things hard for Rob."

What does she think? I'm sitting in the studio with my feet up on the console, picking my nose?

I rinse my bowl and pop it into the dishwasher. "Jason's got it all under control. And they liked me." I don't wait for her response. I quickly dip into the bathroom and put on some glittery lip gloss. I like the way it looked when Pop-Tart— I mean, Kelly—put it on me. It feels good on my lips, too, nice and smooth.

I throw on my iPod and book it to school. I still can't believe I was actually live on the air, not holed up in my room talking to myself! So what if Mom thinks it's only a matter of days before I mess up? All I need to do is practice.

I'm in a daze for my first two classes. SLAM is welded to my brain. I have to say something different tonight. I have to establish my "radio personality." I always hear Rob talking about that stuff, about how you have to build up your persona the same way you have to build up a business. He may have been stupid enough to marry my mom, but he did bring the station from the number four spot to the number two spot in less than a year. He fired half the staff and made sure everyone he brought on board had something different to offer. Why he kept Derek around is still under debate.

I don't feel like conquering the lunchroom today—I have too much to think about. I know Audrey will probably be disappointed if I don't show, but I head over to the language lab instead. Kayla's walking out of the room when I get there.

"Hey, Tere. What are you doing here?"

"Reviewing."

She stuffs her books into her bag. "Let me guess—you take Spanish."

"Nope. German."

"Really? I've never seen you at any of the programs. I've been taking *Deutsch* since freshman year."

I stare at her white sneakers. They're so bright. "Schedule problems."

"Oh. Well, see you in English."

"Yeah." I open the door to the lab.

I walk around the back first to make sure Stacy isn't hiding anywhere. I even peer under all the booths. Then I grab my books and CD from Mrs. Tripp and take the seat with the best view of the door. That way I can see if anyone comes in.

I'm on lesson four already. I'm really getting the hang of this German thing. *Feelings & Emotions*. Just what I need, ha. There's a girl on the page smiling with the word *glücklich* next to her. Talk about a mouthful. The boy with the droopy eyes is *traurig* and the kid yelling is *wütend*. It almost sounds liked wounded. I flip the page until I find myself, *nervös*. Well, you don't need a translator for that one.

Once I get the pronunciations under control, I do a quick scan of the room again, then pause the CD. I let each word roll off the tip of my tongue. At first I say everything in my normal tone, then I read everything with a scowl. I sound like a serial killer. I try the smile next, but halfway through I crack up. There must be something in between.

I spend the rest of the period working on the "in-between smile." It's not quite a smirk, but it's not the fake glamour pics photo either. I like to call it the "isn't it a nice day" smile.

The bell rings midsmile and I rush to Ms. Peters' class. I can't wait to see Gavin.

He's already at his desk. He's got his black Ravers tee on and is busy scrawling in his notebook again with his earbuds in. *Damn, I missed looking at him.* I slide into my seat and drop my bag to the floor. It hits with a thud. Obvious or what?

Gavin looks up and pulls out an earbud. "Hey, Tere. What's up?"

"Just thought I was late."

"You're never late."

True. "I try."

"How was your spring break?" he asks.

"Uneventful. And yours?"

"My mom thought it was a great opportunity for me to clean out the garage."

"That sucks." I bite the inside of my cheek. "What are you listening to?"

He hands me an earbud. "Trena Bay. I'm usually not into mushy stuff, but I heard her on SLAM last night and she's pretty dope."

"You listened? Last night?"

"Yeah, I was scanning the dial and dug the tune that was playing. I like to listen to music while I do my homework."

I'm too stunned to say anything. Did he know it was me? That I'm the one and only Sweet T? I can't believe Gavin was actually listening to me last night!

He puts his hand on my desk. His fingers are long and slender. "What do you think?"

"Huh?" I look down at my own fingers. I'm suddenly embarrassed by my short, chipped nails. I hide them in my lap.

"Of Trena?"

"Oh, right." I stick in the earbud. After a few seconds I say, "I like her voice."

"I think the love show's on every night around seven. You should check it out."

"Definitely."

"If it isn't Dorkstag." I hear an evil witch laugh. I look up. It's Stacy.

"You're not late," I mutter.

"Can't be, thanks to you."

I don't even bother to answer. I bet she blames me for her low IQ, too.

But that doesn't stop her from continuing, "My dad almost ripped me a new asshole when the principal called my house about my tardies." Her face is pulled tight and has a fierceness to it, but if you peer into her eyes there is a tinge of sadness.

Finally Frank waves her over. She sneers at me, then leaves.

"What was that all about?" Gavin asks.

Ms. Peters shuts the door. Everyone shuffles to their seats.

"Long story, but she hates me."

"That's probably a good thing." He brushes the hair out of his face. "But I don't know how anyone could hate you."

"Thanks. That's sweet."

"I mean it. I know Stacy thinks just because you're shy, she can step all over you, but that's B.S." He sets his hand on my shoulder. His touch immediately sends shockwaves through my system.

I look into his eyes, and I know he understands where I'm coming from. He doesn't judge. He grips my shoulder tighter, and I will myself to touch his arm. To let him know that I appreciate his understanding.

I want to stay like this forever, but my perfect moment is interrupted by Ms. Peters announcing that the science teacher, Mrs. Fletcher, had her baby this morning. Then she goes around the class asking us how our group projects are coming along. You can tell who has started working and who hasn't. Kayla, our spokeswoman, speaks for us. "There are definitely a lot of challenges to overcome since we have such an eclectic group, but I think we've come up with some good ideas and I'm looking forward to our presentation."

"Kiss ass much." I hear someone cough in the back.

Ms. Peters tells everyone to get to work, and we push our desks together. Kayla pulls out a binder filled with pastel paper.

I yawn. After staying at the radio station past eleven last night, I could totally use a nap right now.

Kayla lays out her glitter pens and scribbles frantically. Why is she always writing? We haven't even started yet. I peer over. She's just heading the paper. If she does that for every piece, we'll be here until the bell rings. Finally, she looks up. "Okay, I've already been practicing with my cousin's roller skates. What about you guys?"

"I've started on my song, but I don't have anything to share yet," Gavin says.

Kayla turns to me. "And you?"

"Well, as a kid, Helen's hobbies were sailing and tobogganing." I grit my teeth.

"You own a toboggan?" Kayla asks. "You've had over a week. Couldn't you come up with something that you can use?"

Helen worked in vaudeville as a child, but I don't want to give Kayla any ideas. There's no way I'm standing up there blind-folded and doing any kind of singing or dancing. "Well, she was a writer—"

"Duh." Kayla looks at me like I'm crazy.

Okay, think. What would Sweet T do in this situation? *Good evening Miami, up next we have our very first SLAM song in Braille . . .*

"Braille. I could write something in Braille," I offer.

She shuffles the pastel papers. "That's stupid. We don't know Braille."

Gavin grabs her wrist. "Relax, Tere just needs a little more time to come up with an idea."

"But the presentation is in less than a month," Kayla protests.

Gavin looks at me. "The next time we meet, you'll have something, right?"

If I don't keel over and die first.

chapter FIFTEEN

I go straight to the library after school. I have to finish all my homework before I head to the station, and my teachers have piled it on today. You'd think they could give us seniors a break, but no.

I better come up with something for our English project. I don't want to give Kayla a heart attack. I flip through Helen Keller's autobiography and try to get a better sense of who she was. To get inside her head. How would she like to be remembered? Which immediately brings me back to the question, how do I want to be remembered after I leave Ridgeland? At this rate, I won't be remembered, but a part of me wants people to know that I at least existed. I want to carve my name in the tree and write, *Tere Adams was here.*

I wonder if it's ever too late to be somebody. But then I think of Helen and how the older she got, the more of a mark she left. She started off as a helpless mute kid and ended up as an accomplished writer and activist. She spoke English, German, Latin, and sign language and read Braille. She probably would've blasted everyone away at Ridgeland. I know I have to showcase her true talents in the group presentation, but I'm not sure how to honor her yet. I don't want to do any stupid old thing. Who am I kidding; I'm dreading being on display in front of the whole class. And what about Stacy? Is she going to sit there and mock me the whole time?

After staring into space for almost half an hour, the only thing I can come up with is to have Helen spell into people's hands. I don't know if that classifies as a talent, but it's pretty amazing that she was able to communicate that way. Hopefully, Kayla will be okay with it. I glance at the clock and grab my stuff. If I miss this bus there's not another one for forty minutes, and that will put me at the station after Derek's show starts.

When I reach the main hallway, there's a guy running around hugging everyone. He's holding a piece of paper and jumping up and down. "I got in! I'm Harvard bound!"

When he's inches from my face, I step aside, but say, "Congratulations!"

He grins from ear to ear, then moves on to embrace the girl

behind me carrying a huge clay pot. I'm glad I added to some-one's happiness, even if I only said one word.

Of course, as soon as I open the front door, it's raining. Is this some kind of evil joke? By the time I get to the show, I'll look like a mangy mutt. I speed-walk to the bus.

Kelly says hi to me in a normal tone when I walk into the sta-tion, and I actually call *her* by *her* name. She'll always be Pop-Tart to me, but that's something I'll keep to myself.

Before I join Derek, I do a little freshening up in the bath-room. There's no way I can mimic all Kelly's beauty tricks, but I manage to roll on some mascara without smudging it. Then I run a comb through my hair and put on a little lip gloss.

Derek's already sucking down a Red Bull when I enter the studio. As usual, he's exposing too much chest hair and he has his cowboy boots up on the console. Isn't he afraid he's going to hit a button and screw up the whole show?

I shove my backpack over to the side and immediately start checking the commercials. After I'm done, I ask Derek if he needs me to do anything. I figure if he sends me on errands, I won't have to say another sentence to him all evening.

He turns around sporting a huge grin. "I knew you were wait-ing to pounce on me. Want some of this, huh?" He stretches his arms out wide and wiggles his hips.

What would Sweet T say?

"Get real." *You are so disgusting.* I run out of the studio. Outside the door, I bump into Jason. Some getaway.

"Whoa, where are you going?" He rubs his shoulder.

"Sorry, I didn't mean to maul you, but Derek is so nasty." I grit my teeth.

"True," Jason says. "Don't let him get to you."

"How?" I rub my eyes. Great, the one day I wear mascara I have to tear up.

Derek pops his head out the door. "There you are. Can't a guy get some help around here?"

I glare at Jason.

"Derek, I think you owe someone an apology," Jason says.

"Her?" Derek points to me.

Jason eyeballs him.

Derek shakes my shoulder. "T knows I was only kidding, right?"

"Wrong." I sniff. I'm still seething inside with *raserei,* rage.

He pulls at the side of his mustache. "I was just having a little fun."

I walk right past him back into the studio. He follows me inside. "I'll make it up to you, don't worry."

"I'm not worried," I say, even though I am. I take the seat farthest away from him.

Jason whispers into my ear. "Don't forget we have *The Love Shack* coming up at seven, and I'm counting on Sweet T to pull through."

I smile. She's the one that got me to stand up to Derek. Even if I ran out of the studio and leaked a few tears, I still said something. Now if only I could get Sweet T to rough up a few other people for me!

Derek stays clear of me for most of the show. Surprisingly, he cracks very few jokes and actually does his job. He only sends one shout-out to all the ladies, and when he picks up the phone lines, he doesn't invite every girl to join him on Saturday night at Club Foil on South Beach. Only every other girl.

At six, Derek announces that it's teaser time and turns on the mike. "Coming up at seven we have *The Love Shack* with Jason Stevens filling in for Paul Garrison. In the studio with Jason tonight will be Sweet T, the lady of mystery. If you want to know more about her or make a request, give the SLAM lines a call at 1-800-555-SLAM . . ."

My body stiffens. He had to say something, didn't he?

Jason punches me in the shoulder. "Derek's got to talk up the show. That's what spices things up."

He's got a point. I'm just extrasensitive today. I'm still seething from yesterday after my mom basically said I was bound to mess up any second and Stacy embarrassed me in English class again in front of Gavin.

"I guess." It's my turn to pick up a few phone lines. That's when it hits me that Gavin could be listening again. I would love to be a fly on his wall and watch him enjoy the show. Although, even if I were there, I don't really know what I'd see. Him jumping up and down, bugging out to the tunes? I doubt it. I'm sure his earbuds are in and he's just doing one math problem after another.

"92.7 The SLAM."

"Are you the hot chick?" a strange, whispery voice asks.

"What?"

"Are you wearing a blue T-shirt?"

I look down at my shirt just to confirm. "Yeah," I whisper into the phone.

"Your hair is really thick." Okay, now I'm officially freaked out. My lungs are filling up fast with air and I'm having trouble breathing. Is there a webcam in here?

"I know who you are," the caller says.

My hands are all sweaty, and the receiver slips to the floor with a bang.

Derek cracks up. I glance at him just in time to see him shutting his cell phone.

I use what feels like my last breath to utter, "Asshole." Sweet T comes through again.

I look over at Jason for support. He's laughing, too. But when he catches sight of my face, he immediately turns it into a frown. "Man, that was wrong."

"Lighten up, T. It was only a joke. I pull that one on all the interns," Derek says.

I can't believe it didn't register in his pea-sized brain that I despised him after he asked me if I wanted a piece of him. I wipe my sweaty palms on my jeans. "I do not need this."

"We've got to get you out more." Derek brings up his last track for the night. Gracie May with "Dumped."

I better pull myself together for *The Love Shack*. I can't let Derek mess things up for me. I need to pick out some fresh tunes for Gavin. Derek lets me scan through the mp3 files to start off the show. I know Gavin said he likes edgier stuff, so I go with Juice Box and Mintpaste. I also want to introduce something new, so I find a song by a band called Shrinking Violet that's just making it to the scene. They're from Seattle and their single is "Can You See Me?"

I listen to it a few times to make sure it fits into the love format. With the lines, "*If love is blind, then why are you tearing me apart*" and *"you left me in so much pain, I'm bleeding inside out,"* I figure it'll work. Either that or half the audience will be suicidal by the end of the night.

"Have you ever heard of the band Shrinking Violet?" I ask Derek.

He laughs. "Ha, you would like a band like that."

"Like what?"

"Shrinking . . . violet . . . get it?"

Huh? I don't hide the puzzled expression on my face. I look around for the closest weapon—a stapler—in case I need to smack him over the head.

When I don't answer, he continues, "A shrinking violet is a very shy person."

Oh, that's it? I actually let out a sigh of relief. I was waiting for one of his unfunny sexist remarks. "I have nothing to say, then." I hand him the headphones to give the song a listen.

"Clever," he says and slides them on.

I have heard of people being called shrinking violets before, but I didn't really make the connection when I heard the band's name. Anyway, violets are beautiful and the band rocks, so I'll take it as a compliment.

Only after Derek is long gone does my stomach settle. Okay, calling me from his cell was kind of funny, but I'd never admit that to his face. It'd only fuel more pranks at my expense. The *want some of this* hip shake did not register on the humor meter at all. I still can't believe I actually sort of stood up to him. I know girls like Stacy or Kelly would've kicked him in the balls, but just leaving the room was a big step for me.

Two years ago, I was on the Metrorail after a trip to Bayside Marketplace with Audrey and a bunch of band kids. It was pretty late at night, and there were a lot of drunk people coming back from a soccer game. I was smushed in a seat against the window, and a sweaty, smelly guy sat down next to me. I had a couple of shopping bags on my lap and he kept on rubbing up against me. At first I thought it was because the bags were on his side, so I moved them right up to the window. That only gave him more ammo, and he pressed his hairy leg smack against mine. I didn't even try to move. Not once. It was like I was frozen. I never looked at his face, though. He got off a few stops before mine, but I stayed pressed against the window until Audrey yelled my name to make sure I got off with the rest of the band. Everyone was giggling about the night and how much fun it was to play at the waterfront. I was so ashamed about the guy that I didn't speak the rest of the way home. And I didn't tell anyone what happened, not even Audrey.

Jason comes back in the studio after filling up his coffee mug. "Tere, you want to take the lead after this song?"

"I don't know." I bite my lip. I hear Mom in the back of my head, warning me not to screw up.

"We can't get anywhere if we don't take chances." Jason smiles.

"I knew you'd say something smart like that."

"Hey, I didn't receive a degree from the Miami Fashion Institute for nothing," he says.

"You have a degree in fashion?"

"What, you can't tell?" He runs his hands up and down his sides, showing off his crisp white button-down and black Guess jeans.

"You do dress really nice." I look down at my own clothes. Blue tee, worn Gap jeans, and Nikes. And this is my good outfit.

"Thanks, I try." He glances at the clock. "You're on in sixty seconds."

Sixty seconds. Well, it wouldn't matter if he said six thousand, I'd still feel jittery. All I have to remember is that I did it yesterday. I quickly transform back into on-air mode. I take a few deep breaths and stare at the mike. I think of Gavin in his dimly lit bedroom finishing his homework and zoning out to the tunes. I think of Gavin with his hand on my shoulder in class and the warmth that he gave me. I hope he liked the Shrinking Violet single. It was especially for him.

Jason hands me a few love dedications and tells me to read them and say the station ID. Another deep breath, and he gives me the five-second countdown. Now it's all me. *Don't let me down, Sweet T.*

"Hey, Miami, this is Sweet T, hanging out with Jason Stevens on *The Love Shack*. We have a few dedications for you. Happy twenty-first to Lucas from Mimi. April, Juan says he'll love you forever, and Brit can't wait for her baby daddy, James, to get home tonight for some . . . you fill in the blank . . . So call us up at 1-800-555-SLAM if you want your dedication aired." I turn sideways to face Jason. "Man, my heart was pounding like a gorilla."

"Tere." Jason points to the on-air light. He reaches over me and quickly shuts it off.

My face feels hotter than the sun. "Did they hear me?" I gasp.

"Yeah, probably. But you didn't say anything incriminating."

It's not me I'm worried about. He called me by my name. Tere. "Did they hear you?" I'm hyperventilating now and grab Jason's chair for support.

"Hear me what?" He looks confused.

"Say my name!"

"No, definitely not. I was a few feet from the mike. The pickup isn't that good."

My face has not cooled down. Not one bit. I hope he knows CPR.

"Trust me, Tere. If there's not a mike directly in front of you, they can't hear you." He puts a hand on my shoulder. "Breathe. You look like you're about to burst."

Tell me about it. After that, I take a break from the air. Hopefully, Mom didn't hear the part about the gorilla. The last thing I need is her saying that associating yourself with a gorilla is very bad for your image. And hopefully the rest of the world, including Gavin, didn't hear Jason call me Tere.

But after I pick up a few phone lines and no one says anything about it, I feel a lot better. They don't mention my gorilla comment either. They just want to tell so and so how much they love them and so and so that they can have their baby anytime. That's fine with me. Have all the babies you want as long as you don't call me by my real name.

Jason convinces me to end the show. I figure I have nothing to lose. "Miami, we're leaving you tonight with Speed Bump and 'Capture My Love.' Sleep tight and we'll see you here tomorrow night, same place, same time on The Love Shack 92.7 The SLAM." I make sure I shut off the mike right away.

Jason high-fives me. "Whew, we did it."

We're meeting after school at Kayla's to work on the project, so I told Derek I'd be an hour late. Hopefully we'll be done by then. Since Kayla is the only one with wheels, we all meet at her car. It's less than a five-minute ride to her house, so I can catch the bus at my usual stop.

Kayla sets us up at her kitchen table. The kitchen lets in a lot of sun and smells like fresh lemons. The place is gleaming. I'm afraid to press my sneakers against the white tiles in case they leave scuff marks.

I quickly take the seat next to Gavin. He's wearing all black again today; with his dark eyes and black hair, you'd think he'd look like a corpse, but he actually looks hot. The rich black is a nice contrast to his milky white skin. It's like when you dunk an Oreo into a glass of milk.

I stare at his face to see if there are any signs that he knows I'm Sweet T. He doesn't even look over at me. Maybe he's disgusted by the gorilla comment.

I shiver. That studio mike could be the death of me.

Kayla has a new hot-pink folder in front of her, entitled *Internet Research*. Oh, brother.

She doesn't even wait until she sits down to start blabbing, "Okay, so I did a little investigating last night and found the perfect idea for Tere."

Gavin and I both glare at her. We know better than to stop her mid-idea.

"I knew there was more to Helen Keller than you told us, so I googled her and found out that as a child she performed in vaudeville shows . . ."

Damn, she found me out. What's next? She's going to tell me that Helen was a nudist? That's where I draw the line.

"Like a circus act?" Gavin asks.

"Not exactly. Vaudeville is a theatrical act consisting of various performances, which can include singing, dancing, and pantomime."

What, did she memorize the dictionary?

"And?" Gavin folds the corner of the flowered place mat in front of him.

"She can do a mime performance." Kayla yanks the place mat out of Gavin's reach.

I shake my head and mutter, "Ahh."

"Or would you rather *speak*?" Kayla dangles the word "speak" over my head like an evil captor might.

Hmm? An image runs through my head of the first time Helen went to the ocean. She was so excited that she plunged right in. Unaware of its vastness, she had no fear. I need to think of this project as just our group in the front of the classroom. Not me, alone in front of a room full of students. I need to do it my way.

"How about if I spell words into people's hands to communicate with them? Helen did that," I say.

Kayla rubs her chin. Gavin and I both eye each other.

"Yeah, I read that," she finally speaks. "It's pretty neat. You could spell a few things into my hand when we do our introduction." Kayla quickly jots that down.

I look over at Gavin. His hands are resting on the table. He's wearing a silver thumb ring today. I wish I could trace the lines of his palms.

When Kayla's finished writing, she hands Gavin a couple of sheets of blue paper. "What's this?" he asks.

"Just info on Stephen King's band, The Rock Bottom Remainders, if you need any inspiration for your song." She pushes the stapler over to him. This girl must max out her mom's credit card at Office Depot.

"Thanks. I've got a couple of their songs. They're not bad."

"How's your song?" I ask.

"Going pretty well. Not ready for the radio yet."

"What do you mean?"

"I heard a new band last night and . . . no, it's pretty stupid, forget it . . ." He lowers his head and traces the grooves of wood in the table.

"What?" I lightly place my hand on his shoulder. The electric current is back, sending waves through my body. He looks up, and I force myself not to let nerves pull me away from the warmth of his back.

"I heard this cool band, Shrinking Violet, and was thinking how amazing it would be to go from fooling around in your garage to all of a sudden hearing your song on the radio. Big dream, I know," he says.

I want to yell, I chose that song for *you*! I guess that means Jason was right—nobody heard him or me. Phew, I can breathe again.

The phone rings and Kayla runs to answer it.

"Is that the kind of stuff you play?" I ask.

"Yeah, I like to think. Not too realistic, huh?" He looks up at me, and his face is just inches from mine. My nerves are working overdrive. I can hardly stand it. I want to pull him closer and feel his lips against mine. But I remind myself that we are in Kayla's kitchen.

"No, it's great!" I say a little too loud to drown out the thumping of my own heart.

"Thanks. I can't wait to listen to that show tonight, in case they have any other new tunes." I look into Gavin's eyes. They are glowing.

"Which show?" I bite my lip.

"*The Love Shack.* The show I mentioned earlier. Jason's been on this week with some chick."

"Chick?" I'm a chick? Chicken? Hot chicken? KFC Girl?

He blushes. "Sorry, that was rude. But she sounds cute. She goes by the name Sweet T and she has a sexy voice."

"Really?" I say, with a little more raspiness than usual. *Hello, I'm right here next to you.* But of course I can't say what I'm really thinking.

Wait, does that mean he likes her more than me? Is it possible to be jealous of yourself?

chapter SIXTEEN

Mom calls from the hairdresser and asks me to pop the chicken in the oven for dinner. And no, she didn't make it. She bought it at Stella's Marketplace, famous for their gourmet food. She's busy getting highlights at the salon, but says she'll be home soon. I fix a garden salad and baked potatoes, too. Tonight is my first night off in a couple of weeks, and I'm spending it with Mom and Rob. I hope that's not a recipe for disaster.

I'm sprawled on the couch, flipping through channels, when Rob gets home. He heads straight for the fridge to grab a beer.

"Mind if I join you?" He slides into his La-Z-Boy and kicks off his boots.

It's your house, dude. "No."

He stretches his legs out. "Man, I'm starved."

"Dinner's ready. Just waiting for Mom." I catch a glimpse of PJ Squid, shirtless on MTV, lounging in a beach chair. It's a promo for his upcoming album, *Calamari*. Mmm, would I love a bite of him.

"Thanks. Played a round of golf today with a couple of guys from the bank, worked up my appetite."

Slightly more exciting than my day of sleeping until noon, obsessing over whether Gavin likes me, and cramming for my physics and sociology exams.

I hear the front door unlock and Mom's bracelets jangling. She's also gabbing on the phone. She never makes a quiet entrance. "What do you think?" Mom stands in front of the TV, still on her cell. Her two hundred dollar highlights could not be achieved naturally by even the best sunbather.

Be smart, Rob. If you say the right thing, we can eat quicker.

"Beautiful," he says, then gets up and cups his hands around Mom's face. "Makes you look ten years younger."

"Oh, you're so sweet." Mom nuzzles his nose and quickly says good-bye to the person on the other line.

"Looks good." I walk past them to the kitchen. The highlights do make her seem younger, but her ego doesn't need any more inflating, so I keep it at that.

Dinner consists of dishes being passed back and forth and Mom and Rob playing footsie under the table. I might not have known if she didn't accidentally attack my foot first. It's times like this that I could really use a brother or sister. Dog. Anything.

But it's still much better than the old days when Mom and I used to eat alone or when she'd bring home one of her dates. I'd never know if I was going to be the center of criticism or a stand-in for a potted plant. Keeping my mouth shut seemed like the safest bet. Plus, I didn't see why I should bother getting to know her dates if they just came in and out of a revolving door. I was really surprised and skeptical that only three weeks after meeting Rob, she dumped all her other suitors. I guess he knows how to keep her happy. He deserves a gold medal for that.

Rob cracks open another beer. "Tere, the show sounded good last night."

I nearly choke on a piece of chicken and wash it down with some water. "Really?"

"Yeah, the building's still in one piece." He laughs.

Mom glares at me like that was not a joke. I laugh, too, just to show her.

Rob puts down his beer. "But seriously, as you know, we're trying to bring up our Arbitron ratings and it looks like you and Jason taking over *The Love Shack* could help do the trick. Garrison was only filling in anyway, so for now I want Jason to stay put. He brings a fresh sound to the station, and you guys make a good team."

My lips are stretched so wide, I'm afraid they might snap like frayed rubber bands. A small "thanks" escapes from them.

"Are you sure that's such a good idea?" Mom fishes a piece of ice from her glass and slips it into her mouth.

I drop my knife and fork onto my plate and push it away from me. "Why wouldn't it be?"

"I know how you are, and this is not fun and games. Being on the radio is serious business." She crunches hard on the ice.

"You think I don't know that? I love music."

"I understand that. But let's face it, you're not the most social person in the world, and to be on-air, you have to be friendly."

I try to smile, but I feel like it looks more like I'm sucking on an orange. "Give me a chance, Mother." I jump up from my seat.

Rob puts his hand on the small of Mom's back. "Delilah, it's true. Tere knows her stuff."

Mom strokes his face. "Okay, baby. I just don't want her to ruin anything for you."

"Too late," I growl. "You've already done that for me."

"What did you say?" Mom breaks away from Rob.

"You heard me." I enunciate each word like I'm giving the opening speech at a hard-of-hearing convention.

"After all I've done for you?" Mom says.

"Like what?"

"You're such an ungrateful bitch!" Mom fumes.

"Now, Delilah." Rob pulls her out of her chair and onto his lap.

Mom lowers her head. "I'm trying my best."

Right, by calling me a bitch.

Rob turns to me and says, "It'll be okay." Then he pulls Mom's face up to his and gives her a kiss.

How does he know? He hasn't lived with her for eighteen years!

I've had enough. She can't stand the attention on someone else for a second. I run up to my room and no one stops me.

I try to think of all the positive things that have happened to me since I started doing the show. With Jason at the lead and with my music knowledge, we have it going on. And I still can't believe Gavin actually said Sweet T was sexy. So what if he was only referring to my voice and didn't know it was actually me?

I speed-dial Audrey's number and don't even wait for her to speak before I rant about Mom, the Princess.

Finally, Audrey says, "Wow, I don't think I've ever heard you talk for so long. That was two and a half minutes." Her second favorite show, *Love Knots,* blares in the background.

"You were timing me?"

"No, you called during a commercial break. You should get pissed more often."

"Is that supposed to cheer me up?" I toss my teddy bear, DJ, against the wall and watch him fall facedown.

"No, no," Audrey backpedals, "that was totally bitchy of the Princess. But it sounds like Rob's got your back, so don't worry."

"Yeah, I guess. Plus, Gavin likes the show. A lot."

"You told him?" She turns down the volume on the tube.

"No, of course not. But we talked about the show, and he digs Sweet T."

"Ohmigod, Tere. You're a mess. You should sign up for *Love Knots.*"

"Thanks." I pick my bear up and loosen the plaid tie around his neck. Then I prop him up next to me. "I'll tell Gavin someday."

"Wouldn't it be cool if you told him on live TV?"

"No." I hang up.

After I'm off the phone, I download all the Shrinking Violet songs I can find and pump up the volume on my iPod. I'm moving like crazy around the room and don't give a damn. This is mine and Gavin's band, even if he doesn't know it. It's like we have a special bond, but the only thing is, I can't tell him or my cover will be blown. Then *The Love Shack* won't seem so special to him anymore. I burn a copy of the songs for him and shove the CD into my backpack. Mom can't stop me now.

★ ★ ★

This is Sweet T banging out the hits tonight on 92.7 The SLAM. I'm loading up your requests as fast as I can, Miami. Here's Shrinking Violet with "Cold-Hearted Mermaid" . . .

chapter SEVENTEEN

On Monday after school we meet at Kayla's again to work on the project. This girl is a slave driver. She'll definitely end up CEO of some major company. Either that or have a mental breakdown and devote her life to watching game shows.

Kayla hands out more sheets of paper. She has printed out a script for everyone. Of course the presentation begins and ends with her, which is fine with me.

I start out by spelling "water" into Judy Blume's hand at the table, and she pours me a glass. After telling us a short gory tale, Stephen King whips out his guitar. While he's playing, Judy roller-skates around. Then I do my mime act. In the end, we have our own vaudeville show. I have a few speaking lines, but otherwise

Kayla does the majority of the talking. I'm not too comfortable with having to speak, but I keep my mouth shut about it. I don't want Kayla to come up with any more *brilliant* ideas, like having me stuff my mouth with cotton balls.

Our presentation clocks in at thirteen minutes. Perfect, because Ms. Peters said it had to be twelve to fifteen minutes. Kayla says if we run short, she'll just do some skating tricks. Geez, can't wait.

After we do one run-through, Kayla declares it munchie time and heads to the fridge to put the finishing touch on her snack trays. I watch as Gavin swirls his thumb ring round and round. Eventually he catches me and slides the ring over. "Try it on."

The silver is warm from his touch. I pray it's too big. I've always wanted dainty hands like Audrey or Mom, but my fingers look more like hot dogs. I slip the ring onto my thumb. It fits. Perfectly. I want to keep it on, if only for a minute. So I have to think of something to say. Anything.

"Are you going to the prom?" I look away from his face. I immediately regret the question. I already know the answer. But, still, I was hoping he had changed his mind. Hoping that he'd want to go with me.

"No, I'm going to see Speed Bump play on the Beach."

"Oh, that's right." I pick up the pastel pink paper and pretend to be enthralled with the script.

"Yeah, I didn't even realize it was the same night. My brother's coming back from Florida State that weekend. He surprised me with the tickets, so I figured, why not?"

Why not? I could list a thousand reasons, with prom being number one. I kick my sneaker against the coffee-table leg. "Sure." I hand him the ring back.

"I heard they play until the club kicks them out."

I heard people dance at the prom until their feet are throbbing and their lips are sore from kissing all night. Does he even wonder if I'm going? I never even considered attending prom before I met him. I had already crossed it off my list a long time ago.

I can think of nothing to say except, *Change your mind, take me to prom.* So instead, I stare at Gavin's thumb. He does, too.

I wish Sweet T were here. She would ask him to the prom, and the sad thing is, he'd probably say yes. I try to find the words to plead with him to change his mind, but my lips tremble, and I'm afraid if I open up, all that will come out is a puddle of drool.

He slides slightly closer to me, and his thigh grazes mine. There's something about Gavin that puts me at ease. I feel like we've known each other a lot longer than a couple of months.

"Okay," Kayla butts into our silence. "We have cheddar and American cheese, Ritz crackers and Wheat Thins. Miniquiches and my specialty, glazed almond tarts." She sets the tray down in front of us.

Is Betty Crocker serious?

"Thanks," Gavin and I both say.

I wait for Gavin and Kayla to reach for the appetizers before I take a few. Mom says that no matter how hungry you are, you should never be the first one to attack the food tray at a party. I would hardly call this a party, but I don't want Gavin to think of me as a pig. Of course, that doesn't stop me from diving in for seconds.

After we're done eating, Kayla makes us do another run-through of the presentation. She stops us a couple of times, to tell Gavin to slow down on the strumming and for me to make better eye contact, which is kind of stupid since Helen couldn't *make* eye contact.

We're almost done practicing when Kayla's freshman brother bursts into the room.

"What is it, Wizard?" She crosses her arms and glares at him.

He's panting. "They just fired the freshman football coach for bad-mouthing the administration and lying about it."

"What a loser!" Kayla says.

"It's about time!" Gavin hisses.

"Why?" I ask. Since when does the guy that skips prom and doodles skulls on his folder care about the football coach?

"He had it coming," Gavin says.

Kayla's brother scrunches his eyebrows together. "He did?"

"The guy's a liar." Gavin clenches his fist. "I can't stand people that skate the truth like it's no big deal."

My internal temperature drops until I feel like a human icicle. You hate lies? What about secret identities?

Kayla shoos her brother out of the room. But neither of us moves, the fumes from Gavin still simmering.

Finally Kayla says, "Are you on the team?"

"Was. Freshman year." Gavin picks up his guitar.

"And?" Kayla prods.

Gavin strums louder. "Nothing I want to talk about."

For once Kayla doesn't say anything else. Instead, we both watch Gavin play the guitar. He's sexy when he's mad. His hair strikes his cheek as he bobs his head up and down. His eyes are intense, focused on the guitar. I picture him up onstage strumming his guts out to a crowded room filled with screaming fans. I'm mesmerized.

I finally glance over at Kayla's huge kitchen clock. Oh great, Derek's going to kill me. I wish I didn't have to leave. If I could ditch Derek's gig and focus on *The Love Shack*, I'd have more time. But I made a three-month commitment and I don't want him to use it against me. Who knows what scheme he could come up with to publicly humiliate *moi*? I shudder just thinking about it. Time for another fabrication. "I'm late. My aunt's coming for dinner." I stand up and grab my backpack.

Gavin sets down his guitar. "No problem. Give me your number and I'll call you later in case Kayla makes any more changes to torture us."

"Really? That's so nice," I say.

Gavin plugs my digits into his cell.

Kayla stares at us.

"What?" I can't help but ask.

"Oh, nothing, you just seem like brother and sister. It's cute." Kayla smiles.

Damn, crush my heart with a two-ton boulder. Brother and sister. Not cute. Red-hot lovers, much cuter.

I zip open my backpack and take out the Shrinking Violet mix that I burned for Gavin. "I almost forgot. For you."

"Thanks." Gavin smiles. "This is great."

I don't wait for him or Kayla to say anything else—I just rush out the door. When I'm halfway to the bus, I realize Gavin has my number programmed into his phone! Of course, he might never call, but for good luck I pull out my cell and kiss it. It hasn't rung for two days. The only numbers I have stored in it are Mom's, Rob's, Audrey's, and Domino's. I know, lame.

Gavin, not lame.

I overheard Rob talking on his BlackBerry last night about the SLAM power lunch where all the "heads" get together to strategize. That's when they come up with their promotions, giveaways, and crazy stunts to attract more attention. I know they had the big meeting today. I don't know if they can top last year's scheme to boost ratings, though. Garrison dressed up as an old lady and tried to sneak into a Juice Box concert. What makes it even funnier is that he's six foot four and has a goatee.

Derek's clicking away on the laptop when I slip into the studio. I didn't even know he could write. "Thought you ditched," he says over his shoulder.

Tried to. "Sorry, had a school project to work on." I plunk into the chair.

Derek goes on-air for a quick station ID, then resumes typing.

I just sit there like a stuffed elephant. I know I wanted as little contact with him as possible, but this is really awkward. "Where's Jason?"

"I told him he could come in late since he's been working so hard on his show."

This puts me on high alert, and I scoot my chair back in case he wants to try anything. But a second later, Paul, another producer, comes in with coffee. He stays to chat for a few minutes, then leaves to run some copies for Derek.

"Need me to go through the commercials?" I ask.

"Nah, it's been done. I'm doing a teaser for your show in the next break, so I want you to give a quick shout-out."

"Thanks." I nod. Wish Jason was here, but I can handle it. I shouldn't complain, at least Derek's chatting up our show.

"Hey, all you studs out there," Derek says into the mike. "Have I got a surprise for you! Now I'm not talking about you old dudes, this shout-out goes to all the high school guys. Thinking about prom, but don't have a date? Or just want to show up with a really hot chick? Well, if you're musical, I've got the ultimate SLAM contest for you. There's a megahottie in the studio here and she's dateless for the prom . . ."

Where? I look around.

He turns to face me for a quick second and flashes all his teeth. I cringe. "It's none other than SLAM's own teen DJ, Sweet T."

No, he didn't. This nightmare can't be happening to me. I'm

suddenly queasy. "So if you'd like to escort her to her prom, record your own love song and send it to us here at the station," Derek continues. "Vocals have to be sung and written by you. You can catch all the rules that I just finished uploading on our Web site. Dude, if I was only a few years younger. . . . " A few? Try twenty! "The winner also receives a free tux from Alan's Formalwear, Hummer limo escort to and from the prom courtesy of Drive In Style and three hundred dollars spending cash. And the best part: your song will be played on the radio! So good luck!" He motions for me to step up to the mike.

I try to move, but I'm frozen. If I take one step, I might crumple into tiny little pieces. Derek pulls me by the arm.

"Ouch." I wince.

"So, do you have your dress yet, T?" he says into the mike.

"No, not yet." I try my hardest not to sound like someone on her deathbed.

"I'm sure she'll tell you all about the slinky number coming up on *The Love Shack* tonight at seven." He brings up a Mintpaste tune and shuts off the mike.

So basically someone pockets some cash and is driven around in style just to escort me to the prom. This is definitely a scheme my mother would've come up with if only she were smart enough.

This contest has got to be illegal. "I don't think Rob will go for it." I stand up again even though I'm still trembling from head to toe.

"Not to worry, I ran it by him this morning. He loves the idea." Derek yanks the gold chain around his neck.

"He does?"

"Look at the phone lines already. They're ringing off the hook. People eat this stuff up, T."

"Didn't you even consider consulting with me before you offered away my life?" My legs start to give way and I slump back down into the chair. What did I do to deserve this humiliation?

"For a sec. But I knew you'd totally be up for it. This is your chance. You never know who might submit a killer song." Derek pops the plastic lid to his coffee and downs half of it.

"That's exactly what I'm worried about. It could be some total freak, ax murderer."

"I have a friend on the force. I'll have him run background checks on all the finalists." He picks up one of the phone lines and tells the caller to check out everything on the Web site.

I need access to the Internet and fast. Maybe I can erase the whole thing and pretend that it never happened.

Derek picks up the phone again and repeats the same line about accessing all the rules. If I could roll into a ball and die, I would. I can't go through with this, and now I'm totally trapped if Rob's already in love with the idea. Maybe I can come up with a different scenario that would involve me being shipped away to a tiny island only accessible by canoe.

"Don't worry, Tere, you'll have fun, and think of the exposure." Derek grins.

My stomach whirs like a dishwasher short-circuiting and I motor to the bathroom. I reach the toilet just in time and watch my dinner flush down the bowl with my life. How can I go through with this? I know the listeners don't know it's me, but once they find out, I'll be an even bigger loser than I already am. I'll have to wear a full armor suit to school to protect me from the wounds.

The bathroom door busts open and I hear someone calling my name. "Tere, are you in there?"

"Go away," I moan.

"It's me. Kelly. Are you okay?" She knocks lightly on the stall door.

"No."

"The calls are coming in like crazy. You are *so* popular."

I open the stall door a few inches. "What are you talking about?"

"You've got tons of guys that want to go to prom with you. You'll just have to pick the one with the best song."

"But they don't even know me." I lower the lid and sit down.

"Well, they love your voice, so that's a start." She sounds like my school guidance counselor fishing for my good qualities to put in my college recommendation.

"Until they see me."

"It'll be great. I swear." She pulls the stall door open all the way and leans down to give me a hug. I hope I don't smell like puke. She squeezes tight.

No one's ever hugged me like that before. It felt good, even if it came with inflatable boobs.

"I'll be here if you need anything." Kelly smiles.

"I hope you own a body bag." I pry myself off the seat and shuffle over to the sink to splash some water on my face and rinse out my mouth. I turn the water on full blast and when I'm done splashing, my white PJ Squid tee is soaked. Great, now I'm rewarding Derek for being an ass with a free titty show.

Kelly catches on immediately and runs out to snag me a SLAM tee to throw on instead. I never thought she'd be the one to save the day. Boy, was I wrong. Without her, I would've spent the night in the bathroom.

When I'm back in the studio, Derek hands me a printout of the contest rules. I read down the list. The song has to be an original, the guy must be in high school, and it says the tune has to be under three minutes. Also, the person can't have a recording contract. Great, that rules out Lil' Ray and the two youngest hotties from Speed Bump. At least that would've made it worth it. Everything is done anonymously, and I select the winner. Well, at least I get to do something. Then I read down to the end. "What?" I shriek. "I can't meet the guy until prom?"

"I added that part in last minute, made the station's lawyer scramble like crazy. Brilliant, eh?" Derek taps himself on the chest. "People love suspense. And that way the cameras will be rolling and we'll be able to broadcast live on the Internet. It'll really up our Web presence."

And send me back to my room. Forever. "What if the winner hates me?" I say to my sneaks.

"Then just give him what he wants and he'll forget what you look like." Derek laughs.

Why do I even bother talking to him like he's a human being?

I refuse to answer the phones for the rest of the show. I'm trying to let this all sink in, to see the bright side, if possible. At least I'll be going to the prom and who knows? The guy could actually be hot. All expense paid is pretty cool, and maybe this will get Mom off my back. She should be happy, now that she has an excuse to chaperone.

The part that freaks me out the most is that this is totally going to blow my cover. I like being the *mystery* woman. I don't know what to do. Wear a disguise to the prom? But how long could I keep that up? Knowing me, my wig would come flying off when I was attempting to dance or something.

"Hey, Derek." I come out of my coma. "My principal will never agree. She's a stiff."

"I've got Ms. Cuniff by the—" Derek reaches for his balls but stops short. "She said district approval was no problem. The winner has to be a student registered in Miami-Dade County. And we're only going to reveal which school you go to, live, at the prom. When students are buzzing about the contest, they won't know you're among them. So there should be no distraction from learning at Ridgeland." He laughs. "Besides, we're making a donation to the school."

Figures.

"But how are we going to keep this a secret from everyone? If one person finds out . . ." I tap my nails on the console.

"Trust me, the whole thing is under wraps. It'll be awesome."

Teresa Adams sold to the highest bidder, Ms. Cuniff. I never thought I'd go down like this. Three weeks until prom. God, it's going to be a long three weeks.

Every time someone calls about the contest, Derek gives me a synopsis of the conversation. One guy wants to know if I like songs about roses, another wants to know if I have a thing for role-playing. Most just want SLAM to post a photo of me on the Web.

I go on the air a few times with Jason, but mostly I'm trying to let the plan to ruin my life sink in. Jason assures me that the exposure will be good for my career.

For the rest of the night I search for an out. Finally, when Jason's turning the corner to my street, it comes to me like a flash of lightning. What if random people try and stop by the station to catch a glimpse of Sweet T? They might not gain access to the studio, but nobody can stop them from hanging by the front door. Yes, this is my ticket out. There's no way we can keep my identity a secret from the world. Derek will have to think of another way to boost the show's ratings without exploiting my anonymity.

chapter EIGHTEEN

After Jason drops me off, I find Mom and Rob sitting at the kitchen table drinking cappuccinos. There's a bag of biscottis and a plate of croissants in front of them. I stick my head in and mumble good night, but Mom motions me to the table. I'm still pissed at her for calling me a bitch, but I'm too tired to fight. I slump down into the chair.

"Would you like one?" Mom pushes the cellophane bag of assorted biscottis toward me.

She's offering me food past ten? Something's got to be up.

I shake my head. Even though I'm hungry, I'm not falling into one of her traps.

"Listen, Tere. I wanted to apologize for yesterday. I was out of line," she says.

No kidding. I don't budge an inch. I'm not meeting her halfway. She could've raised a heroin addict, but she got me—good girl, former snowball—who spends most of her time in her room.

Mom wipes some froth from her lips with a napkin and continues, "I just didn't want you to fall into a situation that you couldn't get out of."

"Well, you can get me out of one now. Derek announced some crazy prom contest, but I don't see how it can work." I fold my arms against my chest.

She wants peace? Let her work for it.

"That's what we wanted to talk to you about." Rob sets his cup back into the saucer.

"So you agree? It makes no sense." Phew, I lean back into the chair and finally breathe.

"Actually, I think it's a great idea. We're number two in teen demographics, and this stunt is sure to secure us the number one spot. You can have a lot of fun with it."

"Mom?" I look at her, plead with my eyes.

"What? Now you're going to prom!" She sounds like she's announcing the Florida Lotto winner, not the end of my life.

"Or do you mean, now *you're* going?" I say. She's been on me all year to be a chaperone and now her dream has come true, while mine has been squashed. Funny how that works.

"I only wanted to help." She secures the cellophane bag shut with a chip clip.

"I have a bad feeling about this setup. What if the winner is disappointed when it's just me? Not some supercelebrity." I cover my face with my hands.

"That won't happen. We'll get you all dolled up and pick out a beautiful dress. I'll ask Pamela to do your makeup."

Suddenly I'm famished. I reach for the plate of croissants and grab one. Mom pulls the end of it. "Just half. We have a dance to prepare for."

I roll my eyes, grab a second one, and storm out of the kitchen. And I thought she was apologizing? How stupid of me.

In my room I catch a glimpse of myself in the mirror in my SLAM tee. Two months ago I only dreamed of being on the air, and now I have people calling up to say how much they like me. I take a bite of one of the croissants, but reality hits. I have to get glammed up and wear a slinky dress in a few weeks. I toss the pastries into the trash and stick on my headphones. Music is the best medicine.

* * *

Hey, Miami, it's me, Sweet T. I hope you're still out there. . . . It's a quiet night, I have no contests to run, no celebrity gossip—it's just me, you, the mike, and an old track by Pete Baxter before he was with Juice Box, before he was a somebody . . . "Split Open Wide" . . .

★ ★ ★

As I'm walking toward the library after school, I overhear two guys talking about the prom contest. I'm sure they mean SLAM's contest, so I slow down, pretend to be frantically searching for something from my backpack.

"Dude, you should totally enter. Then you'd get to go to the senior prom," the kid with the crew cut says to his friend.

The other guy is barely five feet and weighs about as much as a box of uncooked noodles. "Yeah, that'd be so cool. But I can't sing."

Thank God for that! This is really scaring me. It's going to be a treacherous few weeks until the prom—talk about a long drawn-out death.

I finally zip up my bag when the conversation switches to jockstraps. I'm about to turn the corner when I see Gavin at the far end of the hall by his locker. He couldn't possibly hear them talking that far away. Could he? I thought he was absent since I didn't see him in English class today. He pulls out his notebook and shoves it into his bag. I shuffle his way, hoping he'll turn around and say something. He didn't call. I've checked my cell like a hundred times. I know it's kind of stupid, it's only been one night, but still, I was hoping I'd hear from him.

He looks up. His eyes are like polished stone. "Hey, Tere." He shuts his locker.

"Hi." I pretend to be surprised. Pretend that I didn't know locker 203 was his. "I figured you were sick."

"No, I forgot to tell you guys yesterday that I had a dentist appointment today. Did I miss anything in class?"

"Just Kayla whining. We didn't work on the project today." I rub the tip of my sneaker against the linoleum. It makes a little screeching noise.

Gavin laughs. "Oh, and thanks for the Shrinking Violet tunes. They were even cooler than I imagined."

"No prob." I smile. "I'm mad for Shrinking Violet."

"Me, too. How was dinner?"

"Dinner?" It's only two o'clock.

His eyes narrow. "With your aunt."

"Oh, that. Fine. Good food. Yeah." I nod, trying to convince myself that I didn't really eat dinner out of the vending machine at SLAM last night. "Did I miss anything?"

"Only Kayla stressing over the schedule. She shifted a few things."

"She'll give herself an ulcer."

Gavin laughs again. "Or us. If you have a sec, I'll go over everything and save you from meeting with her."

"I'd love that." *More than you'd ever know.* My homework can wait and Mom's not picking me up for another hour. We stroll over to the picnic table near the school parking lot. Alone time with Gavin—if Audrey could see me now!

We sit across from each other. He shows me Kayla's revised schedule, and I pull out my heavily doodled *I Love Gavin* notebook. I quickly flip the pages, so he doesn't think I'm a deranged stalker.

It turns out Kayla just moved around a few things—a couple more lines for her, a longer skating solo, and a big group hug at the end. I'm really not even thinking about the presentation because the contest has taken over my brain. But if sitting here, talking about the presentation, means more face time with Gavin, I'm all for it. Unfortunately, we're done discussing the project after twenty minutes.

I don't want him to leave, so I point to his iPod resting on the table. "Isn't that the best invention ever?"

"Definitely. Whoever came up with portable music was a genius." He cups the thin black rectangle in his hand.

"I'd be dead without mine." I feel inside my pocket to make sure it's still there.

"So, who's your favorite band?"

"Hard to say. I get totally lost in Speed Bump and Juice Box when I'm having a bad day, but PJ Squid, Gracie May, and Mint-paste pump me up."

"I know what you're saying. I've got music for different moods, too."

A few volleyball players walk by. I scan the group to make sure Stacy's not going to jump out and attack me. Thank God she's not with them.

I pick at a splinter of wood on the table. "So I'm not the only insane one."

"Nope." He pushes his bangs out of his eyes.

I stare back at him and utter, "Good."

Gavin rests his elbows on the table. "You know, you're so easy to talk to. You don't jabber on and on like most girls."

I want to pelt him with questions: *So what does that mean? Do you think I'm cute? Will you ever ask me out?*

But I take the safe approach. "Thanks. I like talking to you, too."

We both blush, and I rack my brain for a way to get out of this awkward but wonderful moment.

Gavin beats me to it. "Do you like Maltese?"

I nod my head.

He scrolls through some songs on his iPod and hands me an earbud. "Check out this track. They can't play this version on the radio."

I already know that he's talking about the thirty-second intro to "Hot Button," where Maltese mouths off about his cheating ex, but I make like it's Gavin's discovery. "Wow. That's heated," I say after the track is over.

"Yeah, he must've been so ticked at that Lyla girl."

"Or maybe he did something to her first."

"I guess there are two sides to every story."

"Mmm." I'm still thinking about how nice it would be to go to the prom with Gavin instead of Mr. X. I could be paired with a serial killer in training or worse, a guy that eats cold spaghetti in his oversized undies all day.

Maybe I should tell Gavin to enter the SLAM contest. I know he can play the guitar well, but he has to be able to sing, too. I wonder why his tune for the project is all instrumental.

"Hey, why aren't you writing a song for the presentation?" I ask.

"Getting up in front of the class and playing my guitar is daunting enough, don't you think?"

"Yeah." I nod.

There goes that idea . . . out the window. I guess I'll have to rely on fate to pick a decent contest winner.

"That's cool." Gavin reaches over and touches the bracelet on my arm. It's braided leather with silver butterflies. His fingers linger and send chills up my spine.

"Thanks. I got it last summer at an art festival in Coconut Grove."

"It's really pretty."

I smile, pretending that he's talking about me, not my fashion accessory. We lace fingers. Before I even have a chance to take a deep breath, he stands up and slides onto my side of the bench. He is sitting so close to me, I hope he doesn't mistake my heart for a ticking time bomb.

I look into Gavin's eyes. They are soft. He scoots even closer, but I am frozen. I take a deep breath and lean forward. I can feel his breath on my lips. *Body, don't fail me now.* I press my lips against his. The touch is magical, lighting up my whole body.

A car horn beeps, and he quickly removes his lips from mine. I look over. Damn, it's Mom. She rolls down her window and waves. Why does she have to ruin everything? Does she know how long I waited for a kiss like this?

I shove my notebook into my bag. "Sorry, Gavin. That's my mom. I have an appointment."

He rises from the bench, too. "I'll see you tomorrow. And don't worry about the project. It'll be fine."

Wish I could say that about the rest of my life. "I hope."

We say good-bye and I run to the car. Mom beeps again when I'm like fifteen feet away. Does she think I'm going to do my penguin run in front of Gavin?

Mom agreed to drive me to the station every day until the contest is over so my cover isn't blown. She blasts the tunes from SUN FM on the drive to SLAM, and I stare out the window. Occasionally she lowers the volume to talk about prom-dress styles or hair accessories, but other than that, we let the tunes carry the conversation.

When we're about five minutes from the station, Mom turns off the radio. "Who was that boy?"

"Where?" I look out the window, hoping there are random boys running across the intersection.

"The one you were sitting with when I picked you up."

"A kid from my English class. We're working on a group project together."

"Right," she confirms to herself. "From where I was sitting, he looked goth."

I don't want to argue with her, but I feel the need to protect him. "Mom, he's not goth."

"Could've fooled me. What kind of person wears all black on a day like this?"

I don't want to share any part of Gavin with her. I lightly trace my lips with my fingertip. I can still feel his lips pressed against mine—soft but firm. "He's a plain old nice guy who happens to like dark colors. You don't even know him."

"Exactly."

You can never win with her.

We pull up to the parking garage and Mom slides her access card into the machine. The bar raises and she zooms inside, right up to the elevator. "I really hope you meet a decent guy through this contest."

"Wishful thinking. This is a blind date, after all." I shut the car door. Voice meets voice. Mystery man hears me on the radio, and I hear him sing. Why can't we just leave it that way?

I try and keep a low profile at the station, but that's kind of hard when Cindy from promotions pops in every five minutes to ask me stupid questions. I was okay with her asking what color flowers and confetti do I prefer for prom, but then she asked me for the measurements of the dance floor. Okay, it doesn't take a PhD in promotions for a person to figure out that maybe the hotel might be the best place to find that answer.

"Has Cindy always been this . . . not so bright?" I ask Jason.

He laughs. "Sometimes she takes her job a little too seriously."

"Yeah." I roll my eyes. "Maybe she'd like to go on the date."

"You know, I think this experience might be good for you." Jason cues up a Moonstar track.

My face drops. Even Jason's turning on me. This is not good.

He puts a hand on my shoulder. "What I mean is, it's like your first step into dating. You're cute. You're eighteen. And you need to have more fun. Consider this prom gig a practice run."

"I never thought of it that way. But I do like someone at school."

"Hello?" He knocks softly on my head. "Then why the hell aren't you going with him?"

"He's seeing Speed Bump play with his brother on the Beach that night."

"Man, that's a bummer. Well, once he hears about this contest, he'll wish he'd went with you."

"Let's hope so." I write Gavin's name on the console with my finger. "Wait, but the prom will be over by then."

Jason cues me, "You're on in thirty."

Gavin, I hope you're listening. The music director added Shrinking Violet to the rotation, so we're not only playing them during the request hour.

"You're on in ten, Tere," Jason reminds me.

I move closer to the mike and breathe deeply. I remind myself that no one can see me. They don't know it's me, Tere Adams, behind the shield of the mike. I'm just Sweet T to them.

The red light goes on and so do I: "Good evening, Miami, you're listening to *The Love Shack* on 92.7 WEMD SLAM-FM. It's Sweet T in the studio with the one and only Jason Stevens. I hope you liked that fast track, 'Sultry Summer Love' by Moonstar. Before that we had Juice Box with 'Lemonade' and Gracie May with 'Stay.' I'm mad for Shrinking Violet and here they are with 'Freeze-Dried Love' . . ." Did I say that already tonight? Geez, I feel like an old lady. Maybe I should write down everything before I go on-air.

Jason's busy with the phones, so I tune him out and let Shrinking Violet take over. *You're going away, you say, but I still love you so, even if you have to go, we'll work it out, we can take it real slow, I'll freeze-dry your love and pull it out little by little when I'm feeling low . . .*

I've played this on my iPod over and over, but, still, by the end of the song, I'm almost in tears. How sad. It's hard enough to find someone to fall in love with, but what if they leave? I never thought about that. Maybe I am better off going to the prom with someone that I've never met. That way we don't have to say good-bye and cling to one memory, one special night. If it doesn't work out, then hopefully the night will fade until it turns to tiny particles of dust.

I feel like an electric current is running through my body. It takes me a second to realize it's only my cell buzzing in my pocket. I pull it out to take a peek at the screen. Maybe it's Gavin telling me to turn on the radio because Shrinking Violet is playing. My heart skips a beat, then drops to the ground. Ugh, it's Kayla, and it can only mean she's calling about our presentation tomorrow. I totally forgot that in fifteen hours I'll be standing in front of the class in a flowered dress that Kayla's mom wears to PTA functions.

Both Kayla and Gavin get to wear normal clothes. If I had known we were dressing up, I would've chosen a more contemporary author. But I guess since Helen couldn't see, she really didn't give a crap about fashion. You have to admire her, though. She spent her time helping others, not popping pimples or wondering if her boobs were perky enough. Speaking of perky, I better listen to the message from Kayla before she calls me again.

It's just a courtesy call to make sure I haven't flipped out and been rushed to the hospital with pre-presentation palpations. *No, Kayla, I have a lot more important things to worry about, like going on a blind date to prom in front of a webcam.* Instead of saying something sarcastic, I text her back that I'm practicing at this very moment. That should keep her quiet.

Toward the end of the show Jason asks if I'd mind grabbing a few phone lines. I know I can't avoid them all night, so I take his post next to the spreadsheet and look over his tallies for the night. As usual, most of the calls are for Juice Box, Speed Bump, and Gracie May, but there are a bunch of check marks next to Shrinking Violet, too. I wonder if Gavin was one of the callers. Does he know about the contest? Did he wish he was going to the prom now? Fat chance. He seemed pretty set on Speed Bump.

I click on the first line. "92.7 The SLAM."

"Can you play PJ Squid?"

"Sure."

Click.

Next caller.

I slump down in the chair and let my body relax. That wasn't bad. I race through the next few calls and add checks by most of the bands that have been requested all night.

"92.7 The SLAM."

"Is this Sweet T?"

I bite my lip. Just say no. Deepen your voice. Call yourself Bertha. Move on to the next caller. But the person sounds so excited.

"Yes," I say softly.

"Holy crap," he practically screams, "I can't believe I'm really talking to you!"

"Why?"

"Because I've been trying to get through all night."

"What can I do for you?" I try to sound professional.

"I want to know what I should write about in my song so I can win the contest."

Gavin and me. His onyx eyes melting me into a pile of love mush. The kiss that could've been if my mother hadn't honked her horn. "Anything. Just be yourself."

"What do you like?" It sounds like he's tapping away on a computer. I hope he's not keeping a file on me. How creepy.

"Music." I have to give him more. I look around the room. All I spot is a bowl and Jason's bag of cold Burger King food. "Soup. French fries."

"Okay." The typing stops.

"Great. Can't wait for your entry. Have a good night." I click to the next line before he can say anything else.

The next caller wants to know if I'm really going to the prom or am I going to make a quick appearance and ditch. I wish.

Even though I love working at the station, I'm almost glad when Jason calls me over to sign off with him and hand over the show to Floss, the overnight girl.

"Sweet dreams, Miami. Stay safe and sleep tight," I whisper into the mike.

But how is that possible when I have to stand up in front of the whole class tomorrow and not talk? It might be worse than actually having an author that speaks. I can't believe Kayla wanted me to stuff my mouth with cotton balls. She got me to wear the dress. That's about the most embarrassment that anyone should have to endure in a lifetime.

After Jason drops me home from the station, I just unwind in my room. Both Mom and Rob are at a new club, which is a real relief because I have no energy left to deal with Mom. There's a note on my bed telling me to let her know when I want to go prom-dress shopping. I should shock everyone and wear my

Helen Keller dress. That'll definitely pump SLAM's ratings up and send the grand prize winner running, while I'd be the number one loser of the whole city.

I crumple up Mom's note and toss it into the garbage. Then I kick off my shoes and fall facedown onto my bed.

Sweet T, what have you gotten me into?

chapter NINETEEN

I wake up early and shuffle out of the house before I have to deal with Mom. Running into her would only mess up my game-day focus. I stayed up until one a.m. last night, polishing my paper on Helen Keller. I want it to be perfect. Not to mention the English project is 40 percent of this quarter's grade.

I have to be Helen Keller today. I have to channel her enthusiasm for life. As I near the school, I stop under a large palm tree and slip her book out of my backpack. I kiss the cover and whisper, "Helen, give me inspiration." I randomly flip open the book and point my finger to a passage. It's the end of chapter 22, when she talks about feeling isolated and beyond her isolation there is light. How there is joy in "self-forgetfulness."

I read aloud, "So I try to make light in others' eyes my sun, the music in others' ears my symphony, the smile on others' lips my happiness." Then I read it again, even slower, letting every word sink in. I have to forget about Mom, forget about Stacy, and focus on delivering a successful presentation. Gavin and Kayla are counting on me, and if Helen's looking down on me, I want her to be proud.

But before I enter Ridgeland, I quickly text Audrey and tell her to meet me under the big oak for lunch. I need to be around a positive force before English class. Things have been so crazy that we haven't hung out in a while. It's nice to have a friend I can trust.

As I'm walking through the main hallway, I close my eyes for seconds at a time and feel around, like I imagine Helen did. I put my hands out on either side as a buffer. I make it halfway down until my foot whaps a hard piece of rubber.

"Ouch, hot," someone yells.

I open up my eyes to see steaming tea dripping down the front of the school nurse's mint-green scrubs. My toe rests on the corner of her sneaker. I quickly remove it.

"I'm sorry. I didn't see you!" I try to mop up the tea on the floor with my sandal.

"It's okay." She fans out her shirt. "But please watch where you're going."

That was definitely a close call. I better try something new. I decide to ignore everyone, instead, which really is nothing new for me. I don't listen when Mr. Porter tells me to hurry to homeroom before I'm late or when Ms. Michaels tries to convince me to sign up to be a senior buddy to the visiting eighth graders.

Of course, Helen had to rely on touch and vibration to know what was going on. However, if I caress everyone that walks by, someone's liable to yell perv, and I don't need to bring any more attention to myself.

I feel a hand tap my shoulder and I shudder. It's small but firm. Before I can turn around, I hear the words Helen wouldn't have been able to hear. "Can't wait for you to bomb today! No talkie, no grade." Stacy laughs.

Sorry, Helen, but I don't see the light in her eyes.

I quickly hold up my fingers and sign the letters *B* and *I* for bitch. Okay, so I never got past *J* in sign language, but she doesn't have to know that.

"What, you've got the shakes now, too, dorkstag?" Stacy sneers.

Before I can answer, Frank, who's linked to Stacy's arm, elbows her. "Hello, we were talking about Trevor's kegger on Saturday."

She instantly forgets about me and turns to Frank. "As soon as my dad falls asleep, I'll leave. Should be around eleven."

I always thought someone like her was curfew free, free to roam the streets at all hours of the night. Seems like her parents are way stricter than my mom. I don't hear the rest of their conversation because Frank has propelled Stacy forward, leading her down the hallway.

I try to erase Stacy's words from my head and float from class to class until it's time for lunch. But I can't seem to break free of her evil grin. When Stacy chooses someone to pick on, she doesn't let up. Thirty more days until school is officially over and I'll never have to see her again.

I pick at my turkey sandwich while I wait for Audrey.

"Hey, girl. What's up?" Audrey flops down next to me.

"This." I pull out the dress I'm supposed to wear in exactly twenty-six minutes.

Audrey scrunches her nose and fingers the polyester garden disaster.

"Told you it was ugly." I quickly shove it back into my bag. "I'll be so embarrassed that I won't be able to move."

"Why don't you wear this with it?" She removes her black cardigan from around her waist.

"It's too small." Audrey is four inches shorter than me and built like a dancer.

"It'll be fine. It's stretchy." She hands it to me. "You don't have to button it up."

"Thanks. And if you have a body double for me, too, we'll be all set."

The back entrance to the band room is flung open and I see Doug, swinging his trumpet case, walking toward us. "Hi, Aud. Hi, Tere." He smiles.

"No more braces?" I ask.

His smile widens. "Just in time for prom."

"Yeah, I told him I'd only go if he got rid of the tracks," Audrey teases.

"Isn't she nice?" Doug grips his trumpet case. "I got to go. I have a meeting with my counselor. Catch you guys later."

A few months ago Doug offered to set me up with one of his buddies for prom, but I said no. I wasn't up for another band date disaster. Funny that now I'm going on a real blind date. At least with a band guy, I would've known what I was getting myself into.

My shoulders are rigid. Audrey pats me. "I'm sure you'll do great. You've had so much practice on the radio."

"Yeah, but I don't see those people."

Audrey takes a sip of her Coke and sets it down. "Helen was blind. So don't make eye contact, and pretend you're speaking into the mike. Make like you're back at the station. Or even better, alone in your room."

"That's not such a bad idea. I knew I was friends with you for a reason."

"Are you going to eat that?" Audrey points to the other half of my sandwich.

"No, it's all yours."

"I knew I was friends with you for a reason, too." She laughs.

Before class Audrey and I pull together mascara, sparkly lip gloss, and eye shadow, and motor to the bathroom. "This is the best mask I can get you," she says applying the eye shadow to my lids. I do the mascara myself. *Short, swift strokes,* I remember Pop-Tart saying. Then I spritz my hair with water, but this time I let the tap run slowly so I don't end up drenched.

I flip my hair back just as the bell rings.

"You look really nice." Audrey smiles.

"Thanks." I pucker my sparkly lips. "At least when they find me dead, I'll look good."

"It'll be over before you know it." Audrey grabs her stuff and heads to the science wing. "See you after school."

I pass the language lab on my way to English and peer in the glass window at the door. Mrs. Tripp is walking up and down the aisle, placing workbooks on each desk.

"Guten Tag," I say to her, even though she can't see or hear me. Maybe Audrey's right: this presentation won't be as bad as I thought.

Okay, then why is my hand shaking as I open the classroom door? And why is my heart playing ping-pong with the rest of my insides? I rush to my seat and try to savor every moment before Ms. Peters makes my death sentence official and we're forced to start class.

I summon Sweet T by writing my radio name over and over in my notebook. I write it in bubble letters, cursive, and 3-D. I figure if I do it enough times, then maybe I'll become Sweet T for the performance.

"Hey, Tere. Are you ready?" Gavin sits down next to me.

I flip my notebook over. "I just have to put the dress on. I'll sneak out last minute to do that. I don't want to wear this thing any longer than necessary."

"I hear you." He nods and leans in closer. "But it's kind of sexy! A woman in full floral gear." He grins.

This is not funny. I will be the one sporting the floral number in less than twenty minutes! "I'm feeling ill." I grab my stomach.

"It'll be fine." Gavin reaches for my hand and squeezes.

His grip is strong. It's soothing to be holding hands. I don't want to let go. I look over at him. He smiles. I'd give anything to kiss those soft lips again, to finish where we left off.

"Just promise me that if I have a mental breakdown, they don't send me to the loony bin in the floral dress," I whisper.

Gavin laughs. "You're going to be great."

Does he know something that I don't know? It seems like he has more confidence in me than I do.

"Okay, class, settle down." Ms. Peters breaks up our party for two.

Gavin and I instantly drop our hands. Kayla plops down next to me. "Where's the dress?" she whispers.

In the incinerator. "Here." I point to my bag.

"Well, hurry," she says frantically.

I nod in Ms. Peters' direction, who is still talking.

Kayla waves her hand back and forth like a drowning swimmer stuck in the middle of the ocean until Ms. Peters stops talking and nods at her. "Can Tere go change?"

God, could Kayla be any louder? I try to sink down in my chair, but there's nowhere to go. The girl in front of me is barely five feet, hardly a boulder of protection.

"Yes, quickly, while the first group sets up," Ms. Peters says.

I grab my bag and rush to the door. When I'm halfway down the hall, I hear footsteps behind me.

I turn around. It's Kayla. "What are you doing?"

"Thought you might need some help."

"Getting dressed?"

"No, just thought you might . . ." She looks away from me.

"Spaz? Ditch? Puke?"

"Yeah," she admits.

Does everyone think I'm a freak? I can handle this. I won't see these people after next month and if need be, I'll move far, far away. I can broadcast my own after-hours radio show for freaks—*Live From the Dungeon,* I'll call it. *"Tune in if you dare . . ."*

"I'll be fine," I tell Kayla and myself.

I quickly change in the stall. I throw on the dress and Audrey's cardigan. I do up the first three bottom buttons, which hides the granny lace around my waist. I'm so glad Audrey gave me this, but if she had given me a garbage bag, I would've thrown that over the dress, too.

"Hurry up," Kayla calls from the door. "We don't want to miss the first group."

I close my eyes. I try not to think about how I look. Instead, I think about how this will all be over in less than an hour, about the same time it takes to get a cavity filled. I hear Kayla tapping her foot restlessly and realize I better open the door before she has someone break it down.

I avoid the mirror and rush out of the bathroom. If Helen couldn't see herself, I don't need to see what I look like either.

When we get back to the classroom, the first group is still setting up. I catch Stacy's empty seat out of the corner of my eye. It would be sweet if she ditched class today.

I take out the script that Kayla printed for us and mentally run through the movements. After the first group starts, I hide the paper half under my notebook. Every so often I glance at the sheet. I know the order by heart, but there's something comforting about having it right in front of me. I peek over at Stacy's seat. Still empty. I breathe a sigh of relief.

I try to focus on Alex and Carrie. They are both writers from the seventies, with funky outfits, too. Although, they're dressed much cooler than me. Part of their presentation is a slide show, so Ms. Peters dims the lights. Why didn't we think of that? Then people wouldn't have to stare at me the whole time. Maybe we couldn've done the whole thing in the dark. It could be like a radio show, voices only. Helen was always alone in the dark of her world. She couldn't even find solace in the radio. I'm sure she would've given everything to be part of the classroom chatter. I wonder if she ever felt nervous in front of a group. Before I know it, there's a round of applause for Alex and Carrie. Then Ms. Peters makes the dreaded call: "Kayla's group is up."

My legs are wobbly, but surprisingly enough, I don't feel as bad as I had expected. Still, I clutch my stomach and breathe deeply so I don't hyperventilate. I steal one quick glance at our script but all the words are a blur. I really only have to say a few lines; most of my performance is mute. I have to be brave for Helen. I can't let her down. She went through too much for me to freak out over a thirteen-minute presentation.

Kayla hangs up the poster board, explaining who we are, while Gavin and I arrange the chairs and table. After everything is set up, I peek at the audience. *Please don't laugh at me.* Then I close my eyes for a quick second and imagine that I'm alone with the mike in the studio. When I open up, I glance over at my seat. Stacy? When did she sneak in? And what is she doing sitting at my desk? I swear she's snickering at me. I try not to look at her, but it's not easy. It's like her contempt is thickening the air. I have to ignore her. She can't ruin my performance.

I plead to Ms. Peters with my eyes. *She can't sit there; why is she sitting there?* Okay, so I'm closer to the front, but why, all of a sudden, during my presentation, does she feel the urge to show up and take over *my* seat?

My eyes lock on Stacy again as Kayla introduces our group. Her stare cuts into me like razor blades, making me shudder. She flips my notebook over with a bright pink acrylic nail and mouths, "Lesbo." I know I read her right, but what's her problem? Ohmigod, she's talking about my Sweet T doodles. Does she listen to the show? Does she think I'm in love with Sweet T?

"No," I mouth back.

She throws her head back and laughs. What am I thinking—who cares? Stacy's in *my* seat, touching *my* things. But I can't let her ruin our performance, all we've worked for. I focus my attention on Kayla, who's skating around me in circles with the biggest fake smile ever plastered on her face.

After Kayla finishes her tricks, it's Gavin's turn to read a passage from Stephen King's *It*. He places a large skull with deep-set light-up eyes, undoubtedly left over from Halloween, next to his seat. He opens the book and pretends to read to it. He uses a deep throaty voice, and every time he gets to a scary part, he makes the skeleton's eyes flash green. The class quickly catches on and ooohs and ahhs each time they see the light. It's a pretty comical combo, and together with Kayla's performance, they definitely fit the bill as a vaudeville show. Kayla would make a great horror movie victim where the evil slasher sneaks from behind and knocks her to the ground.

Next, Gavin pulls out his guitar and jams for a few minutes. All eyes are locked on him. Even Stacy's. He looks so cool up here, just like a rock star. I'm so mesmerized with his playing that Kayla has to whisper for me to sit down at the table. We are supposed to be having a conversation where Kayla talks and I feel the movement of her lips. Kayla holds up a sign as the music dies down that reads *Welcome to Helen's World*. All I can picture in my head is Stacy whispering *lesbo* as I feel the creases of Kayla's well-lubricated lips. I should've told her to lay low on the ChapStick because my fingers are sliding all over the place with the grease. I'm so happy when this part is over.

Now I'm supposed to hold up a prop, then spell the word in the air. I want to spell *Stacy, get the hell out of my seat,* but instead I'm gripping a bright yellow umbrella and spelling umbrella to the class. How this is entertainment is beyond me. People are actually watching. I focus on the poster in the back of the room—it's a little girl on the beach building a sand castle. I wish I could trade places with her.

Stacy flashes my Sweet T doodles to the class, then gives the page a big smooch. Laughing, she tears the paper from my notebook and holds it up in front of her like it's pirates' booty. I scan the class to see if anyone is looking at her. Thank God, no. Not even Ms. Peters. For once Stacy is not the center of attention.

Everyone's staring at me holding up my sandal. I turn the shoe around in my hand and touch the leather, then rub it against my face. I start to spell the letters in the air when I step forward with my bare foot and skid on a piece of paper. The paper from my notebook with Stacy's lipstick marks on it. I look up just in time to see a huge grin on Stacy's face, right before I land flat on my butt.

Ouch, that hurt. I know I come with my own padding, but this floor is concrete. A few soft laughs break out.

I'm hot and cold at the same time. My face flushes red, but my hands are icy. Here I am, sprawled on the floor in front of the entire class. But I will not vomit. I will not cry. Instead, I bite my lip.

"Helen, let me help you up." Judy Blume reaches for me.

Before I latch on, I ball up the piece of paper in my hand and stick it in the pocket of Audrey's sweater.

Somehow I manage to scramble to my feet. My butt aches, but other than that I think I'm okay. I look down at the dress and straighten it out.

"Helen sustained many falls throughout her life." Kayla hands me my sandal. "But as you can see, she steps right up and keeps on going. Falling to her is as natural as sneezing is to us."

A few more laughs erupt. I slide on my sandal and stand there, stiff as a frozen Popsicle. Kayla elbows me in the ribs. I have to go on; I have to say something. I spell the words *thank you* in the air.

"Helen wants to thank you all for coming to see us perform today, but before we go, I'm handing it over to Stephen King for the song finale."

The laughs have stopped. All eyes have moved from me to Gavin.

Gavin tightens the guitar strap across his shoulder and moves his fingers up and down the strings. I love watching his fingers, especially the way his thumb ring clanks against the wood on certain notes. He seems so at peace, rocking away. He doesn't make eye contact either, but somehow it's okay. He looks like he's one with the music. That's how I feel when I'm listening to my iPod. I know I'm not the one making the music, but I'm definitely receiving it.

Gavin's sound is unique: alternative rock, a bit of soul, and a funky beat running through the song. He was really good with his impromptu preview the other day at Kayla's, but this performance is amazing! This instrumental piece would make great "background music," for the station—we could talk right over it, but the listeners would still be entertained.

He finishes off with a short riff. Everyone's silent for a second, then the room breaks into applause. Just like me, Gavin is not used to all this attention and his cheeks quickly turn pink. He looks so cute. He bows and the clapping dies down. It's my cue to blow a kiss and for Judy to thank the audience. Then we move into the group hug.

Finally, it's all over. I want to rip off this dress and run all the way home. At this point being naked sounds more appealing than looking like a 1950s housewife. Plus, I wiped out in front of the whole class—nothing could be more embarrassing. Kayla did a good job saving my ass, but I'm sure people will forever have that image of me landing on my butt in the ugliest dress known to mankind.

I look over at my desk. Stacy's still sitting there. The mere sight of her makes me want to strangle her. How dare she throw a piece of paper on the floor like a stray banana peel in one of those old Bugs Bunny cartoons? Too bad I can't pull a frying pan from out of thin air and flatten her with one flick of the wrist.

"Two wonderful performances so far. I can't wait to see what Juan and Chad have prepared for us." Ms. Peters motions for them to set up.

I slide closer toward Stacy. I will not react. I know that's what she wants.

I take a deep breath and grit my teeth. If I got through the performance, I can get through this confrontation. "You're in my seat."

"What's that, lesbo?" She runs her finger up and down the spine of my spiral notebook.

"Move."

She looks up at me. Her blue eyes are wide and piercing. "Sweet T would never like a loser like you."

"You mean a loser like you," I blurt.

"What?" Stacy was so not expecting me to answer. She looks like one of those wax museum statues. I'm stunned that I said something, too.

She quickly snaps back to reality. "Even your comebacks are lame, lesbo."

I feel a hand on my shoulder. "I'm proud of you, Tere. That was a great portrayal of Helen," Ms. Peters says.

Stacy gets up from my seat and huffs back to hers. I hope Ms. Peters gives her an F.

I survive in my costume for the next presentation. I can't fully relax because I don't know if Stacy will strike again. But she managed to snag someone else's seat next to Frank and is now cuddling up to him. Hopefully he'll be able to hold her focus and keep her out of my hair.

I look over at Gavin a few times, who's busy scrawling in his notebook. I never knew he was such a writer. He keeps on writing lines, then scratching them out. I fantasize that it's a love note to me, that he's going to tear the page away from the rest and slide it over. Doesn't happen.

The bell rings just after Shakespeare and John Grisham take their bows. Gavin hardly notices. He's still writing.

"What's that?" I finally ask.

He quickly shuts the notebook. "Some ideas. It's really nothing."

"Oh." I gather my stuff.

"Hey, you were great today." He smiles.

"You, too."

As I'm gathering my stuff, Frank brushes by me, Stacy on his arm. "Tere, that was an incredible wipeout. It looked so real," he says.

"You should be on one of those stunt shows," Tim yells from behind him.

Are they serious?

"She practiced the fall a bunch of times. She's good." Gavin pulls me toward the door.

"I think she's a faker." Stacy leans into Frank. But Frank doesn't answer because he's too busy telling Tim that he has ugly sneakers.

And Kayla's at the door waiting for us, so Gavin and I make like a brick wall and plow past Stacy and Frank.

"Ohmigod, guys, I think we did really well," Kayla says all in one breath.

"We made a great team." Gavin slings his arms around us both. Then he turns to Kayla. "And that was a perfect save after Tere's fall. We rock!"

Since I'm now pretty much convinced everyone thought the fall was deliberate, I feel good, too. I'd still like to come up with an idea to trip Stacy up in her performance, but what? Throw something at her? No, that's too immature, and I can't get her to slip on a piece of paper because that would make me a copycat. So *not* cool. As much as I'd like to see her mess up royally, I'm not into plotting revenge. Maybe I'll leave that up to Sweet T.

* * *

Good afternoon, Miami. This is Sweet T on 92.7 The SLAM. I'm usually not on at this time, but I'm filling in today. The sky started off overcast, but now the sun is peeking through the clouds, ready to burst. Here's a song that's sure to bring you warmth: Gracie May with "Hang Tight, Sister." Blast this one as loud as you can!

chapter TWENTY

I'm exhausted, so I head home for a nap before going to the station. I don't think Derek will even flinch when I stroll in late. He knows he owes me big since he set up this whole prom contest featuring *moi* as the main attraction.

Mom's in the kitchen when I walk in the house. She's attempting food preparation again. It looks like some type of soup. Pieces of vegetables are strewn all over the counter and bottles of spices are everywhere.

I give her a quick nod and pull out the bread and peanut butter. All I need is some sustenance and a nap.

Mom looks so awkward hovered over the big pot, swirling the ladle round and round. "Did you tell Derek that you'd be late?"

"Yes, I left a message with Kelly."

"When's the contest deadline?"

"Everything has to be in on Monday by five." Four more days and I'll have to pick my suitor. At least I get to be the one to choose him, not Mom, or even worse, Derek.

Mom tastes the soup, then reaches for the bottle of garlic. "I'm just glad you're not going to the prom with *that* boy."

"What boy?" I dip my knife in the jar to scoop out some more peanut butter.

"The goth one. Definitely someone that's going nowhere."

What's her problem? She sees me with him one time and she already doesn't like him. Talk about judging a book by its cover.

"Geez, Mom, will you leave Gavin alone. He's not even going to the prom." I tighten the lid and toss the jar back onto the pantry shelf.

"Well, that's good. I just don't think he's your type." She holds up the spoon. "Would you like a sample?"

My type? She has no clue what my type is. She used to be on my case to get to know the boys in my school better. She always told me how by the end of freshman year she had four offers to go to the senior prom. Eventually she realized that her nagging was no use, that I was not going to follow in her queen bee footsteps.

"No," I grumble, then take a seat at the table and dig into my sandwich. "And if you must know, Gavin's a supercool guy."

"You might think that, but a mother knows."

"Whatever," I say between clenched teeth.

"You don't have to be so ungrateful, Teresa. This opportunity to go to the prom is a one-of-a-kind experience. You really owe Derek for setting all this up."

"Yeah, he's a great guy," I say with my mouth full.

Mom brushes away the hair from her face. "And I don't want you to mess things up and embarrass the station."

"And how would I do that, Mother? Do you really think I'm going to chug ten beers and strip naked?"

"That's not what I'm talking about." Mom stirs the soup. "This is your one chance to find a decent guy."

I roll my eyes and snap at her, "I hardly think entering a radio contest makes someone decent. And I'm eighteen. I'll have plenty of opportunities to meet people."

"Where is this hostility coming from?" Mom whisks the soup into a frenzy.

"I'm sick and tired of you treating me like a loser all the time. Hell, if I could stand up in front of the class and pretend to be a blind and deaf woman, then I can stand up to you." I push my chair away from the table.

"What are you rambling about?"

"You will never even be half the person Helen was."

"Who's Helen?" Mom slams the ladle down onto the granite counter.

"Do you even care?" I rip off a piece of crust from my sandwich and ball it up in my hand.

"I think you better come to your senses and show me some respect."

"Why should I respect *you* if you don't respect *me*?"

"I don't respect you?" She points to herself. "I'm the one who's taken care of you all these years. If it wasn't for me, you'd be nothing."

"Then I'd rather be nothing." I storm out of the house, with the ball of crust still in my hand. I speed down the street like a marathon runner on her last lap.

How dare she make me feel like crap? I push her words out of my head. Every time a car whizzes by, I think it might be her, coming to apologize and drive me to the station. I pass the Starbucks, dry cleaners, and nursing home, but still no red Lexus pulls up and opens its doors for me.

I'm soaking with sweat by the time I get to the bus stop. I slump down onto the bench and watch the ants scurry through the cracks in the sidewalk. Normally this would gross me out, but today I'm mesmerized by all their activity.

I wait twenty minutes for the number 11 to finally show. I'm too tired to even care if someone stakes out the station and corners me at the front door. But I figure I'll look too worn out by the time I reach the building for anyone to even suspect that I'm Sweet T. I look more like I'm coming to clean the place up, not broadcast fresh tunes to thousands of people.

Once the bus is in motion, I close my eyes. I picture myself in a black prom dress, dancing to Shrinking Violet with Gavin by my side. He looks scrumptious in his black tux and crisp white shirt. He pulls me in tight and wraps his arms around me. The warmth of his chest envelops me like the patchwork security blanket I carried around until I was almost seven.

The bus screeches to a halt. I remove my sticky face from the window. Gross. I wipe my cheek on the sleeve of my tee. Not the best place to doze off. I slide out of my seat and make my way toward the front. Luckily I didn't miss my stop.

I'm only a few minutes late when I flash my station badge to the security guard. I look outside around the corner of the building quickly to make sure no one is following me. Unless some insane listener is disguised as the man with the bullhorn proclaiming that the end of the world is near, I think I'm safe. Although, the man could be right about the world coming to an end. Or at least my world.

As soon as I walk in, I grab a Diet Coke from the vending machine. It's going to be a long night.

"You okay?" Pop-Tart pulls off her headset.

"Just a little sweaty. Walked part of the way here."

"Good for you. I need to get back to the gym. My tummy is looking pouchy." Pop-Tart pats her surfboard abs. There's something comforting about her. I hope she never changes.

"Know what you mean." I instinctively cross my arms over my stomach.

I don't even bother freshening up. Derek will have to take me as is today.

He's busy with a caller when I open the studio door. Good, it gives me time to settle. A couple stacks of CDs labeled with different numbers are piled on the console. There's got to be at least forty entries, and we're about four days away from the contest deadline. I didn't know there were so many singing Romeos out there.

When Derek puts down the phone, I ask him if I can go listen to them in the production studio. He gives me the go-ahead, and I set myself up in the next room.

I place the stack of CDs on the table and randomly pluck one. Entrant Number 12, Treehouse Love. Let's hear what he has to say. Will he be good enough?

I slide on a pair of headphones and hit play. A tinny sound fills my ears. *"K-I-S-S-I-N-G, Sweet T and me, sitting in a tree . . ."* I want to like it, I really do, but halfway through the song, I have to pull the earphones off. He's practically screaming. There's a fine line between alternative rock and a guy sounding like he's trying to break windows. Good thing this room is window free.

I move onto Number 8 with a little more hope. His voice is actually decent—it's the content of his song I'm worried about. *"If you don't pick me, I'll slit my wrists into three. Oh, how I love thee . . ."* Eww, I hope he doesn't take it too hard when he doesn't win. This is kind of depressing.

I listen to a bunch more. Some are pretty good. Love is a popular theme, but one guy sings about the environment and another blabs on about his mother. Nice, but missing that sexy edge. Hopefully the next few days will bring in some good stuff. Maybe the soup and french fry caller will come up with something good—ha!

I'm back in the studio just in time for Derek to do a live station ID. "Good afternoon, this is Dynamite Derek escorting you home on the afternoon drive. I've got Sweet T in the studio here, and she's waiting for all those love ballads to come in. She likes it down and dirty, boys . . ." Derek turns to me and winks.

Pig. I should run a contest on my show for hard-up men. Except the prize will be more of a punishment. They have to clean old ladies' toilets with their toothbrushes—something to teach them to be more respectful.

Derek continues, "Don't forget, Monday at five is the prom contest deadline. Check our Web site for details. Here's PJ Squid on 92.7 WEMD The SLAM.

"So, Tere, what did you think of the love songs?" Derek picks up a couple of CDs and waves them in the air.

"I hope the next batch is better." I sigh.

"Harsh critic."

"Have you listened yet?"

"Nope." He twirls one of the jewel cases round and round. "Promotions is going through all of them. Have a whole number system set up. They'll give you the top ten on Tuesday, then let you pick the winner."

"I didn't mind listening to them."

"Yeah, but I'm sure most of them are crap." He pushes the

pile toward the edge of the console, and one CD topples into the garbage. "Whoops, sorry about that, Number 21." Derek waves to the can.

I leap up and fish it out. "That's somebody's dream in there."

He laughs. "You have quite an ego."

"I'm not talking about going to the prom with me. I'm talking about the dream of hearing their song played on the radio." I plop back into my chair.

Derek smooths the ends of his mustache. "They can keep on dreaming, baby!"

"You know, the only good thing about this whole *prom* setup is that we're supporting local artists. Somebody in this stack really has a chance of making it." I run my finger over the jewel cases.

"This isn't *American Idol*." He laughs.

"No, but I believe nurturing talent at every level is important. If you can get your song played on one major radio station, then you're already ahead of the game."

Derek picks up the entry that I saved from the garbage, air-kisses it, and says, "Number 21, I'm counting on you to cut me a deal when you're working delivery for Pizza Hut in ten years."

Dream crusher. I so don't want to hear that. If my mom were here, she would've flashed a huge smile across her face. I think some people are just afraid to see others succeed. Well, I'm not. I'll make sure this winner gets his name out there. He may not be my soul mate, but at least his voice will be heard.

chapter TWENTY-ONE

In a way it kind of bites that the presentation is over, because now the only thing I have to worry about is prom. Those four letters, P-R-O-M, could be the death of me. I wish I was going with Gavin, but I guess we're both locked in. He doesn't want to let down his brother and I don't want to upset the poor contest winner or Rob. I don't care as much about my mom, but I don't need any more grief from her either. My plan is to suck it up until August when I'm off to the University of Miami. Then I'll never have to see her again, even if I'll be less than fifteen miles from home.

I can't wait for English today because I really need a dose of Gavin. He always puts me in a good mood. He's so calm and never lets anyone piss him off. I'm so at ease with him, the words just roll off my tongue when we talk. Of course, this does mean I'll get a dose of Stacy, too, and I need that as badly as I need to smell Derek's cheesy cologne every day. They both clog up my pores.

I pass Kayla in the hall right before lunch, and she has a huge smile on her face. "Tere, we did it."

I stop short and nearly run over a puny ninth grader. "What?"

"I just talked to Ms. Peters. We got an A on the project."

"For real?"

"Yeah." She shakes me. "She said we were a dynamic group and our delivery was superb."

"Wow." I've never done well on an oral report before. "Thanks for organizing everything, Kayla."

"It was a team effort." She hands me a pink flyer.

"Another script?" I joke.

"Just read it," she says, then keeps on walking.

I unfold the paper. *Join us for the annual Deutsch Klub Partei at the German Institute at 4150 Brickell Avenue . . .* Then, in purple pen, she wrote, *You don't have to be a member to come to the party, just a German enthusiast.*

That is *so* Kayla. She should've been a cheerleader. I can't believe she saw me going into the lab once and I'm already an enthusiast. It's pretty sad that besides a few childhood birthday parties that I've attended, this is my first real *partei* invite. But I'm not sure if school functions really count as parties. I'll have to check with Audrey on that one.

I stuff the flyer into my backpack and head to lunch. I have no plans today, but that's fine with me. All I want is some fresh air.

I see Gavin by the far wall, sitting in his favorite spot with his usual crew. I'm dying to go over and say hello. If I don't, I'll be kicking myself all day about it. Before I chicken out, I casually walk toward him.

Gavin's holding a piece of notebook paper and his friends are hovered over him. Maybe they're studying for a test. As I get closer, I see that they're all smiling, and I swear Gavin's blushing. Okay, if they're not cramming for a test, then what else could it be? My heart drops. Don't tell me, it's a love note. But from who? Did our kiss at the picnic table mean nothing to him?

I can keep on walking, take the shortcut through to the band room. I've never approached a guy before and especially not one surrounded by his buddies. My heart speeds up. It's no big deal, I tell myself. Gavin's only a boy. A hottie, but still a boy. His friends seem nice, too, not the kind that would slam me once I left. He looks up as I'm about to pass and waves. "Hi, Tere."

"Hey, Gavin." I stand there with my hands in my pockets, trying not to stare at the note that proclaims someone's undying love for him.

He spies me looking at the paper and quickly crams it into his pocket. "Wanna sit down?"

Me alone with three guys. I try not to think about it and drop to the ground. Maybe I'm jumping to a conclusion about the note. It could be his shopping list or a treasure map.

As if on cue, we all pull out our lunches and the guys start blabbing about school—about how they never thought they'd leave Ridgeland.

"Me, too," I say. "I feel like I've been here for a hundred years."

Gavin laughs. "Well, we know some of the teachers have."

The guys try to figure out who the oldest teacher in the school is. I mostly listen as they playfully argue back and forth. It's a comfortable feeling sitting with them—I don't feel any pressure to talk. Gavin's friends are just as laid-back as he is.

I see Audrey heading toward the oak and I wave and yell, "Over here!" After the third yell, she finally spots me and strolls toward us.

She has a big smile on her face and I know it's for me. Me and Gavin.

Audrey introduces herself, then takes the spot next to me. She joins us in synchronized sandwich eating. Nobody talks for a few minutes while we all chew.

Finally Audrey breaks the silence. "So what do you guys have planned for the big night?"

Everyone stares at her, including me. This is *so* not good. If my heart was beating fast before, it's in overdrive now. Breathe in, breathe out. I will not turn bright red and burst into flames.

She puts her peanut-butter-and-fig creation down. "The prom."

"I'm going with my girlfriend, Anna, from Deerwood," Ted says.

Wow, he has a girlfriend. Maybe Gavin would like one, too. At prom crunchtime, peer pressure is a good thing. I eye him, but he doesn't see me. He's busy wrapping the cord of his iPod around his finger.

"Not the dancing type. I'll probably work." Justin flattens his Sprite can.

Poor thing. Actually, who am I kidding? I'd be in the same situation if I wasn't being set up for total humiliation by Dynamite Derek.

"You should enter that SLAM radio contest and win Sweet T," Ted says.

I immediately jerk my head up from my lunch. He should what?

"Who's Sweetie?" Justin asks.

"Sweet T is a DJ. If you win, you get to go to her prom with her." Ted winks at Jason.

All the blood in my body has risen to my face. I feel like I have the words *Sweet T* branded on my forehead, like there is no way out of this moment.

"Where does she go to school?" Jason asks.

"Nobody knows," Ted says in a zombielike voice.

I elbow Audrey to change the subject.

"So Gavin, what about you?" Audrey points to him.

Not exactly the save I was looking for, but it'll have to do.

"I've got Speed Bump tickets for that night," he mumbles.

Audrey raises her eyebrows. "And you couldn't get out of it? Not even for prom?"

I elbow her again in the ribs. Enough is enough. This is torture. And what if someone asks me if I'm going? I'll have to lie to the whole group. But there's no way I can break my cover now. Not five days before the prom.

Gavin squirms. "It's complicated, but I'm going with my brother."

I feel the need to rescue him and, quite frankly, myself. "So, who's psyched for summer?"

Everyone nods. Ted says, "Summer rocks," and Gavin just smiles.

I wonder what he means by "complicated." How complicated can it be? Unless it's his last chance to see his brother before he moves to Finland or enters the Witness Protection Program? Or maybe he just said that for me. To let me down easy.

I peer over at Gavin's pocket, hoping the crumpled piece of paper will miraculously fall out, but it doesn't.

Audrey's cell beeps. "Time for class."

Justin grabs his bag. "Catch you guys later. Can't be late for Henderson again or I'm screwed."

"Ready for more presentations?" Gavin asks me.

"As long as we don't have to go up again," I say.

Ted and Audrey leave, while Gavin waits for me to gather my stuff.

We weave through the lunch crowd. I keep pace with him so we're side by side. My arm brushes his by mistake. Then I do it again. I don't know if he notices, but it makes me happy.

When we get to class, we find out that Stacy's group is presenting first. Since plain old revenge is out, channeling evil spirits might work. If only I knew how to summon the phantoms. It's probably one of those things that takes a lot of time and concentration, neither of which I have in the two minutes until class starts.

I can muster up my evil stare for her. I purse my lips together and narrow my eyes but can't keep a straight face. How pathetic. I can't even look mean if I tried. I think it's something you're born with—you either have the mean gene or not.

Stacy waltzes in just after the bell rings. She's carrying a bright pink poster board that reads *Welcome to the Best Show in Town* and lists all the names in her group. I'm sure Frank and Tim are thrilled.

"Maybe she'll choke," Gavin whispers to me.

"We can only hope," I whisper back.

I should've known Stacy would pick a romance writer. She's Danielle Steel, Tim is Arnold Schwarzenegger, and Frank is The Rock. Is this some kind of joke? Because I could make a few jokes about this *not* being a remedial reading class. What was Ms. Peters thinking when she okayed this group? She probably just let them do it so they could pass, otherwise she'd end up with them again for summer school.

No surprise that Stacy is dressed like a slut in a short black miniskirt and a tight white tee. She shuffles toward the front of the class in her two-inch black heels. If her dad is so strict, you think he would've vetoed her outfits long ago. I've never seen her first thing in the morning, so I'm not sure if she's one of those people that wears one set of clothing out of the house and then has another hoochie outfit stashed in her backpack for school.

Okay, I could be wrong, but I think Danielle Steel is ancient by now and doesn't dress like the characters in her books. Frank and Tim are both wearing sleeveless shirts and gym shorts. They get a couple of ooohs from their friends and flex their muscles. This only causes more ooohs and a few chuckles.

Ms. Peters flicks the lights for them to begin, and Stacy announces everyone and says that Arnold and The Rock will be starting off with a few exercises from their books.

"No pain, no gain," Arnold says in a really bad Austrian accent. Then lifts up a free weight.

"That's for sissies," The Rock barks and picks up two weights with one hand. Everyone laughs. The muscleheads banter back and forth for a few minutes, trying to outdo each other.

Gavin taps me on the shoulder and points to my desk. There's a little white piece of paper folded in half. For me? Besides Stacy, I don't have any other enemies in this class that I know of. So it's safe to open. Immediately I recognize the slanty writing.

Isn't this lame?

I eye Gavin, and he pretends to be asleep.

I let out a chuckle and quickly cover my mouth. I don't want Ms. Peters to confiscate the note. I write back and slide the paper over to Gavin.

> Stacy should've been Pamela Anderson. Then she could've shown up in a bikini.

He whispers, "G-string."

Eww, that's not an image I want to carry around with me.

He writes something down on the note again and slides it to me.

> I'm just waiting for her to mess up. Liars like Stacy always get their payback. GUARANTEED!!!

I gulp and reread the sentence. The word *liar* sticks out like a bloody corpse. Can you define the meaning of *liar*? Does that include little white lies? Or just big, fat, ugly lies? I don't know what to say, but I better write something. Surely my little radio contest is nothing like the evil lies that Stacy hatches every day. I'm about to write back when I see Ms. Peters looking over in my direction. I fold up the note and force myself to focus on the performance.

"You want strong?" Arnold says to the class.

"Yes!" some scream, while others cheer. Then he walks over to Stacy and scoops her into his arms. "Let me go," she cries.

He puts her down next to the table. "Sorry, sometimes I get carried away."

The class erupts into laughter.

Then Stacy takes a seat at the table where she has set up a small typewriter. This should be interesting.

"I'm so glad you gentlemen could take a break from exercising to join me." She fans herself with a book.

"At your service, ma'am." Arnold salutes her.

"Here, let me help you," Frank says in a deep voice and pushes in her chair.

I know this is mean, but I keep on waiting for Stacy to slip and fall on her ass. I should've brought some Crisco oil; that would've done the trick. Unfortunately, she's doing a great job acting like a debutante. The guys keep on bringing her drinks and anything else she asks for. I could use one of those manservants.

People are really laughing. This sucks. I was hoping that their performance would be so boring that the class would fall asleep.

Stacy runs her fingers over the typewriter like one of those game-show girls caressing the grand prize. Then she tells Arnold and The Rock to pull up chairs. She's reading to them from her latest novel.

"I want you boys to hear it first," she coos. "It has some body-building in it."

They both flex their muscles again and make grunting noises. Everyone laughs. Well, everyone except for me and Gavin. The muscleheads straddle their chairs on either side of Stacy. She pulls out a couple sheets of paper and sets them up in the typewriter. Then she takes a deep breath and reads, "It was a steamy evening on South Beach when Stacy Barnes stepped out of her red Ferrari . . ."

Oh, brother. I look at Gavin, and we both roll our eyes. She's so full of herself, it's not even funny.

Stacy continues, "She wasn't even out of her car for a second when dozens of men rushed over to make sure it was really her. One held out his hand to help her up the curb, while another handed her a bouquet of roses."

I think Danielle Steel would quit writing if she heard this story. I take inventory of the class. Everyone seems to be enthralled. Brian is salivating, Amelia is at the edge of her seat, and Carrie keeps on giving Stacy the thumbs-up. Yes, it's true that a couple of guys are using the time to look up Stacy's skirt, but everyone is paying attention, whatever their motivation is.

Stacy stops reading at the end of the page, tosses it aside, and starts reading the next one. "What's up, hoochie mama? You look hot!" Stacy tears away the sheet. "How did my note get in there? This isn't what I was supposed to read. Frank, Tim, um, ah, I mean, Arnold, Rock . . . Where's the other page?" Her face reddens.

Man, she's losing it.

"I dunno." Tim shrugs.

"That was your part," Frank adds.

Stacy stomps her foot. "This is *not* what I wanted typed up."

She tugs at her hair and huffs. No one moves, including Frank and Tim. She looks under the table, then picks up the typewriter. We all stare.

Stacy holds up the torn paper and glares at it, mouth open wide. I wait for drool to slide down her chin. The whole class is mute.

Stacy has committed the worst crime that a broadcaster could ever commit: dead air.

Ms. Peters finally breaks the silence. "Stacy, please continue with the performance, ad-lib if need be."

"Add what?" Stacy screws up her face.

The class bursts into laughter. Even Frank and Tim are laughing.

I can't stop from smiling. I look over at Gavin, and he's smiling, too. Revenge. And I didn't even inflict it. How sweet it is.

chapter TWENTY-TWO

I feel like I just got convicted of a crime and am awaiting sentencing, not heading to the production room to pick the winner of the prom contest. Cindy and her promotions team weeded through the sixty-eight entries and narrowed them down to the ten best. A few were disqualified for being too long, one was filled with profanity, and another came from a guy who apparently delivered his a minute after the deadline.

He would've made it, except instead of handing over the CD, he decided to hit on Pop-Tart. He spent the next fifteen minutes telling her all the ways he could please her. She listened to his crap and when he was done, she politely smiled and said, "Would you look at the time? The contest closed fifteen minutes ago! Maybe next year, buddy." Instead of getting pissed off, he said, "Can I at least get your phone number?" So she gave him the number to the station's loser line, where guys call in thinking they're leaving a message for a girl but instead their message gets played on the air with the promo—LOSER ALERT! Got to love Pop-Tart!

I set myself up in front of the ginormous CD player and pop in the first contestant, Number 7. I suddenly feel like I'm on a reality dating show. I'd much rather be the host than the bachelorette. Maybe I should be a martyr, too, and pass off the winning entry to another lucky lady. Maybe the one with the best sob story about breaking up with her skeezy boyfriend. Somehow I don't think anyone would go for it.

I slide on a pair of oversized headphones to block out any outside noise. I want to give all these guys a fair chance. I figure when the song speaks to me, I'll know who the winner is.

After the first one, I already have to take a break. Whoever chose "Bees to Your Knees" as a finalist? Is this some kind of joke? Okay, yes, the dude can sing, but doesn't content count for anything? It even has buzzing noises.

Bees to your knees
You make me buzz inside until I come alive.
Bees swarm me until I drop to my knees.
Oh, please pick mees!

The scary thing is he'd probably show up in a bumblebee costume. Of course, he could be a professional beekeeper, which would be interesting since I've never met one. What am I thinking? I'm looking for the most harmless, halfway decent-sounding prom date, not a subject for a show on death-defying jobs. Next.

A quick pass on Number 56, I'm just not into sword fighting and knights winning the love of their dames. Yes, *dame* was the actual word used.

I cue up Number 42 next and even give it a second listen. It has potential. The contestant is strong on the guitar and his singing is upbeat, but not too pop-ish. I'm not crazy about some of his lyrics: *"Hold me close, don't leave me or throw me away like burnt toast, baby, I want you to love me so . . . ,"* but they'll do. It's not like I have to marry the guy. Right?

I keep Number 42 in the Maybe pile and move on to the next few. I ditch Number 22 because we don't see eye to eye on life issues. He thinks men should drink beer for breakfast and women should wear short skirts and bend over to dust the tables. I don't even want to know how that one made it through. Probably Derek's choice.

As soon as Number 61 loads, I crack up. I can't believe he really sent this entry in and actually pulled together decent-enough lyrics to make it to the top ten.

Burger and Fry Girl
Burgers and fries for my girl and no lies.
Soup when she's sick and whatever else she needs.

Treat her like the queen that she is.
Take in, or take out, that's what it's all about.
For my girl, the queen that she is.
Burgers and fries on a silver platter, it will be.

It certainly doesn't make me look very sophisticated, but it's funny that he went through with it. His voice is a little scratchy, but he definitely deserves an A for effort.

The next two entries, Numbers 18 and 61, have the basics. They both have decent rhythm and sing about the prom. Eighteen says it'll be the night of his life, while 61 says it's a stepping-stone to more great things to come. But both lack pizzazz. I could flip the dial and hear a hundred better than them, past and present. Of course, if it has to be one of them, I could flip a coin. I shouldn't panic yet, there are three CDs left. Still, I move both of them to the Maybe pile.

The next entry, Number 13, has a really cool picture of the moon on the cover. I pop it in. "The Moon Stops for You." Neat title. The guitar starts off slow, but once the vocals join in, it's at an even pace. Something about the song sends chills up my spine. At a minute thirty, I start the song again from the top. I don't want it to end. It's that good. Every beat resonates with me. The words are so alive, so real.

The moon stops for you.
Not a cloud in sight

Gleaming down at your pretty face
Just enough glow to make you sparkle.
The moon stops for you.
Who needs the sun when you're around?
You're a natural satellite, always shining bright.

Without this guiding light, others can't see your beauty from within.
You need to step away from your shroud.
Let the light of the stars illuminate you as your heart beats proud.
Like a whisper blowing through the trees, the moon stops for you.

My hand's shaking when I hit play again. It's not just the lyrics, but the voice, too. It's luscious. Deep and soothing. I listen again, savoring every word. It's like a lullaby for every girl who wishes she was with that special guy.

I wonder if the songwriter was thinking about someone specific when he wrote it. I pull off my headphones. I know this is stupid, but I'm actually jealous of her, the girl that the moon stops for. What's she like? What about her mesmerizes him? I bet she's drop-dead gorgeous and really sweet, too. How depressing. Is she alive? Dead? Okay, I have to stop this. He's definitely the one, lucky Thirteen.

I listen to the last two CDs out of courtesy, but nothing's going to blow me away like "The Moon Stops for You." I just hope he's half as good-looking as he sounds. How ironic. I bet he's saying the same thing about me.

I walk right into the studio and hand the CD to Derek. "This is the one."

"Smoking cover." He slides the CD out of the jewel case. "Let's give him a listen."

Neither of us talk. We're both engulfed by the song, staring at the CD player like it might come alive at any moment.

"Wow, talented kid. Good sound," Derek says when the song is over. "Let me give Cindy a buzz to make sure everything's kosher with this guy. Then we'll blast him through the airwaves."

I'm on pins and needles while he gabs to Cindy. *Don't make me go back and select Bee Guy.*

Finally he puts down the phone. "Everything's clear. Shall we?" He points to the on-air button.

I'm as ready as I'll ever be. It's official; the victor has been crowned. There's no going back now.

Derek announces that a winner has been picked and that everyone should stay tuned for the debut. It's strange, but I feel nervous for the guy. He's probably ecstatic that his creation will be broadcasted to thousands of listeners, but he bared his soul and now that's going to be public domain. I hope he's ready.

"The Moon Stops for You" airs at 6:57 p.m. I'm nervous and excited at the same time. I can't stand. I can't sit. I'm a human jack-in-the-box. *"Without this guiding light, others can't see your beauty from within. You need to step away from your shroud . . ."*

I can barely wait the two minutes and fifty-three seconds

before the phones light up and the listeners speak their minds. *Don't you just love him?*

* * *

Good evening, Miami. I've got a new tune for you, "The Moon Stops for You." The artist wants to remain anonymous. But I promise you, this one will leave you thinking. If he's even half as sexy as his voice, you'll melt every time you see him. This is Sweet T on 92.7 The SLAM, signing out for the night . . .

chapter TWENTY-THREE

I wake up in a panic. Only four days left until I meet Moon Guy and three weeks until graduation. But honestly, I can't even think about graduation at a time like this. In fact, I might not even make it to the ceremony if the prom eats me alive. I might have to go into hiding and have my diploma dropped by helicopter to my new home deep in the mountains. If only Florida wasn't such a flat state. The farthest I'll be able to climb into solitude is to the top of Mount Trashmore, our local dump. No, thanks.

I realize I actually need to find something decent to wear for the *big night*. I can't go fish a dress off the racks at Marshalls. I have to snag something that makes me look glam. I still can't believe I'm going with a complete stranger. It's crazy that only

Cindy from promotions and SLAM's lawyer know who he is.

He could be really hot. So hot that my tongue will be swollen from me salivating all night and all the girls will be lining up to catch a glimpse of him. Of course, with my luck, he's covered in warts and suffers from perspiration overload and extreme body hair. But before I freak myself out any further, I need to refuel.

Mom's in the kitchen fixing breakfast. I was hoping to be long gone before she got up. She's in her pink silk bathrobe and matching slippers, waiting for the coffee to brew. I try to avoid her by quickly grabbing the milk and cereal and sitting at the far end of the kitchen table. She's been so nuts lately that I don't want to ignite her flames. I would just take my food up to my room, but I don't want to hear her complain about ants. She's practically having an affair with the exterminator, he's here so much. I haven't even seen an ant in the house for years. But Mom can't stand insects. Okay, I'm sure most people share her sentiment, but the mere sight of a small critter can send her into hysterics that last hours. Her lunacy is pretty humorous considering we live in Miami, where the cockroach could be an official mascot.

I look over at Mom's slippers. I picture thousands of cockroaches swarming around her feet. Before I can stop myself, I crack up. Then I imagine the bugs chasing Mom around the kitchen. This is fun in a sinister way.

She reaches for the fridge and pulls out the soy butter. She sprays it on her toast. I laugh harder as the imaginary roaches inch their way up the countertop. It seems like I haven't laughed in forever, and that sets me off again. Mom just keeps on spraying. I can tell she wants to say something. Another bubble of laughter bursts from my mouth. If Mom doesn't stop with the soy butter, she'll burn a hole in the bread.

Finally she sets down the spray. "What is it, Teresa? Why are you acting so strange?"

That makes me laugh even harder. For once I've made her feel uncomfortable. My jaw aches. I haven't used my happy muscles in a long time. I finally stop laughing and take a long, slow bite of my cereal. I let the soggy flakes melt in my mouth.

She walks toward me but stops halfway. Her face drops. "Are you okay?"

I still don't say anything. How can I? Every time I try to talk to her, she jumps down my throat. I close my eyes and shake my head. A lump rises in my throat, but I force it back down.

My eyes are drawn tight, but I can feel her standing beside me now. She speaks softly, "Tere, we need to talk."

I don't say anything. Instead, I hum to the tune of *"Like a whisper blowing through the trees, the moon stops for you . . ."*

Mom pulls out the chair next to me and sits down. "These past few months, we've really been at each other. I've said things I shouldn't have. Didn't mean."

I open my eyes. I want to believe her but don't know if I can. I look at her oval face. There are a few lines above her cheekbones. She has not masked them with cover-up yet this morning. "What?"

She looks me straight in the eye. "No matter what you think of me, I really do care about you." Then she peers down at her hands. One of her manicured nails is chipped. She's not perfect, after all. "I just don't want to see you get hurt."

"Hurt? How?"

"Being shy can really hold you back from a lot of things in life. I've seen it happen with . . . my mother."

"Huh?" I never would've thought Grandma Susan was shy, standoffish, maybe. She lives in London now so we haven't seen her in three years, but she oozed confidence every time I saw her—or so I thought.

"Your grandmother was only eighteen when she married my father. She was quiet as a mouse for years, never stood up for herself. I was determined not to get stepped on like her and, well, sometimes I see a lot of you in her and it scares me."

"Oh." I stare down at my lap, boring a hole into my jeans as I wait for her to continue.

"I'm sorry if I pushed too much, drove you away. But I didn't know what else to do."

I look up at her. She is still beautiful, even without all the makeup she usually cakes on her face. Without blow-drying her hair for an hour. I reach out to touch her. She takes my hand. "I'm proud of you, Tere."

I'm not prepared for that. For the fact that she really is happy with me. With the way I am. I open my mouth and suck on the dead air. I take another deep breath and continue to drain the oxygen around us. I'm hot and stuffy.

Mom stares at me, eyes wide. I know she wants me to say something, but she waits, patiently. I look back at her, my eyes wide, too. Finally, on their own, the words tumble out. "Thank you."

Then, without notice, tears stream down her face. She sobs little tiny sobs.

Mom can be emotional at times, but I never thought she'd shed tears for *my* love.

I wait, anticipating a recall from her. *I didn't mean it, Tere. I really don't like the way you've turned out.* But it doesn't come. I reach for her hand, and she squeezes tight. Tears slide down my face, too. No matter what, I can't hate my mother.

"I'm sorry, Tere." She wipes her face with a napkin.

I watch her dab her eyes. "It's okay."

"If you don't want to go through with the contest, we can find someone else to take your place."

I sit up straight. "No, I've made it this far. I can do it."

"You're a strong girl." Mom pats my hand. Her slender fingers lay on top of mine. "I've never told you this, but I didn't go to my senior prom."

"You didn't? But the way you always talk about it . . ."

"I helped plan it and counted down the days ever since I was a freshman, but I was already five months' pregnant with you. Four days before the prom, the school found out. They thought I'd be a bad influence on the other girls and expelled me. I received my diploma in the mail. I was so ashamed." Mom picks at her chipped nail, making it even worse.

I do the mental math. "So this very day, eighteen years ago—"

"Yes," she cuts me off. "I don't want you to experience what I did. To feel like an outcast."

"Sorry." I lower my head.

"For what?"

"For being born."

"No," she stops me. "I'm not sorry, and you should never be. I haven't told you enough that I love you. I can't make it up to you; I know that. It was hard raising you alone but I managed . . . survived. But if there's something, anything I can do . . ." Her voice fades out.

"There is."

Mom perks up.

"You can take me prom-dress shopping."

"I'd love that," she squeals.

Rob bumbles into the kitchen in his bathrobe. "Tere, I just got a call from the station. The phones were ringing off the hook last night. They loved it. The winner. 'Moon Shine'?"

My eyes light up. "'The Moon Stops for You.' It's awesome."

Rob sets the newspaper down onto the table and glances over at Mom. A stray tear slides down her cheek. "Did I come down at a bad time?"

I'm compelled to answer for the both of us. "No, it's a good time."

"Really?" Rob takes a step back. "Could've fooled me."

"Tears aren't always bad. You know us girls." Mom sniffles.

"No, I don't. That's the problem." Rob laughs.

"Mom's taking me dress shopping today." I steal the inserts from Rob's paper, hoping to find some cool clothing ads.

I scan through a few of the pages, then head up to my room to shower. I'm having second thoughts about going shopping with just Mom so I call Audrey for backup.

"Hey, Aud." I fling open my closet door. "Remember how you said I should hurry up and find a dress for the prom?"

"Yeah, that was over three weeks ago."

"Okay, well, I'm ready now." I walk into my closet and stare at my rows of sneakers.

"Why now?"

"I picked the winner last night. He's amazing." I spy an old pair of black wedge sandals and dust them off.

"You met him?" Her voice rises an octave.

"No, just his voice."

"What kind of song did he send in?"

"Oh, it's awesome. It's called 'The Moon Stops for You,' and it's so romantic. I almost cried." I cradle the shoes.

"Wow."

"I'm in love already." I laugh.

"Whoa, what happened to Gavin?"

"Nothing." I sit down on the carpet and try the sandals on. "I love him, too."

"You're crazy." She laughs. "So you want to go to the mall?"

"Yeah. My mom wants to take me, but I'd like you to come, too. Safety in numbers."

"Your mom? That's good. You guys made up, then?"

"I guess. She apologized." I pace around my room in the wedges. They pinch my baby toes. I kick them off.

"Then what's wrong?"

I rub my feet. "I don't know. It's weird. She was so emotional. I've never seen her like that before. What if she does an about-face?"

"Give her a chance. People can change, you know."

"True, I just don't want to . . . get hurt." I mumble the last part.

"Take it one step at a time," Audrey offers.

"Hmmm." I'm not too convinced.

"First, let's find you the perfect dress."

"Okay, I can handle that. We'll pick you up in a little while." I hang up the phone before I change my mind.

"I thought we'd start at the Aventura Mall." Mom checks her lipstick in the mirror before she cranks up the car.

"Sure." I nod.

Mom reaches for the radio dial. "Mind if we listen to SLAM?" I ask.

"No, go ahead." Mom lets me take over. "So, I was thinking

of a halter dress for you. Maybe coral or red."

"I guess." I roll my eyes. "Can we wait until we get there? Until I see what jumps out at me?"

"Sure." She pulls at a loose strand of hair poking out of her ponytail.

We pull up to Audrey's *Casa de la Selva*. We call it that because they have so many overgrown trees surrounding their property that you'd half expect jungle animals to jump out at you any minute. My favorites are the mangos. The fruit is juicy, and Audrey and her mom make the best mango bread. Audrey's waiting for us on the front steps.

She climbs in to the backseat. "Hi, Delilah. Hi, Tere."

I fill Audrey in on where we're going, and we hit the expressway. It's already after eleven and all the primo spots are taken, so we park toward the end of the mall lot. I'm nervous. Maybe I shouldn't have eaten breakfast. That could've probably saved me a whole two pounds.

We hit Macy's first. Mom tries her best not to hover, staying a few feet away from us.

"What about this one?" Audrey holds up an eye-straining pattern of swirled yellows and oranges.

"Not." I make a gagging sound.

"Be daring." She pulls out a bright-green silky one that looks perfect for the Victoria's Secret runway show.

A stick-skinny girl with platinum-blond hair is ogling over the same one.

"I'm going to the prom with a complete stranger. Isn't that daring enough?"

Audrey doesn't say a word. She knows it's true.

I pull four blacks off the rack and a turquoise dress just to add a little color. Mom throws in two red dresses, and we parade to the dressing room. I've never had an entourage before. It's usually me following Mom or Audrey around. Being the leader is pretty neat.

I need some breathing room, so I make them sit outside.

I try on one of the red dresses that Mom suggested first. It makes my boobs look like stuffed sausages. Not a pretty sight. I rip it off and throw on a long black dress next. I like the way the bottom of the dress dusts the tops of my feet.

I open up the stall and walk toward Mom and Audrey.

I put my hands on my hips. "Well?"

"It's nice." Audrey looks me up and down.

"Too safe," Mom says.

Audrey bites her lip. "I'd have to agree with your mom. It's not doing anything for you."

"Okay." I turn around and climb back into my box. Stuffed Sausage is out. Safe is out. I rummage through the pile of dresses. There's got to be something *wow* in here.

I try on a couple more black numbers, but they're too everyday. I realize I'm tired of being blah. I reach for the shiny turquoise one. I zip it up and stare into the full-length mirror.

Okay, the color is nice, but it's not me. I'm afraid one of my boobs might pop out. I still have to be myself.

Mom knocks on the door. "Any luck?"

"Be right out." I'm standing here in my pink bra and underwear. I feel so vulnerable. Instinctively I cross my arms over my breasts.

"Try the sexy red one," she says.

I quickly grab another black dress, this one strapless with a pink sash. I zip it up and look into the mirror. It hits me just right at my knees. Not too long and not too short. And I can breathe in it. I feel it in my bones—this dress is it. Of course, the fact that I don't immediately have the urge to tear it off is a good sign, too.

I swish back and forth and sneak peeks in the mirror. *I look good*. The dress de-emphasizes my stomach and accentuates my boobs. It's like this dress was custom-made for me.

It's definitely worthy of leaving the comfort of my stall, so I step out and twirl around. "Ta-da!" I stand in front of Mom and Audrey.

They both look me up and down. Mom pulls at the fabric. I knew it. She hates it.

I look at Audrey and frown.

"It's nice," Mom says.

My eyes bug out. "Really?"

"Yes. It fits you well. They have it in white, too. Let me get it for you."

I put my hands on my hips. "Mom, you can't expect me to travel too far out of my comfort zone. The black is good."

"I like it," Audrey proclaims. "And it's great for dancing."

Dancing? No one said anything about dancing. Is that in my contract? I shake my head.

"Don't worry," Audrey says. "It'll be dark and half the school will be drunk. No one will know if you dance like a toad."

"Thanks, that makes me feel much better." I roll my eyes.

"All right," Mom agrees. "It moves well, and black is always in style."

"Good, then I'm going to change." I point to my back. "Can somebody unzip me?"

Mom gently picks up my hair and loosens the zipper. Her fingers are cold against the skin of my neck. I shiver. "I should just be glad you're not wearing sweats, right?" She lets go of my hair.

"Uh-huh." I hold on to the sides of the dress. I can't believe I'm wearing this to my prom. Unlike my mom, I never thought I'd really be going.

"Sure you don't want to try the shimmery red one?" Mom asks.

I don't bother turning around. "I'm sure." When you find something you like, don't push it.

I quickly throw on my jeans and tee. I hand Mom the dress and meet Audrey over by the handbags.

I pick up a black Juicy bag and read the price tag. Three hundred dollars. Double the price of my dress. "I still don't know if I should go through with this contest. I could become really sick the night before the prom."

"Or Contestant Number 13 could be the man of your dreams." Audrey unzips a blinding purple purse with a pocket for everything.

"I already thought of that, and the other possibilities, too." I pretend to slit my throat.

"It's just one night, and if Gavin's meant to be, it'll happen," Audrey says.

"He didn't even ask if I was going. I'm sure he assumes I'm not, but still . . ." I look down at my shoes. "That can't be a good thing."

Audrey pats my shoulder. "Maybe he didn't want to know."

"I never thought of that." I drape a sheer black scarf over my head.

"See, that's why you have me, to think of the things that you don't."

"Okay, evil twin sister." I hang the scarf back up. "I hope you're right."

"And if I'm not, you can make me disappear with your laser gun." She makes zapping sounds.

"I'll remember you said that." I watch as a plastic-surgery addict runs her fingers over a cream-colored Coach bag and licks her collagen lips.

"Really?" Audrey puffs out her lips behind the woman's back.

We both giggle and run to meet up with my mom. We find her looking at shoes.

"I thought you were paying," I say.

"You didn't think I'd let you wear sneakers to the prom, did you?" she asks.

"No, not really."

She hands me a few boxes, and I obediently try the sandals on. We actually agree on a pair of black strappy two-inch heels. It's a miracle. Hopefully I can dance in them. Too bad they don't come with lessons.

It's not too late to change your mind, half of me says as we wait in line at the register. The other half says, *Oh, yeah, it is.* Still, I'm a bit freaked about the whole situation, but hopefully it's something I can laugh about later. Yeah, like in fifty years, when I've successfully found a way to live harmoniously with the aliens on Mars. Speaking of aliens, does Plastic Surgery Lady know that she'd need a passport to get back to Earth if she ever left the planet?

Mom pays and hands me the shopping bag.

"Thanks." I gulp.

"You're welcome," Mom says and walks toward the escalator. "Now come on, girls, let's grab some lunch." We follow her down a level and end up at The Cheesecake Factory.

That's so unlike her. Maybe she has changed.

We walk over to the glass case with the cheesecakes while we wait for a table.

"Oh, I want that one." Audrey points to a slice of cookie dough.

My eyes go wide. "No, I like Macadamia Nut."

"Carbs galore." Mom waves her finger. "Salads only. You want to fit in your prom dresses, don't you?"

Okay, I was mistaken. The good fairy did not sprinkle my mom with a layer of sweetness.

chapter TWENTY-FOUR

W here is she?" Mom's pacing back and forth in the front foyer like an expectant father on an old sitcom.

"Relax. She's only five minutes late. We have plenty of time." I throw myself onto the living room couch in an attempt to relax. I haven't sat down since the end of school when the bell rang at two-thirty. I don't know why they had to have the prom on a Friday. Everyone was rushing around like crazy, and all my classes were half empty. Even the teachers seemed distracted, discussing where they were going to get their hair done and if their dresses from last year would still fit.

I can't even get comfortable on the couch. My insides are churning, and not because Pop-Tart is late. I'm freaked because if she does show, it means I really have to go through with this. She'll be one more person cheering me on all the way to the finish line. One more person stopping me from ditching the prom and becoming the next face on a milk carton.

Mom peers through the peephole in the front door. "I knew we should've used Pamela."

"Mom, Kelly will be here. Trust me." I hope. I turn to the window and stare at the circular drive. It's still a couple of hours until sunset, but the moon is already in place. Maybe it's a sign. This night is all so surreal. *"Who needs the sun when you're around? You're a natural satellite, always shining bright . . ."*

In less than two hours I'll be meeting my Prince Charming. Okay, maybe that's going a little overboard. I only have to act like he is for the photos and the four hundred other people attending prom. After the last song, we can each ride off into our separate sunsets and never lay eyes on each other again.

A blue convertible zips into the driveway. Kelly's boyfriend is dropping her off since we'll be riding in style in the limo.

"It's about time," Mom calls to me.

"Be nice, Mother," I warn and step up to greet Kelly at the door.

I move in to give her a hug. She puts down her huge makeup bag and wraps her arms around me. "You're going to look awesome, Tere."

"Thanks," I murmur into her shoulder.

Mom's standing in the doorway. "Hi, Kelly, come in." I'm glad she doesn't make any cracks about Kelly being a receptionist, not a licensed cosmetologist like Pamela.

We bolt up to my bedroom. Kelly's eager to get started. My nerves are in overdrive, so I run to the bathroom while she sets up. I splash water on my face and peer into the mirror. "You can do it," I whisper. It's only one night. In less than twelve hours it'll only be a memory. "Just don't make it a bad one, Sweet T." I stare at my reflection.

I'm sad that I won't even get to share one dance with Gavin. Even if he isn't my date, I'd like him to be a part of the experience. He doesn't know the impact he's had on me these past few months. He's helped me come out of my shell by accepting me for who I am. He never questioned why I was so shy, never expected more from me than I could handle. And I can't forget that I shared my first kiss with him, even if it only lasted a second.

Once I'm out of the bathroom, I flop down at my desk that Kelly has set up as her makeup station.

The smile on Kelly's face shrinks when she looks at me. "What's wrong?"

"It's pointless," I say and sigh.

"What?" She lays out a few eye-shadow brushes on my desk.

"Even though I love the winning song, I still wish I was going with someone else. Someone that I know. That's all."

"Could it be the kid from your English class?" She raises her eyebrows.

"Yes." I look down at my freshly manicured toes, painted pink with New Horizons polish. I chose this color, hoping it'd give me good luck. I must be pretty desperate if I'm getting my fortunes off of nail polish bottles. "He's the one going to see Speed Bump tonight."

"Right, that could be a problem." Kelly dips a cotton ball into a bottle of cleanser and wipes my skin.

"Exactly."

She pulls out a powder brush and stops short. "Unless . . ." A huge smile overpowers her face.

"Unless what?" I perk up like she might be the sole owner of a real crystal ball.

"Oh, this is brilliant," she squeals.

"What?"

"Why don't we swing by the concert before the prom and lure Gavin out of there?" She runs the powder brush over my face.

I cough.

"No, I'm serious," she continues. "We've got the limo to drive us around."

"But what if he doesn't want to leave the show?" I slide my silver bracelet up my arm as far as it will go. And what if Gavin does come with us? How would Moon Guy feel being the third wheel? Even if he is the biggest freak on Earth, he still deserves to be *my date*. After all, he won fair and square. Just thinking about whether he's a nerd, a jock, or an underwear model is totally playing with my head. The anticipation is overwhelming. But it's only a three-hour event. People have survived a lot worse. I immediately think of Helen Keller. She spent most of her life in the dark. I'm only spending one night.

"After he sees you all dressed up, trust me, he'll want to leave." No one has ever had so much confidence in me. It's scary.

"I dunno." I slump my shoulders.

"Well, think about it. Now close your eyes." Kelly applies liner to my top lids. If I could keep my eyes closed for the rest of the night, I'd be fine. That way I wouldn't have to read people's expressions when they find out that I, Tere Adams, am Sweet T. I know Helen would say be happy with who you are, but the concept of self-esteem is all so new to me. I've never been the guest of honor before. I'm always one with the wallpaper.

For the next few minutes neither of us says anything. Kelly's busy designing my mask, and I'm playing twenty questions with my nerves. *Will the bathroom be close by? Can you guarantee my stomach won't give way when I'm called onto the stage? Will I tuck my underwear into the back of my dress by mistake? Should I take a detour to the Speed Bump concert and kidnap Gavin?*

Mom pokes her head in the room. "How are you doing, girls?"

"Making good time," Kelly says.

I look up. Mom's dressed already. She has on a red shimmery halter that stops at her knees. "I like your dress, Mom."

"Thanks. I couldn't decide on the color. I also brought it home in white and aqua."

"Definitely red," I say.

"Yes, it's beautiful." Kelly gives her the thumbs-up. "And Tere's going to look gorgeous. You're quite a team."

"Great," Mom says. "Just make sure to keep it bright. She can look a little pale at times."

Wait until I puke, I'll look really pale then.

Mom peeks into Kelly's makeup bag. "Ohh, I like this one." She points to one of the blushes.

I roll my eyes. "Okay, Mom. Kelly has it all under control."

"I know. I was talking about for me." She dips the tip of her finger into the container and tries the reddish-brown color out on her hand. "This is my first prom, too, you know."

I'm so glad Rob is taking her to dinner first or I'm positive she would've ridden to the hotel in the limo with us.

Kelly tells her to pick out whatever she wants to use for herself. Mom takes advantage of that and heads to her room with a few samples.

Maybe Kelly is right. Maybe I should go to the concert, bust open the front door, and sweep Gavin into the limo—it's so movie star–like. But at the same time Gavin never asked me to the prom. For all I know he could be slamming with another girl in the mosh pit. Moon Guy is waiting for me, and any guy who can write lyrics like "The Moon Stops for You" has my vote.

"Thanks for the offer, Kelly, but I'm going to stick with the contest winner tonight," I say. "I owe it to the station. To my listeners."

"That's very admirable of you." She steadies my chin. "Now look up; I'm applying the liner under your eyes."

I thought she'd be more disappointed. Maybe she never expected me to say yes. But it's like Helen Keller said, "Never bend your head. Hold it high. Look the world straight in the eye." And I don't want to go back to where I came from. I need to do this. For me.

It's both terrifying and exhilarating that my secret identity is going to be revealed tonight. I'm scared that people will feel let down when they find out it's me behind the mike. But at the same time, it's thrilling to finally expose the real me. To say this is who I am; I'm not hiding anymore—take it or leave it.

When Kelly's done with my makeup, she pins up a piece of my hair with a silver clip. The rest stays down. I followed all her pre-hair instructions and washed with a special de-frizz shampoo and conditioner. My hair actually looks lively and as an added bonus, it smells like fresh mangos.

I step into my closet and stare at the dress. It's beautiful on the hanger. It would be such a shame to disturb it. I finger the black material. It's so soft, just like I imagine Gavin's hair to be. He's probably on his way to the concert now, wearing a black tee and jeans. Next to him I would look out of place.

I pull the dress off the hanger and slowly slide it on.

"Need any help?" Kelly calls from my desk.

"I can't get this last bit zipped up." I step out of the closet.

She rushes over to help. "Wow, you look amazing."

"Thanks." I blush.

She picks up her makeup bag. "You ready?"

"Do I have to answer?"

We both laugh. She manages to rush me out the door with only a quick "See you at the Marriott" to Mom.

The white Hummer limo is waiting out front. It's gorgeous, like an untouched pearl. I've ridden in a few limos before with Mom and Rob, but they've never sparkled as much as this one. Right now the winner is being picked up in a matching limo. He's allowed to bring a couple of buddies along for the ride, too. I wonder what they'll do while Moon Guy is at the prom. They'll probably raid the snack bar and mini fridge, then have the driver cruise around Ocean Drive. Are we expected to go home in separate limos? I don't even want to think about that now.

I wish I had begged management to allow Audrey and Doug to ride with us to the prom, but they were afraid that having anyone else ride with me might compromise my cover. They don't know that Audrey has known about the contest from day one.

The first thing I do when I get in the Hummer is make sure the window goes up and down, in case I have to vomit.

"This is way cool, huh?" Kelly checks out the stock in the mini fridge.

"Yeah, I wish I could enjoy it."

"Hey, maybe this will help your nerves." She pulls out a bottle and inspects the label. "Sparkling Grape Juice. I should've known they wouldn't give you the real stuff. Want some?"

"No, thanks. I don't think I could stomach anything right now."

"Okay, then." She swaps it for a bottled water and takes a sip. "Maybe on the way home."

"If I make it that far, I can have more than sparkling juice."

"Well, don't worry. I'm yours for the whole night. So whatever you need, I'm here."

"Thanks." I loosen the strap on my sandal. "Does this limo double as a hearse? Hope you don't mind riding home with a dead body."

Kelly laughs. "Oh, you're so dramatic."

Hmm, just wait and see.

We motor along the highway at an even pace. Drivers and passengers stare at the limo. We're neck and neck with a blue Volvo. The man and woman both look over, then start chatting. I know what they're thinking: *Who's seated behind those dark windows?* I imagine the husband saying, "Maybe it's Madonna or Beyoncé." Then the wife says, "No, honey, it's prom season. It's probably a bunch of high school kids."

They would never guess that it's just me Tere Adams, aka Sweet T, and my makeup artist, Pop-Tart. But what they really don't know is the part that's inside me, the part that can't believe I made it all the way to the prom. Technically I have not *made it* to the prom yet; we're still five miles away. But if you had asked me six months ago if I was going, I wouldn't have even hesitated to say no. I didn't think it was in the cards for me. For starters, I didn't have any date prospects, and even if I did find someone, my mom's expectations were so high that I'd never make her happy. I had planned to rent a bunch of old horror movies instead, like *Carrie* and *The Slumber Party Massacre,* and watch them until the sun came up.

We pull onto Rock Hill Road, and my stomach lurches with every bump. We're a couple of minutes from the Marriott, a couple of minutes from my fate being sealed.

"Someone's got to fix all these potholes," I say to Kelly.

"Yes, where is the commitment to making the city streets better? Didn't the mayor make some speech like that?"

"You mean the time he went on TV in the horrible pink suit preaching about making everyone happy?"

"Something like that." She pops the lid on a jar of peanuts. "There it is!" She points to the huge red Marriott sign like I can't see it.

I am not a coward; I will face the music, I keep telling myself as we wait in line to be dropped off. Of course, I'm a little bummed that I gave up the opportunity to see Gavin, but I know if it's meant to be, it'll happen. Just not now.

chapter TWENTY-FIVE

All is fine until we pull up to the hotel entrance. The driver gets out of the limo and opens my door. I feel like I'm fused to the leather seats; my legs are weighted down and my arms are made of lead. This is it. Once I step out of this car, there's no going back.

That's when I see Audrey and Doug walking up the steps toward the lobby, trailing behind the rest of their crew. It's reassuring to see Audrey in her beautiful peach dress. She catches my eye, unloops her arm from Doug's, and rushes over to me.

"You look awesome," she gushes.

"So do you."

"How was the Hummer?" She runs her hand over the body of the car.

"Great, but it would've been better if you had ridden in it, too."

"Tell me about it; there were twelve of us crammed into a limo half this size."

"Hey, at least you got to travel with the band," I say.

"Ha." She laughs. "I'm glad you haven't lost your sense of humor."

The car behind us beeps. I turn around to make sure it's not the matching Hummer limo. Nope. Just a two-seater Porsche.

Audrey leans down into the limo, so she's face-to-face with me. "Let me help you out."

"I don't know . . . if . . . if . . . this is such a good idea," I stammer.

"You can do it." She helps pull me to my feet. "You're ready."

Kelly's still seated next to me but is on her cell. She tells the person to hold. "I'll be right behind you, Tere. It'll be great. I'm just firming up some plans."

I walk with Audrey up the lobby steps. Our classmates are filing in and out. Some people I recognize from over the years; others I've never seen before. The one thing they all have in common is their huge smiles. I have to put mine on, too. It's just hard when you don't know what you're up against.

I wonder if Mom and Rob are here already. I don't see them by the entrance. Maybe they're at the bar, filling up.

I enter the lobby, and that's when it hits me. This is real. I'm at the prom. Many would argue that this is the most important event in their lives so far. The place is magical with its marble floors and winding wrought-iron staircase. A ginormous chandelier hangs from the ceiling like icicles dripping from an evergreen tree in a Christmas greeting card.

I spot a camera as Audrey and I hit the first stair. Ralph, the cameraman, signals for me to come over. He's standing with Craig, the station's roving reporter. I look around for Kelly, but she's nowhere in sight.

"Audrey, will you come with me?" I ask.

"Absolutely." She looks at Doug, who tells her he'll catch up with some of the band members. She clutches my hand and we waltz over to Ralph, who leads us to an outside patio.

"Just want to touch base with you." Ralph sets the camera down on a glass table. "We're still keeping the unveiling under wraps, so we're not interviewing you until after the winner is announced."

I glance around to see if Moon Guy is hiding in the shadows. All I spot is a huge potted plant.

"What do I have to say?" I gulp.

"Don't worry; it'll be quick. We'll introduce you. Then you can say something about being Sweet T. About the winning song. About how it feels to have your secret identity revealed." Carlos dangles the cordless mike in front of me.

Ugh, the big reveal. I have to keep reminding myself that everyone likes Sweet T. That even if they're shocked to see me, Tere, up on the stage, that hopefully they'll get past it. That by the time Monday rolls around and we're back at school, they'll be used to the fact that I'm just another Ridgeland student that just happens to be one of the SLAM DJs. That it will be no big deal.

Audrey clutches my clammy hand. "So what is she supposed to do now?"

Carlos glances at his watch. "You've got about twenty minutes until they close the doors."

"Enough time for me to disappear." I let out a strained laugh. Nobody laughs with me.

"Kidding," I say.

"Okay." Carlos shakes his head. "Jason's already inside. When it's time, he'll say a few words. Then he'll open a sealed envelope and announce the winner onstage. After that we'll call you up and introduce you. Then the winner will perform his song."

"Any hints on what the guy looks like?" Audrey asks.

"Nope," Carlos says, popping the *P* in "nope." "Cindy has everything under lock and key. She's around here somewhere, but you won't get a word out of her."

"No way," Ralph agrees. "That lady's tight."

Only Carlos laughs this time.

"Let's do one last mirror check." Audrey pulls my hand and leads me away.

"Watch the time," Carlos yells after me.

"If you need to go find Doug, I don't mind," I tell Audrey.

"Don't worry, I'll stay with you until you're called up. This is so exciting." She squeezes my hand.

"Yeah, right," I try to add a bit of pep to my voice but end up sounding like a squeaky dog toy.

There's a couple outside the bathroom leaning against the wall. The guy has his arm linked around the girl's waist. She looks up at him and asks, "Do you think Sweet T could go to our school?"

"Doubt it, Jane. I think we would've found out already." The guy laughs.

I hyperventilate. Should I turn back now? Run the other way?

"Yeah, you're right, and there would've been cameras here and bodyguards, too. Besides, there's no one that looks like a DJ at our school," Jane says.

What does a DJ look like? I peer down at my dress. Maybe I should've worn something more elegant or perhaps more rock star-ish? Should I whip out a pair of sunglasses onstage or sport a diamond-studded tiara?

Audrey opens the bathroom door and pushes me inside. As if she's reading my mind, she whispers, "It's too late to turn back now."

I head straight to the mirror to make sure everything is still in place. Audrey hits the stall. I know if I go in one, I'm not coming out until the night is over.

I lean in close to make sure that no unidentified objects have made their way to my face.

The bathroom door swings open and I hear someone yell, "Oh, look, Lesbo's here."

Just my luck. I'm in no mood for Stacy's games. She's wearing a tight lime-colored dress that hugs her in the right places. Her hair is piled high like a snow cone. But somehow she pulls the whole thing off. I sneer at her, hoping she'll go away. She doesn't take my hints. Instead, she marches up to the sink next to me, even though there are three other empty ones. She smells like alcohol.

She interrupts the flow of water with her hand so that the water sprays the front of my dress. "Whoops." She cackles.

"What's your problem?" I reach for a paper towel.

She looks me up and down. "Girl, I'm not the one with the problem."

"Could've fooled me." I dab at the front of my dress.

"You've had an attitude since the first time I talked to you." She snaps her gum.

"I don't know what you're talking about. I've never done anything to you."

Audrey steps out of the stall. "Leave Tere alone."

"I knew you had a girlfriend."

Audrey puts her arm around me. "And so?"

The bathroom door flings open again and three cheerleaders stumble in. One girl is propped up by two others. She doesn't look good.

"You're such bitches, lesbos," Stacy says and flies out of there.

If the cheerleaders weren't gathered around a toilet bowl, they probably would've thought Stacy was talking to them.

"Chicken," Audrey calls after her.

"Why did you say that? Now she'll come back with her posse."

"Forget about that idiot. She's too drunk to remember." Audrey holds open the door for me.

"I'm surprised she was allowed out of the house," I say.

Audrey laughs. "Why, because she's such a threat to society?"

"No, because I heard her talking a couple of times and her dad sounds pretty strict."

"Maybe he doesn't want his little princess to turn into a slut."

"Too late." I point to a hotel phone booth in the corner, where we see the back of a person in a lime dress making out with what looks like Frank.

"Gross. I've had enough." Audrey tugs on my arm. "Come on, you're about to meet the man of your dreams."

"Yeah, right." I follow her up the stairs. "Don't be surprised when they call up Sweet T and I point to you."

"You better not." Audrey elbows me. "Unless he's drop dead gorgeous. Oops, don't tell Doug I said that."

"But let me guess—if he's drop-dead ugly, he's all mine."

"That's what friends are for." She laughs. "Now come on, let's have some fun." She pulls me toward Doug, who's standing by the entrance to the ballroom.

I hear a PJ Squid tune playing even before I enter the room.

It's called "Alone in a Crowd." Why did Jason pick such a sad song? I hope this is not the theme song of my night. I can't run and hide now—the cameras would only follow me into the bathroom and they're not capturing a stall confession.

Kelly's standing by the door with a clipboard, trying to look inconspicuous. No one would mistake her for a teacher or a parent chaperone.

"Thought you'd left," I whisper.

She tosses her hair. "And miss the finale—no way!"

"Are you coming inside?" I ask.

"Yes, as soon as everyone's here, I'm going to rush and change into something a bit more formal. This is the prom, after all."

"Great, then you can take my place."

"I wouldn't dare." She checks something off with her pen.

"Then I hope you'll be able to make my funeral, too." My face is deadpan.

She clasps my hand. "Whatever happens, you'll never forget this night."

That's what I'm afraid of. But I think of my mom who was dying to go to her prom and couldn't. Of the thousands of girls who live for this one night. And Audrey is right—I am ready.

I hear a girl near the door scream, "I think SLAM is at our school! I just saw a cameraman walk by."

Her friend gasps, "No way, where? I don't see anything."

Let's get this over with. I step forward into the ballroom. One foot after the other onto the red-and-black speckled carpet. The decorating committee really did a good job. I know Mom's probably bummed that she didn't get to help, but at least I didn't protest when she signed up as a chaperone. Our theme is Wish Upon a Star. Cheesy, I know, but it's still cute. There are stars everywhere—hanging from the ceiling, adorning the tables as centerpieces, and even the punch bowls are shaped like stars. The colors are gold and silver, so everything gleams.

Audrey shrieks when she hears a disco tune, and I shoo her and Doug off to dance. I want to take in the rush of prom night before I'm called onstage. Who knows what'll happen to me after that? Hopefully it'll be nothing worse than selective amnesia. There are already a lot of couples on the dance floor with their hands all over each other, sweating up a storm. I'm sure Gavin's all sweaty by now, too, but that's probably from stage diving into the mosh pit or rocking out to an old Speed Bump track.

I look toward the stage where Jason's fiddling with the mike. I'm glad Rob arranged for him to be the DJ. It's good to know that he has my back in case people flip out when they find out who I am. Also, he knows what we want to hear and is not going to throw on any sleeper tunes like some of the older DJs might.

After this filler disco song is over, my time will be up. There are a few girls from my sociology class giggling in the corner, and half the track team is filling up their cups with soda and punch. I scan the room for Mom, for Stacy, for anyone that I know—good or bad. Where is Kayla? I could sure use her sunny attitude right about now.

The last beat thuds, and it's a done deal. Sweet T, unveil your-self to the masses. Throw yourself to the wolves. I'm dizzy. I can't see straight. I have to pee really bad.

"Welcome to the Ridgeland High Wish Upon a Star, one-of-a-kind prom," blasts Rachel Wheeler, our senior class president. "This is a very special night for many reasons . . ."

Oh, please stop the torture now. I can only take so much. I cross and uncross my legs. I scan the partygoers again, this time looking for any sign of my soon-to-be date. I don't know what I'm looking for because a guy in a full armor suit would be really easy to spot.

Rachel finally takes a breath and hands the mike over to Jason. "Good evening, senior class." He lets out a long hoot and every-one hoots back. "As Rachel said, this prom is special for many reasons, but tonight we have something truly unique going on. I'm not just any DJ." He holds up a SLAM tee and tosses it into the crowd. "I'm Jason Stevens, your *Love Shack* host from 92.7 The SLAM."

People yelp for more T-shirts and he tosses a bunch out. My neck tenses and I shift my weight from one foot to the other. How long is he going to draw this out? Doesn't he know that I'm freaking out over here? He goes on to explain the whole contest, while I try to forget my full bladder and blurred vision.

A couple of girls near me whisper about how cool this contest experience is, and I see a guy with spiky hair whip out a small video camera and aim it toward the stage. Geez, we're not playing here. This is the real thing. In a matter of minutes, along with the rest of the senior class, I'm going to meet Moon Guy. And they're going to meet Sweet T.

I'm scared. Scared about going up onstage and facing everyone as Tere Adams. Scared that Moon Guy won't like me. Scared that I'll mess the prom up for everyone. And really scared that over eight hundred eyes are staring at me.

"Here you are." Audrey puts a hand on my shoulder.

I'm stiff as a brick now and hardly flinch. "Sorry, didn't know you were looking for me."

"I told you I'd be here for you. Have you forgotten, 'Never Ever, Best Friends Forever . . . ?'"

I smile. "I just feel so—"

"I know." She takes my hand and squeezes it. "But this is your night. You own it."

Jason interrupts our serene moment with a drumroll. "Without further ado, I'm going to announce the winner of the contest, a peer among peers . . ."

"Huh?" My mouth drops.

"He goes to school here?" Audrey seems as shocked as I am.

Holy crap, how could that be? What are the odds of that?

Jason turns to the left of the stage and claps. Within seconds the rest of the students follow suit. I see a dark shadow walking from the far end of the ballroom. Who is he? Someone I've never seen before? I certainly don't know everyone at Ridgeland. At least, besides Stacy, I don't have any enemies, but please don't let it be a super testosterone-filled jock either. I have to remember that this is the guy who sang "The Moon Stops for You," which happens to be a very sweet song.

"Who's that dude?" a guy asks the girl standing in front of me.

"Never seen him before. Shhh," she tells him like she might miss something.

"Ohmigod!" Audrey screams.

What?" My whole body shakes. I instinctively shut my eyes.

"It's Gavin," she spits out.

"No way!" I scream back, not believing her. I immediately turn my gaze to the stage. I have to stand on tippy toes just to see over all the people that have gathered round. How the hell? "Can't be. He's at Speed Bump."

"No, Tere. That's him." Audrey shakes me, like I need to feel any dizzier than I already am.

"But . . . but . . ." She's right. It's him. Same black hair. Same casual stride. Not the same outfit though; I've never seen him dressed up before. "Still, it could be someone else," I say more for myself than her.

But Jason is still talking, " . . . our promotions department had to weed through tons of entries to find this guy, your very own Gavin Tam, singer extraordinaire . . ."

Could there be another Gavin Tam at this school? Stranger things have happened. Where's Kelly? Did she know this? I take a quick look around but don't see her.

The room is quickly flooded with applause.

Audrey snaps her fingers in front of my face. "Uh, Tere, I hate to break it to you, but they just called Sweet T."

"What?" This time I scream, I mean, really scream, loud enough for all the people around me to turn and stare. This is *so* not how I pictured it, none of it. My mind has blanked. If I wasn't wearing this fancy black dress and these toe-squishing heels, I'd have no idea where I was.

"Shall we?" a voice from behind me says. It's Kelly. Only, she's ditched the clipboard for a beautiful lilac dress. Her Pop-Tarts are hanging out the front, like they were strategically placed. She wasn't kidding when she said she was going to change into something formal.

I steady myself by grabbing hold of her arm.

"Let's go, Tere. It'll be fine." She propels me forward.

I glance over at Audrey, then start walking in a daze.

"But he hates liars," I blab. "He listens to the show, and I never told him I was Sweet T."

"That's what you're worried about?" Kelly tightens her grip on my hand. "He's going to be thrilled it's you."

"I hope so."

"Sweet T would stand up straight and smile," Kelly whispers as we walk across the soft carpet, past the tables and goggly eyes.

The room falls to a hush. I arch my back and stretch my lips.

"Sweet T would wave." Kelly winks at a couple of guys staring at her.

"Now you're pushing it." I widen my smile.

She drops me off at the side of the stage. "Remember, you own the audience, not the other way around." Then she steps on my toe with one of her spiked heels.

"Ouch." I wince.

"Just wanted to make sure you were awake." She laughs.

"Point taken," I say. "Sweet T, it is."

Even though the stage is barely big enough to fit six people across, it looks huge. Jason's voice booms from the mike again, "Sweet T, my fair maiden, the grand stage awaits you!"

I'm in such a state of shock that my mind has frozen. I must propel myself forward. I am now a robot. I calculate the steps to the stage. About ten. I march forward. I can do it.

Jason reaches down to help me up the two steps onto the platform. He slings his arm over my shoulder and gives me a quick peck on the cheek. "Sweet T's in the house." I hold my hand up to my mouth to make sure that my smile is still there. It is.

I feel like any moment Mom's going to shake me awake, draw the shades, and tell me to get my butt out of bed. But I look down, and I'm not wearing my usual sweats. I actually have a beautiful dress on that has the Mom seal of approval. The huge lights above me are bright and hot, like I have taken one step closer to the sun. In front of me there are hundreds of familiar and not so familiar faces. If I squint, I can make out a few—their mouths open wide with surprise, their eyes glued to the stage. It's so surreal standing up here.

I look over at Gavin. Did he know it was me all along? Is he really Number 13? He has traded in his Speed Bump gear for a tux. He's so handsome. Why hasn't he made eye contact with me yet? He's focused on the crowd.

Jason squeezes my shoulder. "Many of you might know this supergirl as Tere Adams—" I hear a few people yell, "Who?" and another bunch shout, "Can't be!" I ignore them all and stare at the side of Gavin's head. He's the one I'm here for anyway and doesn't even know it. "Well, she might be Tere Adams by day, but by night she's our own Sweet T."

The crowd is quiet, but then I hear a few gasps, followed by even more *no ways.*

I'm with you guys all the way, I want to yell out. I have no clue what I'm doing up here either! I feel like I'm in some bad high school flick. Actually, it's really not so bad. I mean, my date is my true love, after all. I hope no one casts a spell on him and turns him into an ogre. I glance over at Gavin just to make sure he hasn't morphed. This time he catches my gaze, winks, and says, "You can do it, Tere!"

He warms up my stomach, which is just the right amount of heat to fuel my whole body. I wink back and mouth, "Thanks."

"Tere," Jason whispers to me and points to the mike.

I look up to the glare of the camera striking my pupils. Live on the webcam, Derek must be eating this up right now. Mom, too. Where is she? I scan the audience, trying not to make eye contact. I don't see her or Rob.

My hands are shaking like maracas, but I take the mike from

Jason. This is my duty. I clear my throat. *Sweet T, don't fail me now.* "I'm Sweet T. Tere Adams. I'm so honored to be here tonight. For SLAM. For Ridgeland. For lucky Number 13!"

"Woo-hoo!" Tim from English yells.

"I know this might come as a surprise, but contrary to what some of you think, I do talk, and play music, too." The crowd laughs and so do I. "So let's get down to business. We came here to hear the winning song!"

Everyone claps, then Jason takes the mike from me and points to Gavin. "Take it away . . ."

I quickly try to exit the stage, but Jason pulls me back. He whispers into my ear, "So what do you think?"

Ohmigod, he doesn't know that this is not just any mystery man.

"That's Gavin. The guy I like." I tug on his shirt.

Jason jolts back; one step farther and he could've toppled off the stage. "You've got to be kidding!"

"Nope."

"Wow." He puts his hand over his heart. "This is a real Cinderella story."

"Shut up." I roll my eyes.

"I'm not kidding," he says.

I give Jason a quick wave and quickly step off the stage to watch the performance. I'm dying to hear the song live. Gavin adjusts his guitar, then lifts up his head. Several pieces of hair cover his left eye as he strums the first note. He looks so choreographed. So perfect, like he was always meant to be up on this stage.

My eyes don't want to leave his performance, but I quickly scan the audience. Some people are dancing, some are seated, and others still have their mouths open wide, but everyone is soaking in the performance.

Gavin takes it away, every bit of it. He rocks the house. He doesn't miss a beat and sings his heart out. *"Who needs the sun when you're around . . ."* Many people may have never met him, but they will remember him now.

The clapping erupts the second the song ends. Everyone stands up and cheers. I still can't believe it's him. Out of all the people, what are the chances that Gavin ended up being lucky Number 13?

chapter TWENTY-SIX

I wait on the side of the stage for Gavin. It suddenly dawns on me that just because he won the contest, it doesn't mean he wants to be with *me*. It doesn't mean that the moon stops for *me*. There could be another girl out there that he wrote the song for. I scan the faces around me. Is she waiting in the wings for him?

He walks off the stage and stops in front of me. His eyes are glistening, and he's still catching his breath. I've never seen him look better.

"You look really good," I say.

"So do you. Amazing." He smiles.

Kayla runs to the stage, holding up the sides of her silk tangerine dress. It matches her car. She pulls us in for a group hug. "You're both awesome. I can't believe my buddies are this cool!"

We both laugh. And I breathe a sigh of relief, too.

"I knew you guys were hiding something, but this?" Kayla asks.

"It wasn't planned," I say.

Jason cranks up the tunes and "Spill Proof" fills the sound system. Tons of people rush to the dance floor. Others are clumped in small groups, talking, watching. I've never had the spotlight shine so brightly on me.

Kayla's eyes bug out. "No way. You didn't know that Gavin was the winner?"

"Nope. See my hands? I'm still shaking." I hold both hands up as evidence.

"And you?" Kayla asks Gavin.

"I knew." He gives me a sheepish look. "Not at first, but after a few clues, I figured it out."

He knew? I must have seemed so stupid. No wonder he didn't ask if I was going to the dance. Duh!

"Wow, this is like a real love story." Kayla waves to her date, who's standing alone a few feet away. "I'll check you guys later," she says and darts off to join her Prince Charming.

I squint at the light from the camera above me.

"That's a wrap," Ralph says to Carlos. "We've got some good footage."

I lean in closer to Gavin. "This night is so weird."

"It's weird for me, too. You know what it was like to keep this whole thing a secret?"

I lightly punch his shoulder. "Yeah, you jerk. All along I thought you were going to Speed Bump."

"I was at first." He sticks his hands in his pockets. "But then I heard about the contest and my brother was like, hey, try it. A few days later I figured out you were Sweet T. That was awesome." He grins.

"Thanks." I blush. "Wasn't your brother mad you ditched him?"

"No, he thought this contest was a good opportunity. But don't worry, I brought a little of Speed Bump with me." He loosens his bow tie and unbuttons the first five buttons on his tux shirt.

I laugh. He's wearing a black Speed Bump concert tee under his formalwear.

"That's too cool." I smile.

A couple of girls from pre-calc rush over to me. They're wearing matching white dresses. "We just had to say hello. This is fab," Melinda says.

"Thanks. I think so, too."

"See you on the dance floor." Kate pulls Melinda by the arm.

I turn back to Gavin. "So, I'm dying to know. How did you find out it was me?"

"How didn't I?" He laughs. " 'Shrinking Violet for one. You said to me, 'I'm mad for Shrinking Violet' and then said it again on the air. Don't underestimate a loyal listener."

My face goes flush. I remember the line, too.

Still, I have to ask. "Are you mad that I didn't tell you I was Sweet T?"

His eyes narrow and he draws his lips together. "Pissed."

My heart drops to my knees.

His frown quickly turns to a smile. "Kidding."

"You scared me." I feel for my heart to make sure it's still there. "It's just . . . I thought you hated liars."

"Relax," he says gently. "You weren't lying. You just kept a secret that you hadn't shared yet."

"The station would've killed me if I had blown my cover."

"Tell me about it. They made me sign like a hundred confidentiality forms." He brushes away a piece of hair that has fallen over his eye. "Besides, I did the same thing. I secretly entered the contest and didn't tell anyone when I discovered you were Sweet T."

"No one?"

"Nope." He shakes his head. "Only my brother and my parents knew about the contest. That's it."

"This is crazy. You don't know how nervous I was about meeting the winner. And what if I had picked the bee guy or the burger dude?"

"Burger and bee dude?" Gavin screws up his face.

"You don't want to know. Let's just say, I love your song."

"Thanks." Gavin grins.

I follow his eyes and look over to the side of the stage. It's

Mom. Her forehead is wrinkled and her eyes are wide with suspicion. I totally forgot about her. She's probably been here the whole time, staring at us. Rob's standing next to her with his arms folded. With the blank stare on his face, he looks like he's watching a football game. He is so out of his element.

Mom takes a couple of steps toward us. "Hi, Mom. Hi, Rob." I gulp.

"Is there something I should know?" Mom avoids looking at Gavin.

"No," I say loudly.

She clicks her tongue. "Don't try and pull one over on me. This has *setup* written all over it."

"No, it doesn't. And that's what's so great. It's pure magic." I peer up at the shiny tinsel stars hanging from the ceiling.

"I don't get it." She turns to Rob. "This doesn't make any sense."

"It is what it is, Delilah. Let it go." He looks at me and smiles. "Besides, I think they make a great couple."

I look over at Gavin and grab his hand. Listening to my mom whine must be so awkward for him, but he doesn't say a word. Smart guy.

"You would rub it in." Mom nudges Rob.

"You've got a great voice, Gavin," Rob says.

Mom's face softens. "Yes. You sure do."

Gavin smiles. "Thanks. I really appreciate it."

I lean forward and hug Mom. I have to realize she'll always be, well, Mom. I can only take her in small doses, and right now I've had enough.

But before we run off, there's someone else who really deserves a hug. I wrap my arms around Rob. "You don't know how much being on the radio has changed my life," I tell him. "You've done so much for me. And for Mom."

I glance up at his cleanly shaven face. His eyes are wet. "You deserve it, Tere. You've earned every second of it. I'm proud of you."

"That means a lot." I sniff.

"Now go have fun," Rob says.

"We will." I take Gavin's hand. "Don't wait up for me, guys—the limo will bring me home." Oh, I love saying that! Even if it turns into a pumpkin after midnight, I'm happy to be Cinderella for one night.

I don't wait for Mom's answer. I don't need one. I leave her and Rob standing there while Gavin leads me onto the dance floor. The chance to be alone with Gavin is what I've been waiting for. I'm not letting anyone ruin our night. The song playing is a fast-paced Maltese hit, "Random Night," from a couple of years ago, so we both try to keep the beat. Gavin doesn't seem to mind that all my dancing lessons consist of me "shaking what my mama gave me" around my room with my iPod.

Toward the end of the song we lace our fingers together. I imagine being this close to your crush is how true bliss feels.

You don't care about anyone else around you. You don't care if you dance like an android. Okay, maybe just a little.

Out of the corner of my eye, I spy something that looks like a flying object. I do a double take. Stacy's charging toward us. Hasn't she bothered me enough for one night? One lifetime?

"What is it?" Gavin asks.

I eyeball Stacy, and Gavin glances to his left. "Don't worry. I'll deal with her."

I let go of his hands. "No, I've got this one." The flames are bursting from me like a grease fire on a gas stove.

When Stacy's less than a foot away, I put my hand up to her face. "I've had enough of your crap. I don't know what you've got up your butt, but it's old." At this point I have no idea what I'm saying, but I don't let that stop me. "And another thing, your attitude sucks. I don't know what I did to deserve your abuse, but get over it!"

Stacy's jaw drops and she takes a step back.

I cross my arms and let my eyes burn holes in her skin. She's not escaping.

She blinks. "I just wanted to tell you that you've got balls. To go on the radio and all."

"Huh?" Is that a compliment? An attempt at an apology? Is she that wasted?

"That's all I wanted to say. Have fun, beyotch!" Stacy stumbles off, nearly tripping over her three-inch heels.

Gavin and I are so dumbstruck that we stand on the dance

floor like statues for a few seconds. Could Stacy possibly have a conscience?

"What was that?" Gavin finally asks.

"I don't know. Is there a full moon tonight?"

"You bet." He grins.

It takes a Shrinking Violet tune, "Freeze-dried Love," for us to start moving again. This time Gavin draws me closer until our bodies touch. The heat of his chest soars through me like a rocket. We are fused together and sway back and forth for the entire song.

He whispers in my ear, "That was incredible how you handled Stacy. I'm impressed."

"Me, too." Maybe I do have a little of my mom in me. Scary thought.

I look up at Gavin. At his rich, cherry lips. He pulls me in even closer, slipping his hands around my waist. Our lips touch, and I open my mouth slightly. He slides his soft tongue inside and warms up my whole body. I try not to wonder if I'm kissing right and just wrap my arms around his broad shoulders.

I've never tasted anything so good. I am in heaven.

chapter TWENTY-SEVEN

Good morning, Miami, this is my first early bird broadcast. I feel like I've been running all weekend, but this tune couldn't wait. It was just released and is already number one on the Billboard charts, "The Moon Stops for You" by Gavin Tam. It's the kind of song that melts in your mouth and lingers on your tongue, leaving you wanting more . . . forever.

★ ★ ★

Prom was two days ago, but I'm still walking on air. As soon as I wake up, I pull the photo out from under my pillow. Me and Gavin, bleary-eyed, dancing to the last song, Juice Box's "Spill

Proof." I'm glad I have evidence that the night existed, that and the SLAM webcast. Otherwise I still might think it was all a dream.

I check the call list on my cell. Gavin's name is listed between Domino's Pizza and Mom.

We're two and a half weeks away from Graduation Day. I'm not sure if I want it all to end. It's funny; in the beginning of the year, I was terrified about being the third person to walk on-stage to receive my diploma. Now even if Allison Abel and Phillip Abraham were absent, I wouldn't mind going first.

I'm finally getting used to being in high school. Maybe this yearning for more leaves me at a good starting place for college, even though Gavin and I will be three hours away from each other. I know we'll see each other on weekends, talk on the phone . . . but I'll still miss him.

Mom's not up when I get to the kitchen. She went out with an old friend from high school last night, one she hasn't seen in ten years. I wonder if ten years from now everyone at Ridgeland will only be a distant memory. Not Audrey and Gavin, of course. It's weird. You see certain people practically every day for four years and then, just in an instant, you never see them again. Then and now is only separated by one day.

I make a couple slices of toast and grab my bag. I've got some unfinished business to take care of at SLAM.

"Take my car; I don't need it today," Mom calls from the top of the stairs.

I grab the keys from the kitchen. "Thanks. I'm off to the station. See you later."

She waves good-bye. I really hope she comes through with her promise to buy me a car for graduation. I don't care if it's an old clunker; I just want my own ride.

I listen to SLAM the whole trip. I'm so glad I'll be able to keep working there while I'm at University of Miami. The station is like family now.

It's much quieter on the weekends. There are no bodies rushing around the sales office and no Pop-Tart up front answering the phones. I find Derek in the production room working on a commercial.

"Hey, babe." He slides a CD into the player. "How did you know I'd be here?"

"I've got my sources." And Jason's phone number.

"I thought you were too hot for Dynamite Derek." He brings his finger to his lips, wets it with his tongue, and makes a sizzling sound.

I stand in front of him. "That's what I wanted to talk to you about."

"Really?" He drops his feet from the edge of the console and sits up straight.

"Yeah, you're a sleaze, but with some redeeming qualities." Something about my confrontation with Stacy has left me feeling liberated.

"Gee, thanks." He lets out a fast laugh.

"All I'm saying is, if I never went through with the contest, I would've never—"

"I know, you would've never met your Romeo."

"Well, that's up for debate because I already had a crush on him, but without the contest, I wouldn't have truly broken free from my mask."

"Now you've lost me." He puts up his hand.

"Just wanted to thank you, that's all."

Derek slaps the label of the commercial onto the CD cover. When he sees me looking, he flips it over.

"You're welcome." He smiles a real smile, no sleaze.

"See you tomorrow, Dynamite Derek."

I leave him to finish cutting the Viagra commercial. No comment.

Gavin answers the door in a black Shrinking Violet tee with raised bubbly letters.

"Hey, where did you snag that?" I ask.

"I've got connections."

"Really?"

He leads me back to the family room and hands me a purple version of the same shirt. "For you."

"Thanks." I hold it up. "I love it."

"Yeah, I thought you could use a little color." He laughs.

"Great, Mom." I sit down on the couch. He plops down right

next to me. I lean my head on his shoulder. I'd be content if we could just stay like this forever.

I look over at the end table cluttered with frames. There's a small one up front of Gavin in a football uniform. He's sporting a huge toothy grin. He looks eight or nine. "You were so cute."

"Ugh, I look like such a dork in that picture."

I straighten my back. "You never told me what happened with the coach at school. About how he lied."

"Oh, that."

"You don't have to—"

"No, it's okay. It wasn't even really about me, but Reynolds pissed me off. There was this kid on the team from England, Patrick Olsen—"

"I know who you're talking about." I smile. The kid I used to have a crush on.

"Anyway, he always busted his ass, more than anyone else. Coach kept on telling him that if he played well, he could make it professionally. Then one day I got to the locker room early and overheard Reynolds talking to the varsity coach, telling him what a loser Olsen was, that if he actually thought he would play pro ball later, then he was a bozo."

"That's so mean," I say.

"The guy was a dog. He totally pumped up this kid, then laughed at him behind his back. I didn't want to be around someone like that."

"Did you tell anyone?"

"I spoke with my dad about it. He said it was up to me what I wanted to do. At that point I just wanted out. My dad respected my decision."

"That's really cool." I rub Gavin's back. "Did you say anything to Patrick?"

"No, I couldn't. Who knows, maybe he'll prove Coach wrong."

"Let's hope."

"Enough of me. Shall we?" He gets up and pops in a Juice Box DVD. We don't move until the concert is over.

"So what are you doing this summer?" I stretch my legs across his lap.

"I'll be around, just working at my dad's office." Gavin shifts his arm around me. "How about you?"

"No plans, really. Besides hanging at the station and doing some volunteer work."

"What's that?"

"Reading for the blind."

He runs his finger over the bridge of my nose and in between my eyes. "Ah, you really learned a lot from Helen."

"I did. She was an amazing woman."

He lowers his voice and makes his hands look like claws. "That's awesome. I learned a lot from Stephen King, too."

"Very funny." I laugh.

I deepen my voice, too, and say, "Want to go to a party with me on Saturday?"

"Will there be blood and guts?" He gnaws at my neck.

"No, but there'll be Wiener schnitzel and sauerkraut." I gently press my lips against his.

"Huh?" He pulls back slightly and furrows his brows.

"German Club. Don't ask. I promised Kayla."

"You're full of surprises." He grins.

"Who knew?" Certainly not me.

Gavin leans in closer. "I love listening to you."

"You mean, Sweet T." I laugh.

"No, actually I mean you, Tere. Whenever you speak, it really means something."

I reach for his hand and squeeze. "Thanks. That's so sweet."

"Of course, I love your show, too." He tilts his head and brushes the tip of his tongue against my lips. I close my eyes and gently thrust my tongue inside his mouth. My whole body tingles. I slowly pull out, and he kisses me back. Everything feels so perfect that I'm afraid to stop.

We hear footsteps shuffling down the hall and immediately sit up straight. When no one opens the door, we both breathe a sigh of relief.

I lick my lips, savoring the taste of Gavin. My eyes flit to the pink frame above the TV, and I read aloud, *"Don't be afraid to succeed. You might just surprise yourself."*

"What's the thing you're most afraid of?" I run my fingers through Gavin's hair.

"Not living up to my mom's needlepoint sayings." He laughs.

I elbow him lightly in the ribs. "No, really."

"Not being able to play my music every day." He leans over and brushes a strand of hair from my face. "What about you? What are you most afraid of?"

I sink into his deep onyx eyes. They're warm and inviting, and the snowball that's been inside me for so many years melts away.

And I realize what it is I no longer fear.

Speaking my mind.

shrinking violet

danielle joseph

questions for discussion

1. Does being shy mean you lack confidence? How much of a role do you believe Tere's self-image plays in her being shy?

2. What is your initial impression of Tere's mom, Delilah? Does it remain the same by the end of the book?

3. Tere states, "I'm glad I have Audrey to talk to, but still I can't share everything with her. Not the depths of my soul." Does this change your thoughts on their relationship? Should best friends be able to share everything? Do you think that Tere and Audrey's friendship is one that is lasting?

4. What are your thoughts on the novel's structure considering that the narrative is told from only Tere's perspective?

Do you think you would have the same impression of the characters if it was told from a different perspective?

5. Why do you think Gavin and Tere are so connected? How do you think their upbringing and lifestyle affect who they are?

6. Considering how shy Tere seems, is Derek's decision to make Tere a prize in a contest inconsiderate? Why do you think Rob went along with the idea?

7. Was Stacy's anger at Tere justified?

8. Discuss the theme of wearing a mask in *Shrinking Violet*. To which characters does this apply, and why?

9. Did Tere become more self-assured through being a DJ or do you think it was caused by multiple factors? Explain.

10. Do you believe the book's title, *Shrinking Violet*, to be an apt description of Tere?

11. Is there anything about Tere and her experiences that are similar to situations you've had to deal with? Discuss.

12. What would be the next chapter in Tere's life as she graduates and goes on to college?

reader tips

1. Tere has a real love of music. The music she plays also taps into the emotions she's feeling. Share your top five favorite songs with the book group and what you feel when you play them.

2. Before your book club meeting, look up your favorite author, tell the group why they are your favorite and share something new and interesting about them.

3. Helen Keller was a real inspiration to Tere. Read *The Story of My Life* by Helen Keller.

a chat with the author

1. Was your high school experience at all like Teresa's? Is that when you got involved with radio broadcasts?

   I was shy growing up but not nearly as shy as Tere. I loved being involved in drama, not necessarily center stage, more on the side. I also had a good group of friends that I felt secure in and was able to express myself within that group. Like Tere, I've always loved music and used to spend hours making mixes. Then when I went to college, I got involved with the radio station and loved being behind the mike. There was something comforting about the fact that I was alone in the studio, speaking to thousands of people that could hear me but not see me.

2. You mention many types of masks throughout the story. (The mask that radio provides, the heavy makeup that people wear, the transformations of Teresa's mom with

each new boyfriend.) Why do you think so many people are compelled to disguise or hide themselves? Is there a particular mask that you wear? If so, why?

When people feel insecure about their inner or outer appearance, they often put up a mask in the form of a wall. Some masks help you grow as a person, while others hinder you because they don't allow you to overcome your fears and insecurities. Sometimes somebody who appears to be really put together is actually hurting inside. Two examples from Shrinking Violet *are Delilah, Tere's mom, and Stacy. You really have to unpeel the layers to get to know them. I have always tried not to put up a front and be myself. However, instead of wearing a mask, in certain situations, I hid behind my shyness. Going off to college really allowed me to open up. When you come from a small town like me, it's hard to break free of the mold that you are in. Being on the radio, behind the mic, allowed me to "wear" a mask that enabled me to show my true colors in a positive way. By the end of my time at the radio station, I was much more comfortable speaking to people and expressing myself.*

3. With fashion magazines, music videos, and countless other media outlets, it's often difficult for a shrinking violet to find themselves amid all of that manufactured beauty. What would you say to the Teresas of the world?

I would say the most important thing is to be yourself and not to sell out. You will never find long-term happiness behind a mask. It may not be today, but eventually you will be rewarded for your honesty, for staying true to yourself. If you don't like the way something is going in your life, fix it. Things will not happen overnight, but if you set small attainable goals, you should be able to meet them with success. And don't forget that manufactured beauty is air-brushed!

4. Tere really seems to love hip-hop (though her loves seem to stretch to various genres, from post-punk to "edgy" tunes). Given your radio involvement, are you a rap fan? Who is your favorite musician? (Who is your PJ Squid? Your Maltese?)

I am a big fan of rap/hip-hop music from the old stuff like the Beastie Boys, Run-DMC and A Tribe Called Quest to newer voices like Outkast, Estelle, and Sean Kingston. It's hard to pick just one PJ Squid, or one Maltese, but an artist that I really admire is Wyclef Jean. One of the main reasons is because he does not wear a mask. He is proud of his roots and his heritage and has successfully incorporated his background into his music. He is the total package and gives back to others.

5. What inspired you to tell this story?

I was inspired to tell this story because I think sometimes we box people into certain categories very early on in their lives and that hinders their self-esteem. I don't ever think you should tell someone that if they don't work hard enough, they can't be what they dream of being. Take Tere's mom for instance: If Tere had listened to her mom, she would most likely have never found a home at the radio station, a place where she clearly belongs. If you believe in yourself, that is all that matters. Set your own limitations. Don't let others do that for you.

6. What do you think initially attracts Gavin to Tere? What about Tere to Gavin?

While some people might be turned off by Tere's shyness, Gavin appreciates that when she does speak, she usually has something important to say. He is attracted to her because she is her own person. She's not trying to be the same as everyone else. Tere is attracted to Gavin because he too is doing his own thing and she is intrigued by his mysterious nature. Of course there is a chemical attraction—she thinks he's cute. Plus, music is a great bonding tool and immediately they both are drawn to each other's taste in music.

7. Do you think people like Stacy, Tere's mother, and Derek are partially responsible for Tere's self-discovery? Do you think negativity can have an impact on someone's life in a positive way?

Yes, I do think a lot of the time people are propelled by the negativity in their lives to prove those pessimistic forces wrong. It can definitely affect one's self-esteem, but if you are able to turn a deaf ear to the disapproving voices and really focus on your goals, you can push through any barriers that are set before you. At the end of the day, you only have to look at yourself in the mirror.

8. Do you see Teresa as a modern-day Helen Keller? Do you see parallels between her transformation and Helen's triumphant story? Why did you compare Stacy to Danielle Steele?

I think Helen Keller was one of a kind. She persevered against all odds. And for that she serves as a wonderful role model for Tere. Tere was able to gather strength from Helen's story and use that strength to propel her forward. From reading more about Helen's life, Tere was able to appreciate the gifts that she does have and to make use of them. Both Helen and Tere were able to overcome their own personal obstacles and did not let anyone or anything stand in their way. I compared Stacy to Danielle Steele because Stacy is the type of person who would pick an author to represent, solely based on the author's popularity. Stacy wants to be liked and thinks that money and fame prevail over what's inside your heart.

9. Where did you get the idea for the songwriting contest to win Tere as a prom date? Is that something you actually experienced or witnessed?

The prom contest idea came from the notion that Tere so quickly dismissed the idea of going to the prom and the only thing that could get her there was her love for her job. She also loves to discover new artists and this was the perfect opportunity for her to do so. I have never been a part of a contest like this but was inspired by the likes of American Idol—*how contests like that are responsible for giving people their big breaks. It's great to see people succeed based on their own merit and that is what happened with Gavin. Just like Tere, the idea of being the "contest prize" would be mortifying to me.*

10. Are you working on another novel? Do you have any more stories of Tere to tell, or do you plan to create different characters? Will the focus stay mainly in high school, or would you ever branch out into an older world?

Yes, I am working on another young adult novel, involving a mix of humor, love, and intrigue. It would be a lot of fun to write the next chapter in Tere's life as her relationship deepens with Gavin, as she prepares to head off to college and deals with life at the radio station after her mask has been lifted. I love writing for teens but have been carrying an idea for an adult novel in my head for a few years so I'm sure one day I will sit down and write it.